AMMA AND OTHER STORIES

Amma and Other Stories

OMPRAKASH VALMIKI

Translation and Introduction

NARESH K. JAIN

MANOHAR
2008

First published 2008

ISBN 81-7304-783-9

Published by

Ajay Kumar Jain *for*
Manohar Publishers & Distributors
4753/23 Ansari Road, Daryaganj
New Delhi 110 002

Typeset at

Digigrafics
New Delhi 110 049

Printed at

Lordson Publishers Pvt. Ltd.
Delhi 110 007

Contents

Preface

AMMA *and Other Stories* is the English translation of the collection of Hindi stories entitled *Salaam.* These stories have been well received by readers not only in Hindi but in several foreign languages as well. Their publication in English will enable them to reach a much wider audience.

The stories in this anthology document the acute pain of the world around me. My childhood days were spent in village Barla in Muzaffarnagar district in western U.P., where the misalliance of caste system and feudal mindset has kept human sensitivities at bay. These stories, while depicting the longing for life of characters belonging to this background and highlighting their human concerns, also attempt to underline the intrinsic role of literature.

The characters in these stories—whether they be Kale and Bhoore in 'The Hide of an Ox'; Ramesar and bahuji in 'Eclipse' and 'Biram's Wife'; Sukka, Mukhiyaji and Pandit Ramsaran in 'The Killing of a Cow'; Dinesh in 'Fear', or Harish and Kamal Upadhyaya in 'Salaam'—the sufferings of these characters, their sympathies, concerns, and inner agitations have all emerged as an expression of the experiential reality of life. These characters do not hesitate to give vent to their emotions and their traditional values in an earthy and realistic manner.

The keenness, hard work, profound inquisitiveness and integrity with which Dr Naresh Jain has rendered these stories into English is indeed remarkable. This because Dr Jain has not only tried to capture the spirit of the language but also the inner meaning of the words. Together with this he has exercised full care to retain the contexual specificities of these stories. He has spared no effort to keep the values and the human dimension of the stories intact. Long conversations over the telephone, and his insistence on trying to figure out the meaning of individual words have made this translation significant.

Carrying the dalit struggle and their restlessness across the barriers of language is the fruit of Dr Jain's endeavour. It is to be hoped that the publication of this book in English will add a new dimension to dalit discourse.

It is not a matter of mere formality to thank Mr. Ramesh Jain because if he had not shown readiness to undertake the publication of this book, it wouldnt have been in your hands in its present form.

C5/2, Ordnance Factory Estate OMPRAKASH VALMIKI
Dehradun 248008
Mobile 09412319034
10 January 2008

Acknowledgements

MY ACQUAINTANCE with Omprakash Valmiki's works began with reading an article on his autobiography *Joothan*. I was editing a volume that contained the article. I hadn't read the book but the article had an excerpt from it that shocked me beyond words and made me buy the book and read it. The excerpt related to the beating that young Omprakash received at the hands of a teacher for daring to question the composer of *Mahabharata*. Thus began a relationship that at first thrived over the telephone. It was much later that we met at a function on readings from his short stories and poems and his autobiography at Ram Lal Anand College so thoughtfully organized by Dr D.K. Pabby the Principal and Dr Vijay Sharma and other friends last year.

The one friend who has constantly been by my side and has scrutinized every word of my translation has been Dr N.P. Singh. He has been an ever-willing friend and I can hardly thank him adequately. The translation is so much the better for his efforts. For any error, however, I alone am responsible. I am also very grateful to Dr S.P. Jain who with his usual thoroughness went through two stories from the collection, 'Shavayatra' and 'Umbrella' and made valuable suggestions.

I thank the original publisher of Omprakash Valmiki's *Salaam* for permitting me to translate the stories into English and the Indian Institute of Advanced Study for letting me include the English translation of the story 'Shavayatra' in the present collection.

Ramesh as usual has been extremely supportive. When I mentioned this project to him, he at once agreed. I hope that the translation proves worthy of his trust in me.

In the Manohar editorial office both Bansi Ram and Siddharth Chowdhury were quite meticulous. While the former sifted through the manuscript like a sieve for any error, Siddharth read through both the Hindi original and the English translation and brought the creativity of a writer to bear on his editing. I am thankful to both.

BB/49-C, Janakpuri, NARESH K. JAIN
New Delhi 110058
Telephones: 2550 0179, 2550 4986.
16 January 2008

Introduction

I want words to break the silence,
tell the truth, call
a lie, a lie.

Omprakash Valmiki in 'They are Alarmed'

THE ENGLISH translation of fifteen stories of Omprakash Valmiki is in your hands. Thirteen of them are from the writer's first collection called *Salaam* [Obeisance]. The fourteenth story 'Shavayatra' has been chosen from his second anthology *Ghuspaithiye* [Intruders]. Its English translation with the same title first appeared in *Summerhill* (Issue No. 1, 2006) published by the Indian Institute of Advanced Study at Shimla. The fifteenth story 'Chhatri' [Umbrella] is perhaps his latest story or his latest published story—it was published in *Kathadesh* (November 2006)—and hasn't yet been anthologized. Together these stories give us a glimpse of what it means to be a dalit in today's resurgent India.

I

Who is a dalit? Etymologically, the term *dalit* which is used both as an adjective and as a noun is derived from the Sanskrit root *dal* which means to grind (grain), to split (pulse) open, to crush. This root meaning has been carried over into the metaphorical meaning. Accordingly, a dalit, says Valmiki in his *Dalit Sahitya ka Saundarya Shastra* [The Aesthetics of Dalit Literature], applies to a person who has been broken or torn to pieces, and been oppressed, crushed, trampled upon, exploited, deprived. It stands for a person who occupies the lowest rung of the ladder in the social hierarchy, the person who is recognized to be an untouchable. Valmiki's definition of the term is comprehensive and includes tribals, the so-called criminal tribes, women of all classes, farm workers who work for extremely low wages and bonded labourers (Valmiki 2005:13–14).

Dalit literature is literature in which dalits have depicted their own pain. It is literature that expresses the reality of what they have suffered in their struggle for life. Valmiki himself says: 'It's not art for art's sake; it's literature of life and literature of the desire to live' (ibid. 2005: 14). Two principle tendencies of it are: negation and protest. This negation or protest may be against the system, social discrepancies, religious orthodoxies, or economic disparities. It may be against literary traditions, benchmarks, or aesthetics. Dalit literature is the literature of negation, which is a product of struggle, which has in it the idea of equality, freedom and brotherhood and which is opposed to casteism born out of caste system. The word dalit becomes a symbol of the expression of protest (ibid. 2005: 16).

In his introduction to *Man and Superman*, George Bernard Shaw says that for mere art of art's sake, he would not undertake the toil of writing a single sentence. Much the same could be said for Omprakash Valmiki and indeed dalit writers as a whole. Valmiki writes not for personal enjoyment (nor for that matter for the enjoyment of the readers) but to reveal what has remained under cover so far—the trials and travails of being a dalit in order to awaken us to the harsh reality around us and to be a catalyst for societal change. He writes to express what has come to be called dalit consciousness or dalit *chetna*.

What is dalit consciousness? Dalits, he says, are those who have been deprived of their human rights, those who have been socially ostracized. Their consciousness is dalit consciousness. Like a fast-flowing stream, this consciousness is part of the inner energy of dalit literature. This sets it apart from traditional literature. It is difficult to realize the keen edge of dalit consciousness without understanding the social organization of Indian society. Oppressed by the thousands of years of abuse, exploitation, hostility, and discrimination, the dalit now seems wide awake in his quest for his dignity. Dalit consciousness is an important part of the concerns of dalit literature and it derives its strength chiefly from the philosophy of Dr Bhimrao Ambedkar. Without this consciousness literature would become flaccid and only full of flights of imagination.

This term, perhaps somewhat amorphous and still evolving, has been defined as consisting of pride, self-respect and a vision for the future (Brueck 2006). This consciousness, it is held, is the hallmark of dalit literature and is also a yardstick for judging canonized works of Hindi literature.

The dalit writer has become aware of the power of the printed word. He has also learnt how to use words as weapons. But this weapon is not meant to destroy; its keenness has been fashioned out of the sharp edge of knowledge, wisdom, logic and morality (Valmiki 2005: 32).

The concept of dalit aesthetics is in the process of evolution. His own book on the subject, he says, was meant to present a kind of outline of it before writers, critics, researchers and readers interested in the dalit literary movement. But he acknowledges that it could not be laid down by a single work or a single man; that it is a collective idea and that it is necessary to work constantly towards evolving it. But he categorically says that the texture of aesthetics of dalit literature would undoubtedly be different from either Western aesthetics or the traditional principles underlying the aesthetic theories of heavyweights like Ramchandra Shukl. Moreover, in determining the value of a literary work, the dalit aesthetics would accord primacy to the source and the intention over the artistry behind it. Intention, he said, was what connected any literary work with social contexts. It was important to evaluate literature sociologically. For dalit literature, relations between literature and society were matters of serious concern. Literature, he holds, would be able to fulfil its responsibility towards society only when instead of making it more artistic, we move towards making it socially more relevant. The intention is central in his think-ing. Dalit literature is part of a movement. It is literature for change.

The overwhelming emphasis that Valmiki and other dalit writers place on intention is understandable. But, as his own stories demonstrate, the artistry in his stories is as strong as the content in them. It is this blend that makes them fine works of art.

II

According to Omprakash Valmiki, all the stories he has written so far have had their origin in the life around him.

The stories themselves are meant to be a revelation.

They are all intended to bring to light the indignities and deprivations which the dalits have been subjected to in their day-to-day life for centuries, to sensitize the readers to their sufferings and finally to bring them to a state of preparedness so that affirmative action is possible.

At the heart of the stories lie both anguish and anger. But because of the great restraint exercised by the author, they are remarkably free from lament and rancour both. Dalit pain is there in abundance and it takes protean forms. The presentation of it gives an entirely new dimension to reality which most of the non-dalits probably had a vague idea of but which they hadn't seen presented in literature. In 'Salaam' Valmiki adopts a new device to bring home to the non-dalits the distress caused to a brahmin by being taken for a chuhra. Kamal Upadhyaya asks for tea at a village shop. But since he has come with the baraat of his dalit friend Harish, he is mistaken for a chuhra and is refused tea and is insulted and nearly assaulted.

> Kamal felt as though a dense solitary jungle of humiliation had sprung up round him. . . .Violent hunters were getting ready to attack him with their sharp talons.
>
> For the first time, he personally experienced with intensity what he had only read about in the newspapers but what he had not been able to bring himself to believe: how at one place a dalit youth had been beaten to death, how someone had been roasted alive, houses had been set on fire.

The dalit litany of pain includes several things. Apart from the dehumanizing work of cleaning the lavatories done by dalits, the groom Harish in 'Salaam' is required by custom to go to the houses of their clients to salaam them and receive clothes and utensils; Sukka in 'The Killing of a Cow' must send his bride to the house of the thakur where he serves and when he refuses, he must face his revenge; Kale and Bhoore in 'The Hide of an Ox' must carry away dead animals from the village, for which task they receive no wages. And when they are late in reaching their village, they receive unprintable abuses from Pandit Birij Mohan whose ox had died. 'Amma' reveals the danger of sexual harassment to which the young dalit women are exposed in the houses of the rich and the powerful.

But the pain is hardly ever alone. Along with it there is also the awareness, however dim, of the desire to resist, to fight it out, to try to rise above it. Many of them also exhibit a spirit that refuses to accept their fate as something given, as something unalterable. A prime example of it is of course Amma but there are others too. Four of the five accused in 'The Killing of a Cow' who are barely articulate are grateful for being let off but in their sympathy for Sukka one can see the early beginnings of the questioning of injustice.

Besides their essential humanity, the stories also highlight the modest dreams of dalits and their slim hopes and aspirations. Witness stories like 'The Hide of an Ox', 'The Homeless' and 'Umbrella'. All this sets the stories apart from earlier stories with dalits characters such as Premchand's 'Thakur ka Kuan' [The Well of the Thakurs].

A closer scrutiny of the narrative art of these stories would bring out the artistry behind the stories. Who, for instance, is the narrator in the stories? Several stories use a third person omniscient narrator. We always know where the sympathies of the writer lie but the omniscience of the narrator enables him to probe the minds of different characters as and when necessary and present a composite picture. In the story 'Where Can Satish Go? the omniscient narrator not only shows us the working of Satish's mind but also the mind of Mrs. Pant and how she reacts to the accidental discovery of Satish's caste.

> While coming inside she happened to touch them [Satish's clothes]. Mrs. Pant felt as though an electric current had passed through her, as if something filthy had touched her body. She picked up the long bamboo pole lying in the verandah and with its help threw the trousers and the shirt down.

The exposure of Mrs. Pant's caste bias is so complete that no comments are necessary.

The story illustrates an important feature of Valmiki's art. The writer speaks through the situations he invents and the characters he creates without much outward comment. Similarly, in the story 'The Killing of a Cow', which too has an omniscient narrator, the hypocrisy and the revengefulness of the Mukhiya who is infuriated at being denied access to his servant's newly wedded wife come out through his own words. Though we see Sukka's sufferings and hear his shrieks, we are also given a glimpse of the Mukhiya's mind, who through his mischievous smile, seems to say to Sukka: 'You have now seen the consequences of meddling with me, bachchu?' The last sentence is like the sting in the tail. It completes the indictment of the hypocrisy of the entire village, ruled by the Mukhiya and aided and assisted by Pandit Ramsaran. Notice the last sentence of the story.

> Pandit Ramsaran heaved a sigh of relief, as though the entire village had been absolved of the sin of killing a cow.

To my mind this story contains the severest indictment of the dynamics of a feudal village society—the gross miscarriage of justice administered by the panchayat, the hypocrisy and barbarity of the Mukhiya and the subservient roles played by Pandit Ramsaran and others. Valmiki's last sentences are often notable and carry a lot of thematic weight.

If Munshi Premchand's 'Panch Parmeshwar' presents an idealized picture of the justice of the panchayat, Valmiki's 'The Killing of a Cow' highlights the horrifying reality of it. Incidentally this story can be seen as a testimony to Dr Ambedkar's view (as quoted by Valmiki in his book *Dalit Sahitya ka Saundarya Shastra*) that Indian villages could be heaven for the Brahmins but for dalits they are a veritable hell (Valmiki 2005: 31).

The stories 'Eclipse' and 'Biram's Wife' form a duo, something not very usual in the world of short stories. The story begins in 'Eclipse' and is carried over into 'Biram's Wife'. In the second story Valmiki tries a new experiment in narration—he gives us a double perspective on the wakening love between Ramesar and Biram's wife, something like what William Faulkner does in his novel *The Sound and the Fury* (1929). At times Ramesar believes that by making him sleep with her, the bahuji has made use of him. But the story is told not only from the point of view of Ramesar but also from that of bahuji, his high caste sexual partner. In other words, there are two narrators, two focalizers viewing the same event here. Accordingly, we are told that in spite of her warm feelings for him, she must not give the slightest hint of any contact with him or else there would be hell let loose upon them both, particularly on him. The lone act of sexual union leads to a bond of deep yearning between them but because of the impenetrable social barriers, each must remain imprisoned in his or her ambit. Clearly the softer tones of love and longing are not entirely absent from Valmiki's short stories.

In 'The Beast' we see the events from the point of view of a servant, Jagesar who has been asked to escort his master's daughter-in-law to her mother's home, and note the stages in the slow unfolding of his consciousness as the abandoned wife tells him the reality of both her father-in-law and her maternal uncle. Here we have a surprise ending, which is uncommon in Valmiki's stories, for the newly self-conscious escort announces that he is no Lakshman or Lachhman as he calls him, who had left Sita unguarded in the solitary forest. What the full implications of these words are is left for the reader to figure out.

The story 'Amma' again comes to us through an omniscient narrator and is principally told from the point of view of Amma. But for the first time in these pages we have the omniscient narrator walking out of the text as it were much like Henry Fielding and addressing the reader directly:

> You could call it Amma's story—but not of one particular Amma; for you hardly know how many Ammas you would come across with broom and canister in hand early morning doing the rounds of gali-mohallas, whose decrepit bodies have wilted under the impact of time and like old trees have begun to waste away. Every moment of their lives is moving towards an unseen and uncertain future. All prophecies, intellectual acrobatics and imaginative plans about them just go to pieces or are expected to be a lie.

Such a start is startlingly new but the reason for this is that Valmiki's intention is to present a character that is larger than that he has given us earlier, who is not just one character but several rolled into one and who speaks for all the Ammas. It is a triumph of Valmiki's art that he has been to generate great sympathy for a woman who is faceless and who has been performing a task that is hard and dirty but from which she has shielded all the other members of the family. The story closes as it had opened with the omniscient narrator making a comment:

> Amma's broken down canister and broom lay resting against the wall mocking her.

This ironical comment brings us back to the reality of her life—she must continue to use those very articles from which she has all along wanted to liberate her children.

The story 'Amma' is almost a mini-epic of dalit womanhood. The Amma of the story is an enduring character not only because she has had such a lot to endure in the course of her long life but because she has kept her eyes fixed on the eye of the sparrow—not to let her children touch the broom and to ensure a decent life for them. She reminds me of the character of Mama in the African American dramatist, Lorainne Hansberry's play *A Raisin in the Sun* (1959). In fact, the story has several episodes that could be turned into drama. I wonder if this idea of the dramatic potential of the story has occurred to the writer of 'Amma'. Those who feel interested in the Amma of the story might like to look up the author's poem entitled 'Vey Nahin Jaante' [They Don't Know] in his anthology *Bass! Bahut ho Chuka* [Stop it! That's Enough!] (Valmiki 1997: 81-8), which has a similar character in it.

'Umbrella' presents an interesting variation in the narrative strategy. It is told in the first person and probes a deprived child's longing for an umbrella and his feelings when the school teacher thoughtlessly breaks it.

Dalit literature is not only literature of pain but also literature of change. One finds not merely resentment or what is called *aakrosh* in Hindi but also an inner, articulated or unarticulated urge for change. And a standard tool to bring about this change is through education. Evidence for this is widespread in the stories—'Salaam', 'The Hide of an Ox', 'Fear', 'Where Can Satish Go?', 'Eclipse', 'Amma', 'Twenty-five Fours are a Hundred and Fifty' and 'Umbrella'. Education enters these stories directly or indirectly and is presented as a source of strength. No wonder those who wield power discourage the dalits who aspire for it. But though Valmiki knows how important education is, he doesn't write his stories according to a set formula or to enforce a moral. The references come in naturally and don't look forced.

Perhaps the most touching realization of the need for education is expressed through the unlettered and barely articulate Bhoore in 'The Hide of an Ox', who imagines his chhutku as standing in the line of students and memorizing multiplication tables. But the story that best presents what a dalit empowered with education can do is 'Twenty-five Fours are a Hundred and Fifty'. Here the young educated dalit protagonist is able to demolish his father's long-held myth about the Chaudhri's help given at a time of adversity and shows him up for the fraud that he is. The story could be seen as a metaphor for the exposure of deceit and fraudulent practices indulged in by the dominant castes in relation to dalits over the ages.

Brahminism comes in for censure in various ways—chiefly in the form of characters like Pandit Ramsaran in 'The Killing of a Cow', Pandit Birij Mohan in 'The Hide of an Ox' and Pandit Siyaram in 'Biram's Wife'. But not all the Brahmin characters in the stories are shown to be acting out of questionable motives. There are sympathetic characters too, for example Kamal Upadhyaya in 'Salaam'. The friendship between Harish and Kamal hints at the way Valmiki's mind works in the direction of bringing about societal change. Another positive character is Ravi Sharma (who doesn't appear before us) in 'Where Can Satish Go?' who recommends Satish, a dalit, for lodging at the house of the Pant family. Jasdev in 'The Homeless' too has the right impulses and goes along with the dalit characters to an extent but lacks the courage to go the whole hog. And we have Ramprasad Tiwari who is a constant visitor in Dinesh's house in 'Fear' but without knowing the latter's dalit identity. This variety reflects the variety of possible responses of the Brahmins or non-dalits towards the dalits in society and shows how realistic Valmiki is.

If Valmiki is ruthless in exposing the Brahminism and the atrocities committed on the dalits, he is equally unsparing in his indictment of dalits, particularly for practising untouchability within themselves. This comes out best in his poignant story 'Shavayatra' where, because of the intra-dalit caste hierarchy, a balhar family, the lowliest of the low among dalits, in a chamar village, are made to face the ordeal of cremating their dead without any help from the chamars who stand and watch the 'shavayatra' as mute spectators. Valmiki was severely criticized by fellow dalit writers and critics for this story which, it was said, highlighted a 'domestic' problem of the dalits. In reply Valmiki said, that those who opposed the story didn't know what they were opposing. Their language, he said, was similar to that used by those who represented India at the Durban Conference held during the NDA regime. When, he said, the question of caste was raised at the Conference, those who represented India said that it was an internal matter of theirs. Valmiki categorically says that dalit literature was opposed to casteism, whether within the dalits or outside: 'You are a dalit and you also wish to remain a bhangi, chamar, passi, mahar. This is a contradiction in terms' (interview with Bajrang Bihari Tiwari: *Kathadesh*: March 2005: 66).

Omprakash Valmiki also realizes that the dalits need to come to terms with their dalithood. There are several instances of this in Valmiki's autobiography *Joothan* (1997). It is but natural therefore that the revelation of the true identity of the dalit characters should be a major motif in the stories also. This dilemma is particularly true of characters that are shown trying to better their prospects in life. Witness 'Where Can Satish Go?', 'Fear' and 'Storm'. Of these the last two are built round the fear of discovery. 'Storm' is particularly notable because it points in the direction of change in the form of acceptance of their identity and this acceptance comes from the lips of a school girl. While the father has metamorphosed himself from Sukru to Mr. S. Lal and has kept his family insulated from his poor caste relations, the daughter is shown to be clear-sighted enough to hold the father guilty of separating the children from their roots and she wants to get better acquainted with them. Can we say that a process of manthan or churning is on among the dalits?

I should like to mention another quality of Valmiki's narrative, which I have held back till the last: his use of last sentences in some of the stories. Some of these sentences are:

1. From the distance came the shrieking whistle of the chowkidar, shattering the silence of the night, as though asking—where can Satish go? ('Where Can Satish Go?')
2. Pandit Ramsaran heaved a sigh of relief as though

the whole village had been absolved of the sin of gohatya. ('The Killing of a Cow')

3. The moon, sick of eclipse, was making its way towards fulfillment. ('Eclipse')
4. Amma's broken down canister and broom lay against the wall mocking her. ('Amma')
5. A chamar village and within it a family of balhars! ('Shavayatra')

Here we have the omniscient narrator speak directly to the readers. The epigrammatic quality of the sentences needs to be related to the overall purpose of the stories: to rouse them to the reality of dalit life today. All these sentences except at No. 3 in their various ways light up the main thrust of the story directly or indirectly and are meant to make the readers pause and think.

Valmiki's stories have an interesting variety of narrative points of view; they show a fine sense of restraint; they employ literary devices like irony and satire. They are also remarkable for their bold and unconventional language. The language used is sometimes coarse and on one or two occasions even abusive but it is entirely authentic and helps to mirror the reality of dalit and rural life depicted in them. Here is an example from 'Salaam'. Kamal, a brahmin, has gone to a village as a member of a marriage party of his dalit friend. At a local tea stall he is refused tea on the suspicion that he too is a chuhra. When Kamal tries to speak to them addressing them as brothers, a local bully rebukes him:

> O you impotent city dweller, are *we* your brothers?—*Saale*, mind your language or I will push a rod up your arse and turn you upside down. Go and make an alliance with Jumman sweeper. Such an attractive girl the city people are taking with them. . . .

This speech, even in translation, will give you some idea of the local words and idiom and the rhythm of spoken language used here. Several examples of it could be given. The standard Hindi word for 'impotent' is 'nipunsak' but the village bully has used a more familiar word 'jankha' instead. The word used for girl—'laundiya' is again a local word. The idiom translated as—I will push a rod up your arse—again is brutally real. At times Valmiki himself omits strong expressions as in the story 'The Homeless'. When in response to the kiln owner's son Sube Singh's summons, a co-worker comes instead of Mano, he says:

'Why? . . . . Are you her husband? . . . Or has too much fat accumulated on her. . . ?' Sube Singh said abusively.

A brilliant example of Valmiki's skill with words is in the use of the word *Chopree* in 'Amma'. Following her brush with Mrs Chopra's visitor Vinod, Amma has 'sold' the Chopra household to Hardei for twenty rupees. Here is her entire speech that is full of strong, colourful language and reminds one of Vijay Tendulkar's play *Sakharam Binder* (1970):

You're stupid, you cursed one. You should've dragged the mother's lover into the lavatory. First, you should have stripped him naked and made him take a walk through Mussourie and then made him dance. After that you should've beaten the dog with the broom and taken him to the street. That would've completed the disgrace of the mother-fucker—seeing him run with his ganpati swinging about. He would've forgotten all about romancing. And that Chopree. I know how to handle such women. Here, take this money. Saali! Imagine a mother of two still trying to seek love elsewhere!

Note the masterful use of the name *Chopree*—with the mere change of a vowel the writer is able to express all the contempt that Hardei has for the high caste Mrs Chopra.

This speech may offend the tender sensibilities of Hindi readers fed on nothing stronger than Tulsidas and Maithilisharan Gupt and Jaishankar Prasad but it is so real, so authentic.

I will refer to two other things about Valmiki's language. The first relates to his use of the startling image of a dead cow coming back to life on hearing the shrieks of Sukka while holding the red-hot ploughshare.

> Sukka's shrieks crossing all limits of helplessness and striking against dusty streets and kuchcha-pucca houses, caused the entire atmosphere to shake with fear, such shrieks that might make a dead cow get up and run. Silence pervaded the crowd, the stunned silence of the cremation ground.

The image is so intense that it lifts the story high above the ordinary and will remain etched for ever in memory and could be seen as a metaphor for dalit literature as a whole.

The other thing relates to Valmiki's attempt to reinterpret a mythical character, Lakshman in 'The Beast'. The reference comes in so naturally, so effortlessly that you realize its newness only later. When bahuji asks her escort Jagesar to leave her to her fate and go back, he says: 'No . . . bahuji . . . I am not Lachhman who will go back leaving Sita alone in the solitary jungle. . . .'

That is not all. I am told that the doyen of Hindi criticism Namwar Singh once complimented Valmiki for two things: for presenting the sex scene in 'The Eclipse' without the least vulgarity and for adding a new word to the Hindi lexicon—the word *doon-na*, to roast, used in 'Fear'.

Though Valmiki is avid for change and wants to narrate

into existence a forward looking rational society based on dignity and equality and human brotherhood, he offers no easy or magical solutions. The struggle is long and hard and he wants to continue to play his part in the on going movement for the regeneration of the dalits.

Valmiki is a dalit writer but as we have seen earlier, his stories go way beyond dalits. They are not the only ones who suffer in them. We have already seen how high caste women are also presented as victims as in 'Eclipse', 'Biram's Wife' and 'The Beast'. And it is dalits who 'save' them. We shouldn't forget that Valmiki includes women of all classes among the dalits. At its best Valmiki's writing becomes a cry of pain of all oppressed and dispossessed people, that asks the readers, indeed insists, on some positive action to undo the wrongs.

Like all good short stories, Valmiki's stories produce their impact at the first reading. But it is only later, at the second or the third reading followed by reflection that they begin to unfold themselves. It is then that the different layers of the meaning that we missed earlier come to us. Most of these stories pay repeated readings.

III

All new voices in literature take time to be heard and heeded. So it has been with dalit writers. Theirs have been among the latest voices to be heard. And these voices mean to stay and insist on being heard. Dalit writing in Hindi has been criticized for being deficient in quality and also of being propagandist in nature. But now its warm human qualities are coming to be seen and it is in the process of winning recognition from the Hindi establishment.

Attitudinal changes towards dalits are inevitably on the way. Journals like *Hans* have opened their portals to dalit writing. In fact, *Hans* was among the first to have done so. Valmiki's story 'Bail ki Khaal' [The Hide of an Ox] appeared in the December 1992 issue of the journal followed by 'Salaam' in the August issue of 1993. Two stories of his included in the second anthology *Ghuspaithiye* appeared in subsequent issues of *Hans*. In a recent article published on the completion of 21 years of non-stop publication of the journal, its writer-editor Rajendra Yadav said that *Hans* had always been opposed to the *status quo* and had promoted debates concerning literature dealing with dalits, women, minorities and marginalized groups. He ends by saying that the basic philosophy of literature today is not 'satyam, shivam, sunderam' [truth, holiness and beauty] but torture, struggle and vision and that the mainstream of literature is *not* constituted by the middle classes trapped between tradition and modernity but by the discourses on women and dalits. This he considers to be the biggest achievement of *Hans*. Clearly the print media is opening up to dalit literature (Yadav 2007: 50).

Dalit literature is gaining acceptance in the academia also. According to Valmiki, several universities have included *Joothan* in full or excerpts from it along with poems or short stories or both as part of their syllabi for different courses. The NCERT has included the story 'Khanabadosh' [The Homeless] for senior secondary classes. Other stories of his that have been selected for study at the school or the university level are: 'Salaam', 'Shavayatra', 'This is Not the End', and 'Twenty-five Fours are a Hundred and Fifty'. The situation is bound to change for the better once more translations into English are available.

The situation at the research level is also quite encouraging. According to the information with the author, nearly forty research projects on his writings at the M.Phil. or Ph.D. level in different universities including some abroad are either on or have been completed.

By his own admission Omprakash Valmiki's experience of interacting with students which included both dalits and non-dalits at the University of Delhi, JNU, and at the University of Jabalpur and elsewhere has been very heartwarming.

IV

Valmiki's stories have generally been received favourably in Hindi literary journals. I have seen several reviews of his anthology *Salaam* from which most of the stories have been taken for translation. I will refer to three. These are: Shivkumar Misra's 'Stories in search of the right goal of humaneness' (*Sakshaatkaar,* November 2001), Bhalchandra Joshi's 'Salaam: A Meaningful Presence in Dalit Literature' (*Kathadesh*: February 2003) and Viveki Singh's 'Flowers don't bloom only in . . . [in the gardens of kings]' in *Kasauti.*

Shivkumar Misra's long review of *Salaam* has high praise for Valmiki both as a creative writer and thinker. Taking a comprehensive view of things, he says that the collection has enriched the tradition of realistic short story writing in Hindi: 'All in all, while these stories are dalit stories in terms of their creative skill, sympathy and art, they are a strong link in the tradition of realistic stories' (Misra 2001: 107). Some of the stories which he praises highly are: 'Bail ki Khaal' [The Hide of an Ox], 'Bhaya' [Fear], 'Gohatya' [The Killing of a Cow], the duo of 'Grahan' [Eclipse] and 'Biram ki Bahu' [Biram's Wife], 'Jinawar' [The

Beast], 'Amma' and 'Khanabadosh' [The Homeless]. The story 'Salaam' which gives the collection its name is marred, he says, by trying to attempt too much—by introducing the larger question of what divides man from man. This, he says, comes as an 'anticlimax'. The story 'Andhar' [Storm] is a trenchant attack on those dalits who disown their past. At the end of the story Mr Lal is surprised at the maturity of his school-going daughter Pinki who till now has been completely unaware of the family past but who now wants to live in the real world where she belongs. But the reviewer finds the change in Pinki too abrupt, psychologically too unreal and therefore unconvincing. The haste of the author to reach the right conclusion has, he says, weakened the story from the point of view of realism and psychology both. The reviewer's best compliments are reserved for 'Amma' which he describes as a story that is 'unforgettable, full of human sympathy and poignancy'. 'She is a smiling lotus flower amidst the mire of life.'

He makes two other points. One, he says that the stories conclusively prove the truth of the assertion that only dalits can write dalit literature and that this should put a full stop to all the unnecessary debate about the issue. Two, Valmiki's stories display an openness of approach and suggest a joint dalit-non-dalit struggle against casteism. The fight for social equality, he believes, can only be won through a joint struggle.

The reviewer of *Kathadesh* has called the stories a meaningful presence in dalit literature (Joshi 2003: 94). They are, he says, free from lament over dalit sufferings nor is there in them any sign of aggression in language flowing from a desire for revenge from remembered wrongs. Whatever frenzy or revenge there is woven into the fabric of the stories and not as a result of authorial intervention. The reviewer follows up these remarks with perceptive comments on all the stories, particularly on 'Salaam', 'Bail ki Khaal', 'Bhaya', 'Kahan Jaaye Satish?', 'Gohatya', 'Grahan' and 'Biram ki Bahu'. He concludes by pointing out that along with the stories Omprakash Valmiki opens up those aspects of dalit discourse that need to be deliberated upon in relation to life.

The third reviewer divides the stories into two broad categories—those that have been written with ordinary incidents and characters in mind and those in which we witness some imposition from outside (Viveki Singh: *Kasauti:* 109). Among the successful stories he includes 'Gohatya', 'Grahan', 'Biram ki Bahu', 'Pachchis Chauka Ded Sau', 'Jinawar', 'Kuchakra' and 'Amma'. Of these he considers 'Gohatya' to be the best. It is written, he says, with such tightness and with such depth that it rises to the level of poetry.

The biggest quality of the stories, says the reviewer, is that the style is very restrained. Whether it be the representation of sexual relationship or of resentment, the writer has exercised admirable control. He goes on:

> He [Valmiki] possesses great ability to depict characters and also the ability to write the right kind of dialogues, which make his stories so full of life. His characterization is not only of a high standard but is also minute. And his dialogues are so dramatic that it seems as though the character was standing right before you. I would like the readers straight to go to the stories and see these qualities for themselves.

The reviewer believes that if the dalit writers confined themselves to dalit life, it might result in a narrowing of their vision and that if they broadened their perspective, even their dalit writing would become more comprehensive. He ends by saying that the publication of this anthology shows that a new era in Hindi writing has already begun, which will bring about a qualitative change in it.

V

At the end a few words about the translation would be in order. Translating from one language to another, particularly in a different cultural zone, is always challenging. So it has been with me. Frost once said that poetry was what was lost in translation. Fortunately short stories are much less untranslatable.

While translating Valmiki's stories I was conscious of the fact that a translator had what A.K. Ramanujan calls a double loyalty—to the language in which the text was being translated as much as to the language from which it was being translated (Ramanujan 2001: 231). My aim was to use a language which while being faithful to the original would also read well in English. In *re*-presenting a text I had to represent it as closely as possible. This is what I have tried to do in the translations. It was like walking on a tight rope.

Valmiki's language is distinguished for its authenticity and its closeness to the language spoken by the characters, particularly those belonging to the unlettered section of society. This language is heavily based on its use of the local register, which gives it a distinctive local flavour. This local flavour it has not always been possible to carry across into English. But I have tried to retain some of it by not translating certain terms of address such as chaudhri, chacha, tau, bhai, bachchu, etc. Sometimes words that indicate a low level of education like 'iskool' for 'school' and 'Lachhman' for 'Lakshman' have been retained. This has been done to ensure greater authenticity. To enable those not quite familiar with these terms, a fairly exhaustive glossary has been provided.

Also, it has not been possible to provide an English equivalent to the uneducated speech of many of the characters. As a result, Sudeep's father in 'Twenty-fours are a Hundred and Fifty' and numerous other characters in the stories use more or less standard English instead of the equivalent of the language they actually use. This is one limitation that has to be accepted. But the hope is that not all is lost. Of course, it is impossible to reproduce in English the colourful language used by Hardei in 'Amma' but the translation does manage to give some idea of the liveliness and the punch in it. This applies to other stories also.

A word of explanation about the titles of the stories is necessary. The titles of two of the stories have been retained. 'Salaam' stays for it has a special meaning for dalits, that are entirely absent from a possible alternative 'Obeisance'. 'Amma' also stays because it has an intimate resonance all its own and its meaning is clear to all. So also the title of 'Shavayatra'. The last story of *Salaam,* 'Khanabadosh' deals with a dalit woman's desire for a home of her own but the English translation of the title 'Nomads', though perhaps more accurate, doesn't carry the suggestion of the need for a home. Nomads move about especially to find grass for the animals or travel with no fixed aim. The story on the other hands deals with dalits who dream of having a home of their own. Hence the title,'The Homeless'.

All translations from the stories and comments by critics are mine.

REFERENCES

Brueck, Laura R. 2006. 'Dalit Chetna in Dalit Literary Criticism', *Seminar* (558) [on Dalit Perspectives: A Symposium on the Changing Contours of Dalit Politics], February.

Faulkner, William. 1929. *The Sound and the Fury*, London, Wintage, rpt. 1995.

Hansberry, Lorraine. 1959. 'A Raisin in the Sun', in *The Norton Anthology of African American Literature*, ed. Henry Louis Gates Jr. and Nellie Y. Mckay. New York: Norton, rpt. 1997, pp. 1728-89.

Joshi, Bhalchandra. 2003. 'Salaam: Dalit Sahitya Mein Saarthak Upasthiti' [Review of *Salaam*], *Kathadesh*, February, pp. 94-5.

——. 2005. 'Dalit Sahitya mein Vichaar Sampann Pratibadhdhata' [Review of *Ghuspaithiye*], *Kathadesh*, October, pp. 90-2.

Limbale, Sharan Kumar. 2004. *Towards the Aesthetics of Dalit Literature: History, Controversies and Considerations*. Translated from Marathi by Alok Mukherjee. New Delhi: Orient Longman.

Misra, Shivkumar. 2001. 'Aadmiyat ki Sahi Manzil ka Sandhan Karti Kahaaniyan' [Review of *Salaam*], *Sakshaatkaar*, November, pp. 98-107.

Premchand. 1994. 'Thakur ka Kuan' [The Well of the Thakurs], *Premchand Rachna Sanchayan* [Selected Writings of Premchand], ed. Nirmal Verma and Kamal Kishore Goenka, New Delhi: Sahitya Akademi, rpt. 2002, pp. 222-4.

Ramanujan, A.K. 1999. 'On Translating a Tamil Poem', *The Collected Essays of A.K. Ramanujan*. Gen. Ed. Vinay Dharwadker. New Delhi: OUP, rpt. 2001, pp. 219-31.

Shaw, George Bernard, 1903, *Man and Superman*, London: Constable, 1931, rpt. 1952.

Tendulkar, Vijay, 1974. *Sakharam Binder*, in *Five Plays*, Delhi: OUP, rpt. 1992, pp. 123-98.

Tiwari, Bajrang Behari. 2006. 'Dalit Chetna ka Sakshaatkaar: Omprakash Valmiki ki Kahaaniyan', in *Kathadesh*, November, pp. 31-3.

Tripathi, Vishwanath. 2007. 'Dalit Kahaniyan' [Dalit Stories], *Pragatisheel Vasudha*, no. 73, April-June, pp. 183-9.

Valmiki, Omprakash. 1997. *Bass! Bahut ho Chuka*. [Stop it! That's Enough!]. New Delhi: Vani Prakashan.

——2000. *Salaam* [Obeisance]. New Delhi: Radhakrishna. Paperback edn. 2004.

——2003. *Joothan: A Dalit's Life*. Translated by Arun Prabha Mukherjee. Kolkata: Samya and New York: Columbia University Press. Original Hindi edition published by Raj Kamal, New Delhi, 1997.

——2003. *Ghuspaithiye* [Intruders]. New Delhi: Radhakrishna.

——2005. *Dalit Sahitya ka Saundarya Shastra* [The Aesthetics of Dalit Literature], 2001; rpt. New Delhi: Radhakrishna.

——2006. 'Five Poems.' Translated by Naresh Jain. *Chandrabhaga: A Season of Indian Writing*. New Series, no. 14.

——2006. 'Chhatri' [Umbrella], *Kathadesh*, November, pp. 34-7.

——2006.'Shavayatra' [Funeral Procession], *Summerhill*, vol. XII, no.1, pp. 30-4.

Viveki Singh. 'Nahin Phoolte Kusum Maatra . . .' [Review of *Salaam*] *Kasauti*, 9, pp. 108-13, date not known.

Yadav, Rajendra. 2007. '*Hans* ke Ikkees Saal' [Twenty-one years of *Hans*] presented by Ashok Misr, *India News* [Hindi], 4-10 August, p. 50.

Zelliot, E. 1998. 'The Roots of Dalit Consciousness', *Seminar* (471): pp. 28-32. [A Symposium on the Voices, Visions and Political Assertions of Dalits.]

INTERVIEWS

'Omprakash Valmiki se Dr Pallav ki Baatcheet' [Ompraksh Valmiki talks to Dr Pallav] Undated. Copy in manuscript form with the translator.

'Omprakash se Shivbabu Misra ki Baatcheet' [Omprakash Valmiki talks to Shivbabu Misra] Undated. Typescript with the translator.

2005. 'Brahmanvadi aur Saamanti chehron ko theek se chitrit karna hoga' [The brahminical and feudal faces will have to be depicted correctly], (Suprasidhdh Dalit Rachnakaar Omprakash Valmiki se Bajrang Bihari ki Baatcheet') [Well-known dalit writer Omprakash Valmiki in conversation with Bajrang Bihari Tiwari], *Kathadesh*, March, pp. 62-7.

1

Salaam

BY THE TIME the marriage ceremonies were over, it was two at night. Most members of the marriage party were asleep. Only a handful of them stayed with the bridegroom in the marriage mandap. In an excess of enthusiasm, Kamal Upadhyaya remained with Harish at all places. Everything was being done under his supervision as though he were a member of the family. Such was the intimacy between Harish and Kamal.

After the marriage ceremony the two started looking for a place in the verandah where they could rest their backs and stretch their legs for a while. So many people lay asleep crowded and cramped in the small verandah. There was no place left anywhere where one could lie in a relaxed manner.

Only the school verandah could be procured for the stay of the marriage party. Pradhanji had said yes to the opening of the school rooms. But at the eleventh hour, the headmaster had gone away to visit a relative of his. Even after a great deal of running about, the keys could

*'Salaam' (Hindi), first published in *Hans*, Delhi, August 1993.

not be obtained. Ultimately, the marriage party had to be put up in the verandah itself. The previous night someone had removed the handle and the valve from the hand pump. There was no other arrangement for drinking water there. Only two earthen pots could be procured with great difficulty.

As for light, there was only darkness. The faint yellow light from the street lamppost changed into darkness as it reached the verandah.

Harish took off the heavy trappings of the groom and rested his back against the wall. Making room for Kamal, he said: 'Straighten your back for a while. You must've got tired. . . . You must be finding it quite odd here.'

Kamal said while putting his socks and shoes away carefully: 'It's just a matter of spending the night here, it'll pass somehow. I'd only read about villages. I've seen one today.'

'How do you find it here?' Harish drew Kamal near.

'What's there to say! The situation is miserable. How patient are these people!' Kamal heaved a deep sigh.

Near the corner of the verandah were two elderly persons who were still awake. They were talking intermittently. On hearing Harish and Kamal talk, they turned to them. One of them said: 'Bette, Harish, this friend of yours—has he come to the village for the first time?'

'Yes, uncle.' Kamal said in reply.

'What caste?' the elderly person asked to continue the conversation.

'Tau, isn't it enough that he's my friend and has come with my marriage party?' Harish expressed his resentment.

The old man had served under an English officer. Whenever he got an opportunity, he tried to show off.

'Have I said something to insalate [insulted] you . . . that you have taken it so ill?' The old man became silent.

'Tauji, why should I mind what you say?. . . I'm a brahmin. . . . Please ask me whatever else you want to.' Kamal was polite.

'Go to sleep, Kamal . . . It'll not be long before it's morning', Harish tried to change the topic.

Kamal tried going to sleep. After remaining quiet for a while, he said: 'Harish, have you gone to sleep? . . . What will happen in the morning?'

Harish's eyes were heavy with sleep. He said drowsily: 'Morning? . . . What do you mean?'

'Harish, I'm in the habit of getting up early. I may sleep at two but I wake up sharp at five. Mother gets busy with her puja from five. Her clatter makes me get up too. This has now been going on for years. Mother hands me a cup of tea early in the morning. I'm so used to it that if I don't get tea by six, I start feeling heavy in the head.' Kamal told him about his problem.

'How will you get tea here at six . . . ?' Harish expressed his helplessness.

The old man had lighted a bidi, which shone in the darkness. He said to Kamal: 'Babuji, there is a shop outside the village. You could go and see it yourself. You might get tea there.'

'Have you seen the shop? How far is it? Kamal asked eagerly.

'It's quite near. I purchased a bundle of bidis from that shop yesterday in the evening. The street in front—go straight along. There is a road at the end of it. The shop is right there,' the old man said.

Just as it was morning, Kamal went out in search of tea. The street was almost deserted. Stray people were going about with their heads covered with cloth in an odd manner. The bustle of the night was nowhere to be seen.

The pavement, made of upright bricks, was slippery. Tiptoeing his way to avoid the water from the overflowing drains, he reached an open, sandy spot at the end of the street. Across the road was a shop with a thatched roof. On one side of it was an oven. There was a platform alongside.

A wooden stall on the platform had betel leaves, zarda, and tobacco bags. There were also two-three discoloured containers there. Dense black smoke was rising from the red-hot coals in the oven, whose pungency he felt in his lungs. On the wall hung a calendar showing a faded half-naked picture of a cinema star, which had become dirty because of dust and smoke.

A big kettle of aluminium lay near the oven, which had got blackened. There were a few dirty glasses, cups and plates, and a glass jar containing some biscuits. The round cooking utensil was black from outside and brown from inside. A swarm of flies buzzed about nearby.

A fragile old man in dirty, greasy clothes sat on his haunches on the platform smoking a bidi. The veins on his hands and feet showed up as though someone had taken flesh from the body and pasted it on to his skin and bones.

Nearby lay an old bench, whose condition seemed more miserable than that of the old man. Kamal tried to sit on the bench. It creaked. He somehow managed to sit on it and said to the old man: 'Can I get tea?'

'Sure. But it will take some taim.' The old man took a last puff of the bidi.

Kamal was watching everything in the shop with curiosity. He thought of his mother. If he had been at home at that time, his mother would have given him a hot cup of tea. While preparing tea his mother used to recite some shloka or the other.

A gust of smoke filled Kamal's face and eyes. Taking out a handkerchief he covered his face and nose with it. The bitter taste had gone deep inside him.

'How much time will it take for the tea . . . ?' Kamal asked inquisitively.

'In just a while. The oven is heating up. Please sit down,' the tea-stall owner said assuring him.

The tea maker began to mend the fire with the help of an iron rod.

'You seem to be new here, babuji. Where are you from?' the tea maker said to start a conversation.

'From Dehradun,' Kamal said with simplicity. His attention was fixed on the smouldering fire in the oven.

The mention of Dehradun startled the tea maker. 'A marriage party has also come from Dehradun,' he said as if asking a question.

'Yes, I've come with the same marriage party.'

'That baraat has come to the house of sweepers.' The tea maker's curiosity had changed into open hostility.

'So what?' asked Kamal.

The tea maker at once shut himself up. His silence made Kamal feel uncertain.

The tea maker's demeanour had changed.

Moving away from the oven, he started attending to odd jobs here and there. Sometimes, he would pick up a box and place it elsewhere, or transfer water from the earthen pot to the canister. The oven had become red-hot, flames were rising from the embers but there were no signs of tea being made anywhere.

Kamal's throat had begun to get dry. 'The oven has

flared up. Please make a cup of tea for me,' Kamal said politely.

The tea maker continued being busy doing other things as though he hadn't heard him. Kamal's patience was giving way. He said: 'Please make the tea.'

The tea maker replied from where he was standing, '*You* won't get tea here.' The tea maker's tone was dry. Sensing this Kamal asked sharply: 'But why? Just a few minutes earlier you had said yes.'

'I'd said it. And now I'm saying, you won't,' the tea maker said harshly.

Kamal was taken aback by the tea maker's behaviour. Even so he spoke politely: 'But what's happened, bhai saheb? Won't I pay you for it?'

The tea maker came and stood straight before him. With hands on hips and chest thrust out, he said: 'This money you go and show off in the city. What with the little money you have earned, you think you own the entire world. . . . This is a village, not the city. . . Sweepers-cobblers don't sure get tea here at my shop. . . . Go elsewhere for tea.'

Kamal's nerves were in a flutter. He stared at the tea maker with red-hot eyes. Hardening his voice he said: 'If sweepers-cobblers don't get it, who else does?'

The tea maker again pretended not to hear him and seemed to be busy elsewhere. To Kamal he seemed an uncivilized barbarian. Gathering courage he asked him: 'What's *your* caste?'

The tea maker flared up: 'What've you got to do with *my* caste?. . . Now even sweepers-cobblers have begun to ask for your caste. . . . It's kaliyug here, kaliyug.'

'Yes, kaliyug is here. Only for you, since you don't want to disclose your caste . . . now listen—my name is Kamal

Upadhyaya. You must be knowing the meaning of Upadhyaya, or shall I explain it you? . . . Upadhyaya means a brahmin,' Kamal said angrily.

'A baaman in the marriage party of sweepers!' The tea maker said with a harsh laugh.

'You can befool people in the city . . . I can tell the caste of a person at once just from his looks,' the tea maker boasted.

The passersby who heard the exchanges stopped to enjoy the fun. It was morning time. Soon quite a number of people collected there. The sight of people gathered around infused a new energy into the tea maker's old bones. His voice started getting more strident.

Ballu Ranghar's son Rampal too saw the crowd and stopped abruptly. He came towards the tea shop to find out what the matter was. The old tea maker was rebuking a city dweller. He at once asked, 'Chachcha, who is he?'

Just as he saw Rampal, he became more belligerent: 'He's a sweeper. He claims he's a baaman. He has come to Jumman sweeper with the marriage party. Now you people decide. If he's a baaman, why has he come in a party of the sweepers? To drink urine? He's concealing his identity to get tea. I told him plainly—at Budhu's shop no tea for the sweepers-cobblers. Go look for it elsewhere.' The old tea maker tried to garner the onlookers' sympathy.

Rampal was a 'stalk-thin wrestler'. Sunken cheeks, prominent bones, thin moustaches, hair greasy with oil. No one could guess from his entire demeanor that this man of 'one and a half bones' held sway over the whole village.

As they saw Rampal, all whispering ceased. Kamal too felt himself trapped in the chakravyuha. He looked around at the people standing there. In order to oppose them, he started speaking, 'Brothers. . . .'

But even before he could complete, Rampal rebuked him: 'O you impotent city dweller, are *we* your brothers?—Saale, mind your language, or I will push a rod up your arse and turn you upside down. Go and make an alliance with Jumman sweeper. Such an attractive girl the city people are taking with them. Arey, if the girl had been married off in some village, it'd have benefited people like us.' A derisive laughter erupted from him. To this laughter, the people standing around added theirs.

Kamal felt as though a dense solitary jungle of humiliation had sprung up round him. He started trembling to his roots. He saw the people standing nearby. Violent hunters were getting ready to attack him with their sharp talons.

For the first time, he personally experienced with intensity what he had only read about in the newspapers but what he had not been able to bring himself to believe: how at one place a dalit youth had been beaten to death, how someone had been roasted alive, houses had been set on fire. Whenever Harish read out news bits like these to Kamal, the latter would repeat only one argument: 'Harish, banish inferiority complex from your mind. The world has gone places and you people have remained stuck at the same place. See the light of the rising sun. Learn to trust yourself. If you make your own way in life through education, all hurdles will disappear automatically.'

But at this moment every word of Harish's was turning out to be true.

Kamal again plucked up courage and protested: 'Is this the traditional hospitality of the village? You are talking of a girl of your village in these terms? Isn't she a daughter of the village?'

Before Kamal could say anything further, Rampal shrieked beyond his strength: 'Go away quietly. Or else no one will go back alive . . . nor that girl neither . . . .' Rampal pushed Kamal out of the shop with the thatched roof.

Kamal didn't want to rake up trouble. He kept control of the rising temper in his chest. He thought of Harish. Realizing the delicacy of the situation, he felt it was only right to keep quiet.

From the road he came to the sandy path. Every vein of his was aflame with anger. A bunch of boys had started following him. They were trying to mock him.

'Chuhra-chuhra-chuhra. . . .' They were shouting loudly. Every word pierced his body like a knife.

Escaping from the boys Kamal turned to the street. He quickened his pace and almost ran to reach the marriage place. He was gasping for breath. And he was terribly upset.

Thousands of ants still seemed to crawl all over his body. Every pore of his body seemed to burn like lava.

Harish asked him as he saw him: 'What's the matter? You seem downcast?'

'Nothing . . . I'm all right.' Kamal breathed deeply.

'Where did you go? You've been away long. Tea has been arranged. We were just waiting for you,' said Harish.

Kamal sat resting his back against the wall. Silently. As if he were moving about alone on the narrow pathways of thought. Seeing him thus lost, Harish asked him: 'What's the matter? You seem a little distressed.'

'No, nothing . . . just a slight heaviness in the head,' said Kamal evasively.

* * *

A fifteen-year-old incident came back knocking at his consciousness. Just the memory of it caused a shiver in him.

That day Kamal had taken Harish straight home with him from school. His father had gone out of town. He had introduced Harish to his mother. Mother had given them both something to eat. Harish had hardly put a morsel in his mouth when Kamal's mother said to him: 'What does your father do, son?'

'Ji, he's a safai karamchari in the municipality,' said Harish simply.

On hearing Harish's reply, Kamal's mother just blew up. She gave her son a resounding slap on his cheeks.

'I don't know from where he catches hold of these kanjars and brings them home. Be warned. Don't you bring any such bastard home in future again. . . .' The assault on Kamal was unforeseen. Kamal had not wept, nor had he able to show any resistance. He had only stared shocked at mother's angry face.

Mother had driven Harish away after heaping abuses on him also. Mother's reprimand and rebuke had hurt Harish badly. For the first time, he had realized that Kamal and he were different. There was a gulf between the two. He recalled the words of his neighbour Sugana: 'Bette, friendship with a baaman won't suit us.' But he had not given any heed to Sugana's words. Kamal was his very own, like a close relation. In fact, much more than his own people. This incident had left several scratches on Harish's consciousness.

After Harish's departure, mother had continued grumbling. The entire house was washed again. The ground was sanctified with a sprinkling of gangajal.

There had developed a crack in his consciousness as a child. He had gone and lain down in his own room quietly. Numerous questions troubled him. Why after all did his mother behave in the way she did? In what way was Harish deficient? He hadn't eaten throughout the day. Mother had tried hard to convince him at night, told him about the propriety of things but he had continued sitting unmoved. Mother had failed in all her attempts to persuade him.

'Bete, their sanskaras are flawed, they are low people. You get bad ideas when you sit with them. . . .' Mother had told him much besides. But Kamal's experience had been entirely different.

When he started getting tired of mother's arguments, he finally asked her: 'Have you ever been to their house? Ever met them? Then how do you know they are bad?'

Mother looked at him in surprise. There was no anger in Kamal's eyes. Something there was that was melting away like ice. Something that she wanted to catch hold of but wasn't able to.

Defeated, mother had made a compromise, which always remained unknown to Harish. She had kept some utensils apart for Harish. From that time on till today Kamal seemed to be moving in a dark street where there was not a fragment of light. He always felt as though he was being false to Harish.

* * *

Finding Kamal lost in his thoughts, Harish interrupted him: 'Lost in thoughts? . . . Here is the tea. Take it!'

A village boy was holding two glasses of tea. Kamal took one of them from him. As he sipped tea, his spoilt mood started mending. After he had finished, he felt a slight relief in his headache also.

The sun had risen high overhead. There was a lot of hustle and bustle in the marriage home. Special arrangement had been made for lunch. A skilled cook had been called in from a nearby town to cook naan and meat. A stout he-goat had been slaughtered. The smell of cooked meat and hot spices filled the courtyard. Some people had starting drinking right from early morning. There was a lot of noise around. Children were creating their own racket. The elderly members were recounting their own days amid the rumble of their hookah. Women were busy differently. Harish's mother-in-law had put a new head cloth over her old dress. She was supposed to go with the bridegroom for the 'salaam' visit.

Harish's father seemed a little upset. Kamal wanted to know the cause of it but he was evasive. Something had been afoot from the morning itself. Kamal was beginning to have some inkling of it. But no one talked about it openly before him.

Harish's father-in-law Jumman was a government servant at Rishikesh. The family stayed in the village. Their lifestyle was traditional. Harish's mother-in-law did the cleaning in several households. Jumman's elder daughter lived with her father at Rishikesh in government accommodation. Following the ways of the neighbours, Jumman had sent her also to school. Soon enough she had passed her high school examination. She had also become graceful. Good environment had brought about a great change in her. She stood out from among the girls of the entire village. She was also the first girl of the village who had passed high school.

Most of the houses where Harish's mother-in-law worked were those of the Ranghars. In conformity with the traditional practice Harish had to go to the doors of these Ranghars for 'salaam' before the departure of the marriage party. This was a ceremony, which had been in force for, one doesn't know, how many centuries.

Harish's father had said 'no' straightaway—'We won't send our son for salaam.'

Several messages had been received from the Ranghar families. The community elders were giving their own arguments to explain the propriety of the practice.

'It's an ancestral practice—it can't be given up in a day. They are big people. We'll have to go for salaam. And if you have to live in water, it isn't proper to make an enemy of the crocodile. And this also serves as a pretext for getting clothes, utensils as per tradition.'

Harish too had said plainly: 'I don't need such clothes or utensils. I won't go to the doors of strangers for salaam.'

Whenever Harish saw a groom or a bride going from door to door, he felt as if his self-respect had been shattered into fragments and was being scattered around. The groom on his rounds along with the band seemed to be a meek, submissive creature. 'A son-in-law or a newly wedded wife, going from house to house for salaam is a practice, which ancestors and not we have made, which it is not proper to give up in this manner. We have to live in the village. There are numerous needs', Jumman said emphatically.

Harish said pungently: 'Think whatever you like . . . I look upon this practice to be a conspiracy to crush our self-confidence. This ceremony of salaam must be stopped.'

On hearing his voice Kamal advanced towards Harish. Seeing him approach, Harish became silent. Harish's face was taut with tension. 'What's the matter, Harish?. . . Tell me about it!' Kamal asked inquisitively.

In every activity Kamal had been a constant companion of Harish's, right from home to this place. But on this occasion he felt left out.

Harish's father placed his hand on Kamal's shoulders:

'It's nothing, bete. Please sit there. I have got a cot spread out for you in the courtyard under the neem tree. Make yourself comfortable. These are some community problems. We shall sort them out. . . .'

Kamal felt as though he was really an outsider. He looked at Harish nervously, who hinted to him with his eyes to keep mum. Kamal went and sat on the cot.

* * *

By noon the news had spread all over the village that Jumman's son-in-law has refused to come for salaam. The Ranghars of the village had started to assemble at Ballu Ranghar's chaupal. It appeared as though someone had disturbed the water of a pond with a stone. The circular waves had spread up to the banks. The Ranghars were moving about fuming.

Ballu Ranghar's 'stalk-thin wrestler' Rampal was going about haughtily with an increased show of strength after driving Kamal Upadhyaya from the tea shop. He had told his tale of bravery to the entire village. How he had caught red-handed a sweeper who was trying to get tea from a tea shop after concealing his identity. He was a baraati, so he had let him off. If some one else had ventured to do this, his bier would have been in preparation. People would listen and have their fun and also add something of their own to it. By noon the talk had spread over the entire village.

Sensing the gravity of the situation Ballu Ranghar himself came to Jumman. As he arrived, he straightaway reprimanded Jumman and his wife in front of the guests.

'Jumman, why hasn't your son-in-law come for salaam so far? If it's your daughter's marriage, we too have our rights. Whatever is traditional will have to be practiced.

Our womenfolk are sitting, waiting at home. Bring him over soon. . . .'

Taking off his headdress, Jumman placed it at Ballu Ranghar's feet: 'Chaudhriji, whatever punishment you will give me I shall bear. Kindly let the girl formally depart. The son-in-law is an educated boy. He isn't familiar with village practices.'

'That's why I say—don't send the children to school. They don't have to become a balister. Moreover, it makes them high and mighty. They fit neither here nor there. Already, you have caused the village to lose face by making your daughter pass the tenth class examination. Where was the need to educate the girl? You're spoiling the atmosphere of the village. Now your son-in-law is refusing to come for salaam . . . try to bring him round . . . he must come early for salaam,' Ballu said decisively.

Whimpering like a child Jumman implored him saying, 'Chaudhriji, kindly protect my honour . . . I am your slave . . . my living and dying, everything is with you. I shall do whatever you ask me to. Kindly permit the daughter to leave ceremonially. I rub my nose at your feet. . . .'

Ballu Ranghar went away fuming with anger. While going he said by way of warning: 'Tell these city dwellers—a crow can never become a swan.' After he had gone, Kamal asked Harish: 'Who was he? Why was he threatening in that manner?' Harish motioned him to keep quiet. All were frightened into silence. Preparations for vidai began immediately after Ballu Ranghar's departure. Jumman had instructed the women of the community: 'Finish the tika ceremony quickly, without any noise. The Ranghars could create a row anytime.'

In a moment the entire bustle of the marriage changed into stunned silence. The loudness of this silence was making Kamal Upadhyaya restless. He was feeling suffocated. He looked at Harish. The light of the rising sun of self-confidence and pride was shining in Harish's eyes. Each pressed the hand of the other enthusiastically. Each beamed assurance to the other through his eyes. Tender green leaves were swaying in the breeze, as though they were offering encouragement.

The marriage party was fed quickly. Kamal and Harish after taking their meals sat down on the cot under the shade of the neem. A ten-year-old boy was standing facing the wall. His face showed signs of anger.

An old man came to the courtyard looking for him. He had a naan and meat in his hand.

'Deepu, O Deepu . . . where's he? This boy is very troublesome. Born in the house of sweepers, he is trying to speak like a baaman.' Finding him standing near the wall, he rebuked him: 'You're hiding here . . . I've long been looking for you. Come eat this roti . . . just see how good the meat is,' the old man tried to persuade him.

'No . . . I won't . . . my urine will eat it.' The boy said haughtily.

'But why? . . . what's wrong with it? The old man asked sharply.

'I won't eat the roti made by a Musalman,' said the boy retreating.

'Musalman? . . . which Musalman?'

'The gara who is sitting making rotis there.' The boy pointed to the cook who was making rotis.

'That one . . . he is a Hindu . . . go and see for yourself.' The old man started dragging the reluctant boy who was trying to hang back. He was shouting: 'no . . . he's is a Musalman. I won't eat the roti made by him . . . I won't.'

'Abe, you tail of an owl! Have a look at least once.

Then speak.' The old man dragged him to the oven where naans were being baked. The sound of the boy's shrieks continued to be heard.

'No . . . no, I won't eat the rotis made by a Musalman . . . I won't . . . I won't.'

Kamal and Harish stared at the boy aghast. The self-confidence that had been born just a while earlier seemed to get muted under the shouts of the boy. They both got lost in the thick jungle of silence. They looked at each other and breathed a deep sigh.

2

The Hide of an Ox

THE MORNING had advanced into midday, yet there was no trace of either Kale or Bhoore. A search for them was on everywhere. An ox which belonged to Pandit Birij Mohan had died on the pathway near the well in the centre of the village. Hardly had Pandit Birij Mohan's ploughman set off for the fields with his oxen and plough, very early in the morning when he urged the oxen by clacking his tongue. The ground near the well was slippery. One of the oxen slipped and fell down. The ploughman tried hard to make it stand up. The ox was old and weak. It had been hurt near the ribs and it died.

Pandit Birij Mohan came running as soon as the news reached him. The death of an ox at the time of ploughing of fields was no less than a disaster. It was as if a lightning had struck the Pandit.

It was necessary to remove the ox from near the well. A search for Kale and Bhoore started. These two were the

*'Bail ki Khaal' (Hindi), first published in *Hans*, Delhi, December 1992.

only people in the entire village who could take the carcass of the dead ox outside.

As long as the ox was alive, there was no problem. The ox that had helped to grow food till yesterday suddenly became impure on dying. Let alone touch it, even standing near it was no less than a sin.

The sun had climbed up high in the sky. Flies had started to buzz about the carcass of the ox lying near the well.

No one knew where Kale and Bhoore had gone. Pandit Birij Mohan himself had been to their house as many as three times. Every time the answer was the same—they have gone somewhere. They had suddenly become important for the entire village.

As it became hotter, the dead ox lying near the well started giving out a foul smell. There was despair-filled tension in the village. Everyone was cursing Kale and Bhoore. There was no place in the village where they were not looked for. Where had they gone after all?

The village had come to realize their importance. Whenever anyone lost his cattle, it was their responsibility to carry it outside. For this they received neither any money nor grains. This work their ancestors had been doing for the last several generations without desire for any gain. They would skin the dead animal and take it to the city. The cleaning and dyeing of hides was a fairly big business in the city. Many well-known businessmen were engaged in it. Kale and Bhoore lived by whatever the hide brought them.

The village elders were very worried about the dead ox. What would happen if the carcass kept lying there till the evening? No one had drawn drinking water from the well since the morning.

The midday sun had started declining. The shadows had started lengthening. Hope appeared bright in Birij Mohan's eyes dispelling despair. From the street opposite were coming Kale and Bhoore. Their faces looked dull and their eyes thrust deep inside their sockets. The palms of their hardened hands were broad and fleshless. For this reason the veins of their hands stood out prominently. Both of them had tied round themselves part of a white soiled dhoti that came up to their knees. Instead of a shirt, they wore an old greasy bandi-like vest full of holes. Every part of their body reflected their poverty. They went straight to the ox. Bhoore had a longish stout bamboo pole in his hand.

'Where were you, you bastards? We've worn our knees out looking for you. . . . You're coming now like a maharaja . . . who will remove the ox . . . your father?' Pandit Birij Mohan was furious.

Without replying Kale took the thick rope from his shoulder and placing the front legs of the ox together started tying them. The legs of the ox had become stiff. He had to apply extra pressure to put them side by side. After tying the legs fast, he tossed the other end of the rope to Bhoore. Bhoore tied the hind legs together. He motioned Kale to pick up the bamboo pole.

The entire village watched their workmanship. In no time they stuck the pole through the tied legs of the ox and lifting it like a palki started carrying their burden with a slow rolling gait.

The villagers heaved a sigh of relief.

In the south-west end of the village was a small seasonal watercourse that remained dry throughout the year except during the rains. They dumped the ox in that watercourse. They were quite exhausted. They rested for a spell. Kale took out the last remaining bidi from his pocket. They then smoked it together. Four or five dogs had also followed them from the village, which were hovering near the ox. Bhoore was watching the dogs very intently lest they should bite the ox. Kale untied the rope from the legs of the ox.

Bhoore's son had come with knives and daggers. Taking them from chhutku, Bhoore said to him: 'Go back home, chhutku. We shall go straight to the city from here. We'll be late coming back. We shall get the household stuff also from there.'

Kale took the dagger from Bhoore and ran his finger over the sharp edge to test it. The edge wasn't sharp enough yet. He began sharpening it on a stone lying there.

Beginning from the mouth of the ox, Bhoore gave a long cut down to the stomach and the back. They were skilled in the art of peeling the skin of dead animals. Whatever be the animal involved, they were able to peel its skin off like a banana. The skin was removed with such expertise that it did not suffer the slightest damage. Even the slightest cut anywhere meant reduced payment. This art they had learned from their father.

Both applied themselves to the task in hand. The heat of the sun remained unabated. Every pore of the body had become soaked with sweat. Hardly had half of the skin been taken off when a group of vultures began descending from the sky. In no time several groups of vultures began to hover over them. Sometimes they would drive the dogs away, at other times they would shoo the vultures off, or several vultures would all at once swoop, down upon the ox. The dogs too lay in wait for their chance. They were also helpful in keeping the vultures at bay. When a dog attacked a vulture, the vulture running away on its paws made a queer sound.

The peeling off of the skin took a lot of time. Evening was still far away. Taking the freshly peeled off skin they moved a little away from the ox. As they did so, the vultures fell upon the ox. The sounds produced by the vultures made the entire atmosphere frightful. The vultures still continued to come down from the skies.

They turned the moist skin upside down and spread it on the ground in the watercourse in order that the blood sticking to it might dry up.

They were now very tired. They even didn't have any bidi which they could smoke. These days they lived in straitened circumstances. Rolling up the skin they wrapped it in an old torn chadar and tied it into a bundle. Kale picked up the bundle and placed it on Bhoore's head. They started moving towards the main road. There was a small bridge where the watercourse intersected the main road. They came to the bridge along the watercourse. The wetness of the skin in the bundle on Bhoore's head seeped down.

Bhoore put the bundle down on the bridge. They began waiting for a conveyance to reach the city. Noticing that they carried an animal skin, no one would permit them to board a bus. The bus passengers with cloth on their noses would shout them away. Only an empty truck or a tonga would take them to the city.

The evening was now drawing nearer. They saw a truck coming in the distance. From the bridge they came on to the road. The truck was coming towards them at a great speed. They gestured to the truck to stop. The truck continued going ahead belching a lot of smoke. Bhoore waving the smoke away from near his mouth with both hands uttered a filthy abuse, which remained unheard in the roar of the truck.

They again sat down at the bridge. The distant sound of the tinkle of the bells worn by cows was drawing near. The cows were returning to their village. This cattle wealth of Lallu the cowherd was the largest. The villagers felt relieved after they had entrusted their cattle to Lallu. He took particular care while the cattle crossed the road. The traffic on the road had become heavier. There was always a danger of some accident happening.

The bells round the neck of cows and the rising dust deepened the dusk of the evening. The worries of Kale and Bhoore sitting at the bridge were also deepening like the dusk. They wanted to reach the city quickly so that they could sell off the skin and purchase household things. It was several days since the hearth had been properly lighted. They were dragging on somehow. It was after two months that this old ox had died, which had rescued their drowning hopes for a time.

Kale seeing the herd crossing the road said: 'What times are these! Cattle also don't die.'

'Ever since the animal doctor came to the village, the sohra has taken away our livelihood.'

The arrival of the veterinary doctor in the village meant almost total ruin of their profession. They were often forced to go without meals. Even otherwise the village baniya did not give them things on credit. Who could they ask for grains? In the eyes of the village they were the most useless creatures, those who peeled away the skin from dead animals.

Sitting at the bridge they were lost in their thoughts. Kale wasn't able to understand many things. The more he tried to make sense of them, the more confusing they became.

'We should give up this work, Bhoore.'

'Why . . . if we give it up, who will do this work? Will the dead animals keep rotting in the village?'

'Let them rot. This foul smell drowns us neck-deep. Who cares! No one even lets us sit near them.'

Kale again said after some time: 'And that Lala of the city. He says all kinds of things. Last time when we had gone to him with the skin of the buffalo, remember what he was saying?: "Take this small packet. Give it to any cattle and it will surely die. That government doctor also won't be able to do anything." A devil that Lala, a very devil.'

Two or three trucks had gone by without stopping. As evening drew nearer, their worries were increasing. They had to go to the city and also get back. Kale was quite irritated. Fixing his eyes on the long road, he said: 'Come, Bhoore, let's go somewhere else. I hear there are big factories in Delhi, Ghaziabad. We should be able to get a job somewhere. . . . You saw Mamchand's son Salek, didn't you, when he came last time. Here he used to go about stark naked. And now . . . now he's started to wear coat and pant—keeps English-cut hair . . . wears a wrist watch—what did he call the watch—"Hemtee. Otmat"—it moves on its own, day and night . . . doesn't make any sound either.'

To Bhoore Kale's words sounded as if he were hearing someone speak miles away. His thoughts were centred round those village children who went to school with their bags, screaming with delight. Innumerable times standing near the school, he had seen small children memorizing multiplication tables. He imagined that some day his own chhutku would also stand amid those children learning multiplication tables. He had even talked with the schoolteacher. He just had to earn a little more money and he would send his chhutku to the school this year. He didn't even have adequate clothes to go to school.

They had been sitting at the bridge for long now. They hadn't yet got any conveyance that would take them to the city. Whichever vehicle they tried to stop would just speed away. As the shades of the night got deeper, their boredom also increased. An ox had died after so many days. If they didn't reach the city in time, the skin could even start to rot. They would lose whatever little money was to come to them. Their worry was getting deeper than the darkness around them.

From the distant fields came the sound of a she-calf lowing. It had perhaps fallen behind in Lallu's herd. Now fully alert the she-calf came running. It came to the main road running at the same speed, without stopping. In the twinking of the eye it collided with a speeding truck and fell down. . . . The sudden application of brakes made the truck also wobble. It barely escaped turning over. Both of them also let out a scream suddenly.

The truck stopped after travelling some distance. Bhoore ran towards the truck hurling abuses at the driver. The driver sensed the danger and pressing the accelerator increased the speed of the truck. Bhoore gave an earful of abuses to the truck driver. Quickly picking up a large clod of earth from the side of the road he aimed it at the truck. But the truck had sped away. The large clod fell on the hard road and scattered into several pieces.

The she-calf was lying on the roadside writhing in

agony. Its head had fallen to one side. Kale caressed the back of the calf. While caressing its soft smooth back, Kale felt as though it were not a she-calf but a child who was in agony. Kale looked at Bhoore. The latter was still standing at some distance abusing.

Kale called out to Bhoore: 'Bring a little water, Bhoore, if you can find it. Hurry up. See how it is suffering.'

Bhoore started running about here and there in search of water. He went far on the dry watercourse. Some two or three dogs were still gnawing at the remaining bones of the ox. As they saw him coming nearer, they started growling at him. He avoided them by climbing from the watercourse to the field. The fields were also dry. There was no trace of water anywhere.

Seeing the she-calf suffer Kale was not able to decide what he should do. Suddenly he thought of the doctor and he called out to Bhoore: 'Come quickly, Bhoore. . .We've to fetch the doctor. The she-calf's been very badly hurt. . . .'

Bhoore came back empty-handed. He was soaked in sweat. The running about had made him gasp for breath. Breathing heavily he said: 'There is no water anywhere.'

Kale was caressing the back of the she-calf as though he were putting new courage into it. The blood from the she-calf's mouth had started seeping into the ground. In the dark the colour of the blood seemed to be darker. 'What will the doctor do now, Kale? . . . See, how much blood has flowed out.'

'Don't try to show your cleverness, Bhoore . . . You stay here . . . I shall go to fetch the doctor.' There was urgency in his voice.

Kale got up to go to the village. The village was at a distance of a kos from there. The darkness had spread and had turned into a black dense enveloping mantle. Only a few lights could be discerned. Kale started with quick steps. He had hardly gone ten-fifteen steps when he heard Bhoore call out to him: 'Come back quickly, Kale.'

Kale hurried back.

'What's happened?' Kale asked on return.

'Just see . . . he isn't moving,' Bhoore said with trepidation.

The body of the she-calf had become stiff and still. There was no movement anywhere. They were looking at each other quietly. Silence pervaded between them.

Kale broke the silence. He got up.

'Stay here, Bhoore. I shall go and come back after giving the news in the village.' There was disappointment in his voice.

The sudden death of the she-calf in this manner had caused them a great deal of distress.

Kale cast a glance at the bundle of the skin of the ox on the bridge. The skin tied in the chadar had begun to give out a foul smell. He breathed heavily and set off for the village—to give them the news of the death of the she-calf.

3

Fear

THEY HAD been wandering about from morning into noon. They had searched through several bastis of the city but they hadn't yet succeeded. Finally, exhausted, they reached a basti on the Sahastradhara Road. Situated on the bank of a stream, it was a basti of some ten-twelve families. Quite isolated. It might have been a river once but now it was only a rainwater stream. On its level banks, bricks and stones had been piled up to erect walls. Old soiled tin sheets on these ramshackle walls gave the semblance of a house.

Kalu's house was on the right just after entering the basti. He had occupied comparatively more space. He had also erected a pigsty in the courtyard. There was a wide-mouthed deep pit in the ground, in which some eight-ten pigs pushing one another out of the way, swooped on food, making audible sounds. A piglet was trying to reach the pit from under a big fat pig. The fat pig hitting him with his snout pushed him away. The squealing piglet began to move round Kalu. Kalu got

*'Bhaya' (Hindi), first published in *Hans*, Delhi, October 1994.

vexed at the misdemeanour of the fat pig. He hit the pig on its back with a bamboo stick uttering a foul abuse.

Both of them came and stopped outside Kalu's courtyard. They parked the scooter outside. Seeing fat rounded piglets move about amidst pigs, their eyes brightened. Just as they entered the courtyard, Dinesh said to Kalu: 'We need a piglet.'

Kalu, looking them up from top to toe, said: 'Take whichever you like.'

'Your charges?' Dinesh asked the price.

'Has it to be offered in puja?' Kalu wanted to know.

'Yes, we need it for Mai Madaran's puja,' replied Kishore who had come with Dinesh.

'Right . . . four hundred rupees. One price,' Kalu said bluntly.

As soon as Dinesh heard the price, he was non-plussed: 'This is too much. . . .' Ignoring Dinesh's words, Kalu got busy in getting the pigs away from the pit. The piglets had rushed to the left-over food.

Both Dinesh and Kishore became downcast. They just stared at each other blankly.

After wandering about all day, they had reached the conclusion that their demeanour and the way they talked jacked up the rate. They had burnt a lot of petrol in moving from one basti to another. Even then they hadn't succeeded anywhere. Someone on the D.L. Road had told them that Kalu had four-five piglets.

'Charge a reasonable price. . . .This will not yield even five kilos of meat,' said Dinesh by way of haggling.

'If you need only five kilos of meat, there are plenty of shops in the market . . . you could buy from there. It will work out to be cheaper,' Kalu said glaring at them.

On finding them bargaining, Kalu's wife also came out. Kalu's tone had slightly offended Kishore: 'If we had to purchase from the market, why would we have come here?'

'Bhaiji, be reasonable,' Dinesh made another attempt.

'Four hundred is what I will charge. You may ask once or ten times . . . ,' said Kalu emphatically.

Dinesh stared at Kishore. The question—What do we do now?—seemed to be pasted on their faces. Kishore too felt that four hundred rupees was excessive.

Kishore whispered: 'I think let's take it.' Dinesh made one last attempt: 'Reduce the price somewhat . . . we've come from far. You should give some concession because of caste brotherhood.'

Ignoring the request, Kalu said to his wife: 'Put my cycle outside. They won't buy it. I guessed the moment I saw them. They are wasting their time as well as mine. They are pant-shirt wearing babus. They have come here because they are in dire straits. Or else they wouldn't come to these bastis even to piss. After studying, they are now intent on getting to be baamans. But these 'in-laws' can't even be baamans. If you agree to four hundred, fine . . . or go, look for it somewhere else.'

Every word of his got stuck in Dinesh's throat like a bitter pill. On some other occasion, he would perhaps have retaliated also. But, restraining himself, he said: 'All right . . . here are four hundred rupees . . . catch the piglet for us. . . .'

Dinesh handed the money to Kalu. Four notes of a hundred each—he counted them several times. He examined them carefully holding each against the sunlight. He also turned them over. Putting the money in his pocket, he said: 'Catch hold of it . . . the one that is moving about with its tail raised.'

Dinesh, hesitating, said politely: 'Bhaiji, this piglet we have to offer it at Mai Madaran's puja . . . we live in a colony . . . we can't kill it or roast it or cut it there . . . please do all this here.'

Kalu's eyes, becoming rounded, bulged out of his rough hard face: 'The charges agreed to are for a live piglet. Killing is not included. Even so, if you have some problems, I shall charge fifty rupees extra for killing it.'

Dinesh asked in surprise, 'Fifty more?'

'Then do it at home . . . I don't have so much taim [time]; it's not easy taking someone's life. Fifty is too little. You belong to our community . . . if some bania-baaman had come, my rates would have been different,' said Kalu harshly.

Kishore had been standing quiet for quite sometime. He was finding Kalu's ways very provocative. He asked him: 'Do bania-baamans also come to purchase . . . ?' Kalu offered no reply. He just glared at him obliquely.

'All right . . . we shall pay fifty more. . . . Please catch and prepare it quickly . . . ,' Dinesh said helplessly.

'You people sit down . . . I will be back in ten minutes. I have to go to the Rinspana Bridge . . . I have some urgent work. I've given time to someone.' Kalu took his cycle and went out of the courtyard. They just stood agape. He had gone away without giving them any opportunity to say something.

Kalu had been gone half an hour or three quarters of an hour. There was still no clue as to his whereabouts. They had become bored waiting. Dinesh, calling out to Kalu's wife, said: 'Where has he gone? We are getting late.'

'What can I say? . . . just wait a little longer,' she replied from inside. Once or twice, she came out too. But she went in without saying anything.

Every moment was becoming burdensome. They had so much to do at home. Preparation for the puja too had to be made. In any case it would be evening by the time they reached home.

On finding them sitting there, the children and the elders of the basti had gathered together in the courtyard. All gazed at them with strange eyes. An almost suspicious atmosphere had started building up. Dinesh was getting even more restless than Kishore. He was feeling uneasy in this atmosphere.

More than an hour had passed while waiting. Dinesh was getting upset. With his voice full of sarcasm, Dinesh said for the benefit of Kalu's wife: 'Where has he gone? How long shall we wait here? We have even handed him the money.'

'Now I don't know . . . where he's gone. That's how he is . . . one doesn't know when he'll be back . . . you catch that piglet and take it with you. . . .' Kalu's wife replied in her normal manner.

Dinesh and Kishore gazed at each other blankly. They were not able to decide what they should do and what they shouldn't. They couldn't kill the piglet in the colony. Because then they would have to do the roasting also, which it was not possible at all to do in the colony flats. If people saw it, it would be a spectacle for them. Whoever didn't know earlier would also come to know. Several times Dinesh had been a witness to the hatred that existed between people in the name of caste. If people treated him also in the same way—the very thought of it made him shiver.

He asked Kalu's wife: 'Is there anyone else who could dress it?

'No, there is no one here . . . only he does it . . . no one else knows.' Kalu's wife gave a straight 'no' for an answer.

Dinesh's temples began to get hot. Again and again he felt annoyed with his mother. What a mess to have fallen into? He had tried to convince her: 'If, mother, you have to do puja, do it with flowers and halwa-puree . . .' but she refused. She kept on repeating the same thing: 'While he was alive, he didn't permit us to worship Mai Madaran, but at the time of marriage my father had said plainly that Mai Madaran was worshipped in their home, a practice which she would continue. "You would have to worship Mai Madaran there." Your father hadn't said anything that day. But later on, he changed. Can one give up one's gods and goddesses, Dinu bette? Is there any future for a tree that is cut off from its roots. And then, we must do puja in our own way. What is there to be ashamed of in this?'

From the time the maternal uncle had tutored mother, she had started talking in the same vein. Dinesh had never taken part in a puja of this kind. He had certainly seen it once or twice in his maternal grandfather's place. Father's acquaintances were confined only to the factory. Relatives meant only the maternal kins. Dinesh had inherited the same sanskaras that his father had.

He had spoken of it in subdued tones to his maternal uncle also: 'All this, mamaji, cannot be done in the colony. We have to live with others. If someone notices it, what will he say? A mohalla or a basti is quite another matter. There everyone belongs to the same community.'

The maternal uncle had said, boiling with rage: 'With all your education you still remain as foolish as ever. Does it make sense that we change our ways of worshipping just because others don't like them . . . ?' The maternal uncle had caused panic by telling tales of Mai Madaran's fury. Mother had got frightened. Something untoward might happen.

When they were leaving home, the maternal uncle had given special instructions to them about choosing the piglet carefully. It shouldn't be castrated and there should be no cuts or tears on the ears and the tail.

Kishore, finding Dinesh lost in his thoughts, interrupted him: 'Lost in your thoughts? . . . let's start. We'll catch and kill the piglet ourselves. After roasting it, we will do the cutting and slicing.'

'I've never done a thing of this kind,' Dinesh expressed his inability.

'What is there in the killing? My father kills with just one stroke. The dagger has only to be thrust into the chest,' Kishore said simply.

'But I have never done all this before,' Dinesh said with hesitation.

'Nor have . . . I have surely seen father doing it. Only *you* have to do it. Because the puja has to be done by you,' Kishore argued.

After a great deal of argumentation, Dinesh outwardly agreed, though his inner self was not ready for it. He felt as though he was about to commit a sin.

With the help of Kalu's wife, they tried to isolate the piglet from the bunch of pigs. It was proving difficult to get hold of it. Several times it jerked its way back into the knot of pigs. The mother pig growled on seeing Dinesh and Kishore. This frightened both of them. For the crowd of on-lookers, they had become a spectacle. The children and the old people were beginning to laugh at their actions.

Once or twice Dinesh tried to catch hold of the piglet. The piglet, wriggling out, ran away. Mother pig snapped at Dinesh. He barely escaped falling down. This made even Kalu's wife laugh. Suppressing her laughter, she said: 'It is beyond you, this work. . . . You only know how to push a pen in office . . . see, you can't even catch hold of a piglet. . . .'

Hearing this, Dinesh got irritated. Both Dinesh and Kishore were sweating profusely. Kalu's wife suggested: 'Catch the piglet by its legs, not by its waist. Just pick it up and rush into the door in front. I shall shut the door and bolt it.'

Dinesh somehow managed to isolate the piglet from the other pigs. Just as it got separated, Kishore held it by its hind legs and picking it up, rushed into the room. Dinesh too ran behind. Kalu's wife at once pushed up the bolt. All this work was done in the twinkling of an eye.

At the squealing of the piglet, the mother pig, looking fierce, made a sudden attack; it continually struck against the door. It seemed as though the door would break. The other pigs too had started squealing together. The atmosphere was frightful. Dinesh was truly frightened out of his wits.

Kalu's wife, beating them soundly with a stick, shut up all the pigs in the pigsty. They were still squealing. From inside the house came a choking sound from the throat of the piglet. Kishore sat pressing it with his knees. Kalu's wife came near them after lowering the bolt. As he saw her, he asked for a knife. She brought a big knife used for fruit. As soon as he took it, Dinesh's heart began to sink. He was passing through mental torture.

'Before killing it, apply turmeric on its ears and invoking Mai Madaran's name, sprinkle water,' Kishore said applying the right pressure on the piglet.

Kalu's wife brought turmeric. Applying it to the ears of the piglet, Dinesh recited Mai Madaran's name.

Shutting his eyes, he thrust the knife into the piglet with all his force. At that moment savagery had descended upon Dinesh's face and eyes. His eyes had become red in colour. Just as the knife struck, the whole house shook with the shrieks of the piglet. The walls smeared black with soot also shook with fear. Dinesh had struck the knife with such ferocity that it had gone right through the piglet. A stream of warm blood had gushed out. The blood was collected in another vessel.

The piglet squirmed and fell silent. Dinesh had not yet recovered his normal self. His eyes were still riveted on the lifeless form of the piglet.

Kishore pushed the vessel full of blood to one side. The other problem was of roasting. Without being roasted in fire, it was not possible to cut and slice it. They looked at Kalu'a wife with questioning eyes. She simply said: 'There is a lichi orchard in front. Bring in dry leaves from there.'

Kishore said to the children wearing dirty clothes standing around: 'Bring in dry leaves. I shall give you five rupees.' On hearing about the money, the vaanar sena gathered together a pile of dry leaves in no time.

After lighting the fire, they started roasting the piglet. The smell of burning flesh spread all around. They were roasting the piglet turning it over in the leaping flames. After roasting it well, they took it to the tap outside to wash it. After rubbing and washing it thoroughly, they sat down in the courtyard to cut it up. This was a new experience for Dinesh. Kishore was busy cutting it up in his unskilled way. Kalu's wife helped them eagerly.

After cutting it up quickly, they put the whole thing in

a sack. They put the sack on the scooter and started for the colony.

The entire process had exhausted them completely. Apart from the marks of ashes and soil, their hands and feet had got covered with blood stains.

It wasn't long before the dim light of dusk would descend. The redness of the sun was beginning to spread on the horizon.

Dinesh had been very vigilant before stopping the scooter. He was extremely alert. Just as the scooter stopped, Kishore went in with the sack hastily. At that time there was no one outside the flat. On the road were some children absorbed in their play. Even so, Dinesh was terrified as though he had brought in stolen goods.

Dinesh closed the door as soon as he came in. He feared lest someone should drop in right at that time. If someone came, it would cause serious complications. It would be difficult to conceal all this paraphernalia.

Mother began preparations for the puja. Kishore and the maternal uncle were busy cutting the meat into small pieces.

Dinesh's entire attention was fixed on the outer door. The slightest sound of footsteps alarmed him. He had told everybody that no matter who came, the door was not to be opened. The biggest cause for worry was Ramprasad Tiwari. He was a frequent visitor. Sometimes he would even have his meals with them. On the days when he stopped to have his meals, mother would avoid using garlic in vegetable preparations. Meat was cooked only occasionally. That too on those days when it was known that Tiwari would not come, or that he had gone somewhere else. In all these years Ramprasad Tiwari had not come to discover that these people were S.Cs. Many times Ramprasad had employed abusive language in protest against reservations. Besides, he had used foul language for Baba Saheb and Bapu. At such moments Dinesh either kept mum or tried to change the subject. Even otherwise Dinesh tried to avoid such issues.

In spite of all this, there was a great deal of intimacy between the two. Dinesh also knew that the day the caste factor came between them, their intimacy would prove to be a bubble of water.

His greatest anxiety also related to Ramprasad Tiwari. If he came, how could he be put off? He didn't even wait for the door to open. He would walk straight in. He didn't feel easy unless he had scoured every corner of the house. So, Dinesh's worries were increasing. He felt as though he had fallen into a trap of his own making.

He had put off the children of the neighbourhood on some pretext. But it was not so easy to send Ramprasad Tiwari away.

Every moment was no less than a torment for Dinesh. His mental restlessness was changing into a state of depression.

As the preparations for the puja went on, his heartbeats also increased. Mother had placed the earthen lamp after lighting it in a room near the wall. The puja things were also set there nicely. Cinders of cow dung cakes were also arranged in front of the earthen lamp. On instructions from the maternal uncle, Dinesh ceremonially poured ghee into the cinders. In a short while, the 'jot' on the cinders flared up. Mother, covering her head with her anchal, bowed low. She received Mai's blessings, made a ceremonial offering of batashas, cooked meat, baked animal liver, and small pieces of roti. A strange smell of ghee filled the entire house. The puja was about to end when the bell rang. Along with the bell, Dinesh's heart beat faster. He felt as though there was an earthquake. He looked at his mother with fear and surprise.

Mother said: 'Go and see who is it?'

'Who else . . . but the same Tiwari,' said Dinesh, in a depressed tone. 'Just send him away from outside . . . tell him I am not in. If he comes in, it will be disastrous . . . ,' he said laying stress on every single word. He felt as though his heart was sinking.

Mother opened the door a little. It was of course Ramprasad Tiwari, standing there. Betel juice leaked from his right lips. Mother mechanically replied through the half-opened door. 'Dinesh has gone somewhere. He'll return late.'

'Where has he gone. . . ?' asked Tiwari.

'He didn't tell us where . . .,' mother tried to put him off.

'Where has he been since morning? During the day, I saw him coming out of the malin basti on the Sahastradhara Road. There was also a sack on his scooter. I hailed him too. But he didn't stop,' Tiwari said with astonishment.

Mother remained silent. In stead of prolonging the conversation, she tried to put him off. Finding her silent, he said: 'O.K. give me a glass of water, then I shall leave. . . .'

'Hold on . . . I will get it.' Mother turned towards the kitchen in haste.

Dinesh was listening to the entire exchange from the puja room. Every word of Tiwari's was making its way into his heart like an arrow.

After drinking the water and returning the glass, Tiwari said: 'There is a strange smell around . . .'

Mother kept mum. 'Right, I shall leave . . .' he went out quickly. Mother, shutting the door, heaved a big sigh.

Tiwari was gone but he had left a dense silence behind him.

Dinesh felt as though someone had drawn out all his blood from his body. He became restless. Tiwari had seen him coming out of the basti on the Sahastradhara Road! This realization troubled him deeply.

Everyone had gone to sleep after taking their food. But he was awake with deep dejection. After Tiwari had gone away, his mind was filled with sadness. His confusion increased. He felt as though every moment someone was piercing him with sharp thorns.

His eyes were heavy with sleep and exhaustion. But still he was not able to sleep. There was turmoil in him. What will happen when he meets Tiwari tomorrow!

He tried to sleep. He had hardly closed his eyes when he woke up in agitation. He fancied that he saw the mother pig with her red eyes and long teeth standing before him. Behind her was Tiwari coming towards him with a knife in his hand. Tiwari's eyes were filled with hatred combined with scorn. Out of fright he switched on the light. His ears could hear the squealing of the piglet.

Nearby his maternal uncle and Kishore slept in deep sleep. He tried to control himself a bit.

He broke into profuse sweating. His throat began to go dry. He tried to drink water from the kitchen. He felt as though the whole kitchen was full of the odour of the burning skin of the piglet. He came back without taking water. Lying down in his bed, he tried to sleep.

Just as he closed his eyes, the images of the mother pig and Tiwari again swam before his eyes. Mother was asleep in the other room. She also got up because of the light. She called out: 'You haven't yet gone to sleep, Deenu! You have to go to work tomorrow.'

The sound of the mother's voice fell into Dinesh's ears

as though it were coming from miles away.

Dinesh's eyes became misty. He felt as though the mother pig was about to pounce upon him and that Tiwari was advancing towards him fiercely with the knife in his hand. Terribly scared, he called out to his mother.

His call became a scream, which awakened everybody. Mother also got up in alarm. She ran to him: 'What's happened, Deenu?'

Dinesh's eyes were red, burning like cinders. His body was trembling. His face looked terror-stricken. Mother tried to touch his forehead. Dinesh jerked her hand away.

He screamed: 'There . . . look. She is there . . . just look . . . Tiwari is there too . . . he's come to know . . . he'll tell them all . . . all . . .' he was shrieking.

His condition made his mother also scream. Dinesh got up and ran towards the door. Kishore and the maternal uncle tried to catch hold of him. But he rushed out with such speed that they couldn't stop him.

Opening the door, he came out on the road. He began to run fast. The maternal uncle and Kishore were also running behind. The lights of the flats nearby had been switched on.

Dinesh was running unconscious of where he was going. The growl of the mother pig and the cruel laughter of Tiwari were chasing him. An unknown fear had settled in every vein of his body. He kept running. His shriek was lost in the silence of the night.

The maternal uncle and Kishore were trailing far behind. The yellow weak lights on the road, becoming saddened, were making an effort to combat darkness.

4

Where Can Satish Go?

THOSE WERE the shivering cold days of December. Sunlight delicately seemed to play hide-and-seek. The cold wind getting past several layers of clothing pricked the skin like thorns.

Mrs. Pant after having attended to small household chores was reclining on the bed covered with a quilt, knitting a sweater for her daughter.

Solitude intensifies the cold. The daughter was about to come home. Sonu always demands food as soon as she comes. She doesn't wait even for a second. So she has prepared chapattis and vegetables for her and kept them in the kitchen.

Someone knocked at the door violently. It seemed as if the doors would break open and fall down. The rattling of the doors was continuously increasing. Mrs. Pant got up in irritation. Sonu never ever knocks in this fashion. Sonu's father and the tenant Satish also do not beat at the door like this. Even otherwise Sonu's father never comes

*'Kahan jaaye Satish?' (Hindi), first published in *Lokmat Samachaar*, Diwali issue, Nagpur, 1993.

home before six and Satish is home by four and a half. Who, then, could it be? It was in this state of perplexity that Mrs. Pant opened the door.

A stranger couple, man and wife, stood at the door—both old, worn out, and shabbily dressed. The woman's face beaten down by time looked dried up and lustreless. From the face of the man one could tell that he had come straight after a long illness.

Mrs. Pant, her face flushed with anger, said: 'What's it?' Mrs. Pant's demeanour disconcerted them both, as though they had been caught red-handed while committing a crime. Signs of distress could clearly be discerned on their faces.

Finding them standing mute in this manner made Mrs. Pant even angrier.

'Who are you? What do you want . . . ?'

The man vainly tried to muster courage: 'Namasteji. . . .'

Both of his lifeless hands automatically came together. Without replying to his namaste, Mrs. Pant thundered:

'What's the matter? Why were you beating at the door like brutes?' The man trying to muster courage again swallowed a lot of spittle: 'Is there a boy named Satish living with you here?' He also tried to give an indication of his height with his hands.

Mrs. Pant was startled on hearing the name of Satish: Why were they looking for Satish? she reflected.

'Yes . . . he lives here. But what work do you have with him?' Mrs. Pant asked out of curiosity.

'Ji . . . ji . . . he . . .' The man just stammered. The woman standing nearby took the thread of conversation into her own hands: 'What work, bhainji? It is six months since we have seen him. Pl ease just call him.' Signs of timidity could clearly be seen in her eyes.

'At the moment he isn't here. He's gone to school. He

will be back by evening . . . but who are you?' Their clothes and their entire appearance threw Mrs. Pant's inner self into confusion.

The man tried to speak: 'Ji . . . he . . .' The woman nudging him on the elbow asked him to be quiet: 'Bhainji, what shall we say? When one's fate plays false, one has to wander about one doesn't know where. Our entire life has gone bad. We have been looking for him for the past six months and he is here. Let him come. We shall wait outside. . . .' She wiped the corner of her eye with her dirty upper cloth.

'Arey, you'll keep sitting—at my door like beggars . . . but do explain: Who are you? Why have you been looking for him for six months?' Mrs Pant tried to probe the questions rising in her mind.

The man's hesitation had now turned into abject humility. 'I am his father . . . and she is his mother.' The words came out of his throat with great difficulty.

Mrs. Pant was shocked as though the sky had crashed down about her. Satish was *their* son . . . how can that be possible? She wasn't able to believe it. She tried to be her normal self: 'Why did he leave home and come here? Was there a quarrel?' Mrs. Pant was curious.

The woman said, wiping her tears: 'I don't know, bhain ji, what was in his mind? He had learnt just a little and he was neither here nor there. We had simply told him there was no use in studying and that he should do something . . . if he gets some job . . . we could then marry him off quickly . . . but he left home without saying anything. We went about looking for him a lot. . . . We came to know now that he was living here.'

Mrs. Pant recalled the day when Sonu had tied a rakhi round Satish's wrist and there were tears in his eyes. From that day onwards Satish stayed in the house not as a tenant but as a member of the family. He had won not just Sonu's but everyone's heart.

The words of the woman had rattled all the beliefs of Mrs. Pant. It was as though all values had crashed about her. She found herself trapped in a strange cyclone. Treating them with indifference, she said: 'He is not at home at the moment. When he comes, I shall tell him. Where do you live?'

'Ji . . . in this city itself. At Indresh Nagar near Kanwali Road.'

'In this city. . . ?' Mrs. Pant expressed surprise.

'Ji . . . bhainji. . . .' The woman replied looking at her.

'Now then, you go . . . I will send him as soon as he comes,' Mrs. Pant said trying to put them off. She was scared lest Mrs. Gupta in the neighbourhood should see them standing there. She would make minute inquiries. She didn't want her to know that they were Satish's parents. She was very scheming, Mrs. Gupta. She enjoyed being a peeping tom in other people's houses. When Sonu had tied a rakhi round Satish's wrist, how haughtily had she spoken! 'Strangers are after all strangers, however much you might tie them with slender threads. I have no trust in relationships of this kind.' The fear of Mrs. Gupta was hovering over Mrs. Pant like a ghost.

'Bhainji, we have not come to trouble you a bit . . . . the boy has disappeared from home for the last six months. Where have we not looked for him! Balesar comes to do the cleaning in your street. He lives near our house. He it was who told us that Satish lived in a house bearing this number.' The man made an unsuccessful effort to gain Mrs. Pant's sympathy.

'Bhainji, you are a woman yourself . . . you can guess

the pain of a mother . . . please let us stay here till he comes. We shall go away with him.' The woman said humbly.

Mrs. Pant's temples started to get hot. Satish, a bhangi, stayed with us!! She felt as though she was losing her consciousness.

The footfalls of Sonu from outside and her 'Give me food, mummy. I am hungry' woke her up from her drowsy state. For a second she hesitated on seeing two strangers at her door. Then she hurried inside.

Mrs. Pant followed Sonu inside without saying anything to them. The door still lay open. Satish's trousers and shirt were drying up on a wire stretched across the courtyard. While coming inside, she happened to touch them. Mrs. Pant felt as though an electric current had passed through her, as though something filthy had touched her body. She picked up the long bamboo pole lying in the verandah and with its help threw the trousers and the shirt down. Using the pole, she shoved them towards a corner of the courtyard like rubbish. Mrs. Pant was shaking with anger.

Noon passed into early evening. Satish had not yet returned home. For them the last four hours seemed like several years. Without speaking to each other, staring into nothingness, or scratching the earth, each enmeshed in his or her memories, they kept their gaze fixed at the entrance of the street. The passersby in the street would cast a glance at them and move on.

Mrs. Pant's entire attention was riveted on the door. Mrs. Gupta could appear any moment. She was apprehensive that she might cause some problem. She wasn't able to decide what she should do. She was furious with Ravi Sharma. It was he who had brought Satish to them. Didn't he know who Satish was? If he knew, why didn't he tell them? Why did he mislead them?

Sonu was busy doing her homework. On hearing the sound of a scooter, she ran: 'Mummyji, papa's come.'

Parking his scooter in the courtyard, Sudarshan Pant asked: 'Who are these people sitting outside the door, Gaura?'

'Satish's mother and father. . . .'

'They seem to belong to some low caste? Where is Satish?' Sudarshan said with surprise.

'He hasn't come back yet.'

'How long have they been sitting outside?'

'Since noon.'

'Like this . . . in the street! You could have asked them to sit in the courtyard!' Sudarshan said with sarcasm mixed with surprise.

'Yes . . . this is all that remains to be done. The ways of our ancestors have all been destroyed. We have kept a dom in our house. Sonu has even shared the food with him. I don't quite understand what penance will there be for it . . . if Mrs. Gupta had the slightest hint of this, she would beat the drum in the entire town . . . Mrs. Pant has kept a dom in her house, as a tenant. If I had known, I wouldn't have permitted him even to enter the house. As he comes back, throw his things outside. His clothes have started giving off an offensive smell.' Mrs. Pant's rosy complexion had turned coppery. Her eyes were burning like coals.

Sudarshan Pant went outside. 'Where have you people come from?' Sudarshan Pant asked a straight question.

'From Indresh Nagar . . . near Kanwli Road.' The man replied to Sudarshan looking at him with blinking eyes.

'All right . . . you can go now . . . as soon as he comes, I shall send him back.' Sudarshan Pant talked bluntly. He turned to go inside. Stopping he said: 'Look, you don't have to come here. Respectable people live here.'

The woman's eyes were full of tears: 'We shall be very grateful to you, sahib. The child left home out of anger. Please persuade him to go back . . . please tell him, everybody at home is worried.'

They started going back with faltering steps. Time after time they kept looking back. Satish might perhaps come all at once. Their old worn out bodies got lost in the gloom of the street.

Satish returned home late. He had gone straight to the factory. The factory owner Mr. Aijaz was a gentle and an upright man. He was happy to see Satish struggling. He himself had risen from poverty. When Satish first went to him to ask for work, he had patted him on his back: 'Keep up your spirits, son. You will certainly reach the goal you wish to reach. Education is a blessing of God. Get it and move on.'

For the last six months Satish had been going to school in the morning and had worked in Aijaz Sahib's bulb factory in the afternoon till nine or ten. He would get twenty to twenty-five rupees every day. Out of this he met his expenses for school, food and lodging. In Pant's house he was staying in a store measuring five by six, where after putting a small cot, there wasn't any space left even to move about. Even otherwise he had very little by way of luggage: a bag full of books, two pairs of clothes, a mat, a chadar and a quilt. The quilt he had got made recently.

Today he had gone straight from school to the factory. There was some extra work there. When he returned home, the door of the courtyard was closed. The noise of utensils could be heard from the kitchen. He gave a gentle tap on the door. Mrs. Pant shouted from the kitchen itself: 'Look, perhaps it is him . . . tell him . . . to remove his things and vacate the room at once.'

Sudarshan bleated: 'Where will he go at this time of the night? He's still a child . . . he can go in the morning . . . arey! He has given so much love to your daughter . . . he is a brother to her . . . will you turn him out like this?'

'Shall I send him off then with band and music? . . . Is there only a dom left to be a brother for my daughter? . . . this is too much . . . I shall not let him stay in the house even for a minute. . . .' Mrs. Pant's sharp voice was clearly audible outside.

Satish felt as though someone had bound every inch of his body with hot iron chains. His nerves started becoming taut.

'I shall bring Ravi Sharma over in the morning. We shall talk about the whole matter in his presence. . . .' Sudarshan Pant tried to put her off.

'What is there to talk to Ravi Sharma about? . . . I shall not let him also enter my house any more. . . . One doesn't know whether he is a Sharma or not. . . . For all you know, he may also be a chuhra-chamar. . . . The more you indulge these people, the more they will squeeze you. . . .' Mrs. Pant's anger was at its peak.

'But Satish isn't like that. . . . Did you notice any misconduct on his part? What reply will you give Sonu when she asks about him in the morning? She's asleep now. How many times did she ask about Satish before going to sleep? Do you have any idea of what it would mean to her?'

'I don't know anything. Ask him to leave at once. . . . He stayed here concealing his caste for so long—isn't that enough?' Mrs. Pant pronounced her final judgement.

Satish was soaking in sweat even during winter. There was a strange kind of agitation in his heart. He wanted to cry out. He felt like giving a strong kick to the door; he went back a little to do so. But he checked himself. He heaved a deep sigh and retraced his steps. His whole being was full of aversion.

He started for the bulb factory on foot. From the street he had come on to the main road. The roads were deserted. When a stray car or scooter whizzed past, the gust of cold wind made him shiver even more. The flickering lights on the road were unable to dispel the darkness that had lodged itself in his heart. He was exhausted and hungry. In the morning Mrs. Pant had given him a paratha. Ordinarily he cooked his own food in his small room, but today being in a hurry, he had not been able to make anything. Since he had gone straight from school to the factory, he had not been able to eat anything. Yes, he had a cup of tea from the tea-stall near the factory. On his completing the work, Aijaz Sahib had given him fifty rupees which he had kept carefully in the inner pocket of his trousers. He had to buy a book costing thirty-five rupees. Many kinds of ideas were disturbing him. Covering his ears well, he pulled his muffler up to his nose. It was getting to be very cold.

From Sudarshan Pant's house the bulb factory was at a distance of about six kilometres on Kolagarh Road. At ten o'clock at night there was no chance of getting a vehicle for which he could pay fare and which could take him to the factory. A three-wheeler would not go there for less than fifteen-twenty rupees. He set out on foot. The darkness over the Bindaal river bridge was unusually dense. The ascent of the Mall Road was plunged in darkness. The gadiya lohars were chatting over a fire lit to ward off cold at the triangular space between Chakrata Road and Mall Road. He cast a glance at them and moved on.

His feet had got benumbed. Even so he was trying to move fast. There was a hope that Aijaz Sahib would still be in the factory. He used to return home from factory at about twelve o'clock.

When Satish reached near the factory, there was dead silence all around. The sound made by crickets was quite clearly audible in the dark. The lights in the houses near-by had gone out. The twisted tin gate of the factory was half closed as always. Several piles of glass pieces, caps of broken bulbs and filament wires lay scattered all over. Avoiding them he made his way inside. It was quite hot in the factory shed: there was practically no effect of the outside cold there. The yellowish bulb in Aijaz Sahib's room was still on.

The cobwebs hanging from the tin roofs of the cave-like rooms were intensifying the atmosphere of the night. The things lying scattered near the furnace gave the impression of a waste-dump or a kabaari shop. Ahmad and Santa were still absorbed in their work. They eyed him from a corner of their eyes but kept working.

In the fiery glow of the furnace Ahmad's face looked like that of an ape. His health had deteriorated considerably during the last three months. The bones of the face stood out prominently. The eyes had started paining. The atmosphere of the bulb factory was such that no skilled worker was able to work there for more than two or three years. He either fell ill or left on his own.

The upkeep of the factory was very poor. Aijaz Sahib

was a nice man all right but did not pay any attention to its management. His own room was no less than a store.

Aijaz Sahib was startled to find Satish in the factory. The bag of books was slung on his shoulder just as it had been when he had come to the factory from the school at noon.

'You haven't gone home yet, son. . . ?' Aijaz Sahib asked out of curiosity.

He stood speechless. He was not able to figure out where to begin talking.

'Sahib . . .' He wanted to say something. But words got stuck.

'Yes, yes . . . speak up . . . what is it? You seem upset.' Aijaz Sahib was looking at his face intently. In the yellow, dim light, he appeared terribly helpless and tired out.

'Sahib . . . can I spend the night in the factory?' Satish said in low tones. To Aijaz Sahib it seemed as though Satish were standing far away in the dark. His voice was quivering, which he had been able to recognize.

'What? You will stay in the factory the whole night? But why? You won't go home?' Aijaz Sahib asked several questions all at once.

'Which home shall I go to, sahib . . . ! I left father's home because he wanted to get me a job as a safai karamchari in the municipality. He was running about to get me the job in his place. He had even talked to the sahib in the municipality. It was all a matter of two thousand rupees. My father had already planned to get the money from his fund. By paying two thousand rupees, I would hold a broom for my entire life. He wanted that I should give up school and take up the job instead. I do not wish to be a safai karamchari, sahib. . . . I want to study. In the mohalla where we live, I feel suffocated. Not because they are all poor or small people, but because I wish to free myself from the kind of life they are leading. They have got used to their problems so much that they have come to consider them to be their destiny. A feeling of inferiority has struck root inside them. It is only by escaping out of this inferiority that one can experience the world around. Like the iron piece buried in the earth for thousands of years, their thinking has also got rusted.

'Ravi Sharma is my teacher. He teaches Mathematics. He it was who got me a place to live in Pantji's house. I have received so much from the Pant family. They have a daughter, a small one. She studies in the seventh standard. When she goes out of the house in the morning wearing the school uniform, she seems like a veritable fairy. She had tied a rakhi round my wrist, sahib . . . but today . . . they came to know what my caste is . . . sahib! Does being a bhangi result in the snapping of all ties?. . . I wish to get rid of this bhangi-pan, sahib. I haven't deceived them, sahib. . . . I had told everything to Ravi Sharma massahib. Pantji never enquired from me, so what should I have told them?. . . My examinations are drawing near. . . . I need a place to stay. Sahib, have I been born only to be a safai karamchari? I wish to say something more. . . .' Words were coming out from his choked throat as though it were under a great deal of pressure.

Aijaz Sahib was listening to his words with great care. There was an onrush of tears in Satish's eyes.

'Look, son, you are a hardworking, honest boy. If you work, I pay you. You don't oblige me, nor do I. Beyond this, I have nothing to do with you. Work and get paid. If Mrs. Pant has turned you out, or if you have left your parents' home, there is nothing I can do. And then, I am a man of business. You and I are related only through business. Beyond that there is no connection between us. This is your problem; you have to tackle it yourself. What can I do? I haven't set up an ashram where anyone might walk in at will. And then, where is any place in the factory? Try somewhere else. I have full sympathy with you . . . but I cannot let you stay in the factory.' Aijaz Sahib refused in plain words without being wordy.

Aijaz Sahib's words caused Satish's trust to crack like glass. He had come from such a long distance in the hope that he would at least find shelter for the night. But he had not realized then that Aijaz's hollowness would become apparent so soon.

He felt as though he had got trapped in the flood of darkness from all sides. He looked at Ahmad. He was still sitting near the furnace making cells for the bulbs. It seemed to him as though in place of Ahmad there was some shadow that was on the move.

Satish came out of the factory with weary steps. The darkness had got even more profound. His steps on the lonely road were slow and spiritless. He was just moving without knowing where he was to go. From the distance came the shrieking whistle of the chowkidar, shattering the silence of the night, as though asking: Where can Satish go?

5

The Killing of a Cow

THE NEWS of the death of the cow had spread throughout the village like fire. Whoever heard of it was just left staring with disbelief and regret. From the day Mukhiyaji had purchased the cow, it had been the subject of conversation in the village. The cow with small horns was indeed beautiful. Strongly built and a milch cow. The most special thing was that Mukhiyaji had purchased it himself. The choice of such an eminent, respectable man of a good family could not be faulted. The sudden death of such a cow was like causing a commotion in the placid life of the village.

As soon as Pandit Ramsaran heard the news about the cow, he ran towards the haveli. He reached there gasping for breath. The women in the haveli were weeping and wailing. Mukhiyaji was moving about in anger from one side to the other. Every fibre of his body was filled with resentment. The red lines on his face had got deepened.

Pandit Ramsaran, realizing the delicacy of the situation, filled his eyes with tears. Taking on a tearful manner,

*'Gohatya' (Hindi), first published in *Nishkarsha*, Sultanpur, March 1990.

he said: 'How did all this happen suddenly, Mukhiyaji?' Mukhiyaji looked at Pandit Ramsaran. He said almost shrieking: 'I shall have everyone sentenced to jail with hard labour, or else my name is not Baldev Singh. A cow has been killed, Pandat, a cow. . . !'

'A cow killed . . . !' Pandit Ramsaran let out in shocked surprise. He took a deep breath. In controlled tones he said: 'There is no sin greater than the killing of a cow, Mukhiya. The killer of a cow doesn't find a place even in hell. Who is the rascal who has butchered a veritable Nandini?'

The wailing of the women became even louder as they heard Pandit Ramsaran. Many women from the neighbourhood also came and sat down.

'These low-born people, Pandat, will ever remain low-born. It is *their* doing. There is no place left any longer for religion and piety in the village. It's the killing of a cow today . . . tomorrow it will be child murder. I am the son of a *thakur* . . . if I don't have his hands cut off, . . .'

'Please don't get into a temper, Mukhiyaji . . . cool down . . . what's happened? please tell us,' Pandit Ramsaran tried to pacify him.

'Kallu had taken the cow for grazing in the jungle near the river bank. There are many wild boars in the jungle. Someone had thrown explosive material coated with flour in order to kill wild pigs. The cow ate it up by mistake. As soon as the cow pressed it in her mouth, the bomb exploded with a bang and the cow died then and there . . . .' Mukhiyaji's voice became hoarse.

'Don't delay, Mukhiyaji, report the matter to the police. You are on cordial terms with the daroga. He will surely trace out the low-born culprits,' Pandit Ramsaran counselled Mukhiyaji.

'I shall go to the police later, Pandat. First I shall punish the bastards myself—in front of the entire village.' The veins on his temple became taut. He continued after a pause. 'This seems to be his mischief only . . . my cow is dead and gone, Pandat . . . but I shall teach him a lesson. . . .' Sukka's emaciated face came to his mind. It had happened only eight-ten days before.

Sukka had been the Mukhiya's servant for the past several years. From the time even before moustaches had sprouted on his lips. From work in the fields and on the threshing floor to work at home or outside, he did everything with complete sincerity. He never opposed Mukhiyaji in anything. He was a man of few words. But two months back when he was married, there was a change in him. The shadow of silence on his face cleared off like fog. He kept his bride with such affectionate care as though an invaluable diamond had suddenly fallen into his lap. His bride was indeed like that. She aroused the dormant self-confidence in Sukka. In spite of being unlettered she familiarized him with the right and wrong of things. And this was the reason why the Mukhiya had suddenly started appearing to him to be so cruel and hateful.

The news about Sukka's wife's beauty and her self-confident temperament reached the Mukhiya's ears also. He was eager to have a look at her.

That day Sukka had come from the field with fodder. He was busy preparing to give the fodder to the cattle. Mukhiyaji interrupted him: 'It has been two months since your bride came but she hasn't yet come to the haveli.'

Sukka saw Mukhiyaji from the corner of his eyes. He probably wanted to guess Mukhiyaji's intentions. He said nothing.

Finding him keeping mum, Mukhiyaji knit his eyebrows in anger: 'Abe, have you put oil in your ears? Or are you intoxicated with bhang? I have asked you a question.'

Sukka went on working quietly. Mukhiyaji's patience was about to give way. He said rebuking him: 'Have you gone dumb? Or your wife has worked magic on you? Send her to the haveli tomorrow. . . ,' Mukhiyaji ordered him.

Finding a change in Mukhiyaji's demeanour, Sukka stopped working. Chewing over his words, he said: 'She will not come to the haveli.'

'Will not come to the haveli! . . . Do you know what you are saying?' Mukhiyaji felt that it was not Sukka but some stranger who stood before him who was denying his existence. Mukhiyaji's eyes began to emit sparks. The twisted frown got deepened.

'Stay within your bounds, Sukka. Don't try to fly off. It's an ancestral practice.'

The weak person sitting inside Sukka was turning over to the other side. Gathering his weakening self, he said: 'It's when I work, Mukhiyaji, that you give me two handfuls of rice. She will not come to the haveli.' Saying this he went out of the haveli.

Sukka's departure in this manner wounded Mukhiyaji's ego. It was a challenge. The Mukhiya considered it to be an insult. The desire to take revenge settled in his heart.

The wound of that day suddenly became green again. He said to Pandit Ramsaran: 'Pandat, go and call the Sarpanch. These bastards' heads need to be crushed underfoot. The matter relates to the killing of a cow.'

The next day the panchayat met on the platform of the temple—the Mukhiya, the Sarpanch, and the other members of the panchayat. Since the matter concerned the killing of a cow the entire village had gathered together—one member from each family. The brahmins and the rajputs sat on the platform; chamars, sweepers, barbers, washermen, water carriers—sat below. Pandit Ramsaran sat by the side of Mukhiyaji. He had come with a newly washed ramnami wrapped round him. An elongated tika was visible on his forehead from afar. The sarpanch was the oldest in years. White moustaches in a wrinkled face had been particularly trimmed sharp for the day.

The Mukhiya standing up said humbly: 'Brothers, panch parmeswar, members of the panchayat, whatever happened yesterday is a blot on the face of the village. It is the duty of the panchayat to punish the devil who has perpetrated the heinous act. Killing a cow is prohibited in our shastras. I am the Mukhiya of this panchayat. Only you have made me the Mukhiya. But today in this panchayat I give my seat to Sarpanchji because the case concerns me. I want justice—I have full faith in him.'

Pandit Ramsaran supported Mukhiyaji: 'Brothers, Mukhiyaji is a truthful, honest man. That is why he has entrusted his case to Sarpanchji. Killing a cow is a capital sin. The whole village will have to do penance for it. That's why it's important that we punish the person who is guilty of this deed. The shastras aren't false. In the shastras the cow is spoken of as a mother. The person guilty of the murder of mother should be given the sternest punishment. God lives among the panch-es. Whatever the panch-es will decide will be acceptable to all.'

Inevitably, whatever Pandit Ramsaran said carried conviction. Lala Shivdayal had come leaving his wife to do duty for him at his retail shop. He was in a hurry to get back. So, in his haste he said: 'Let's know, who is guilty?'

The people supported what the Lala had said. The Sarpanch motioned the people to remain quiet. Addressing Mukhiyaji he said: 'Who do you suspect, Mukhiyaji?'

Mukhiyaji sternly said: 'Those who go to the dense jungle on the river bank to hunt wild boars, and place explosives coated with flour. They alone who hunt wild boars are the killers of my cow.'

'Please tell us their names, Mukhiyaji,' said the Sarpanch, pushing the matter forward. There was stunned silence in the assembly. All were eager to know the names.

'Now what names shall I name, Sarpanchji . . . everyone in the village knows them,' Mukhiyaji said releasing a deep breath.

'Even so you will have to tell the names,' said the sarpanch, repeating.

'It would be better, Sarpanchji, if they themselves got up and confessed their sin,' said Mukhiyaji loudly, looking towards the sarpanch, so that every person in the assembly should hear him.

Whispering started in the crowd. There was only one question that knocked in the mind of all: 'Who has done this deed?'

When even after a considerable lapse of time no one stood up, Mukhiyaji screamed: 'What do these people know of piety and integrity? The rascals are born low and will so remain. They should be flayed alive and stuffed with straw. . . . Balesar, Jokhu, Ragghu, Chimra, and Sukka here. Only one of these five is responsible. . .'

All the five turned pale. They were alarmed at being named. There was uproar in the crowd. The eyes of each person got filled with contempt and hatred for the five.

They were guilty of killing a cow. An unforgiveable sin.

Sukka's mental state became even more pitiable. His eye-brows became taut. His lips were shut tight. The jaws had become so constricted that his face had started becoming rigid. He felt as though the noose of the rope was just about to be wound round his neck. He saw villainy in the eyes of Mukhiyaji. The entire sequence of events of the past eight-ten days, after being revived, evaporated like steam. Deep agony rose up in him. Opening his eyes in the broad daylight, he tried to see the people around him. But no face appeared distinct. In the crowd of indistinct faces, he entreated the panchayat: 'Mai-baap, I have never hunted the wild boar till now. Nor do I know about explosives, how they look. . . . I haven't killed the cow.' His inner fury had subsided out of fright even before it could find an outlet.

Each of the five offered a similar explanation. They entreated, they wept. But in front of the Mukhiya's rebuke their voice became muted. He said to the five: 'Speak the truth. Who had placed explosives in the jungle?'

All the five spoke together: 'We don't know, huzoor. We are innocent.'

'If he who has done this deed confesses his sin, his punishment can be reduced,' appealed the Sarpanch once again.

When there was no response ever after this appeal, the Sarpanch announced his decision.

'All right then. Here are five chits. Pandit Ramsaran has written the names of all five on them. The person whose chit gets drawn will be pronounced the killer of the cow. . . .'

After the words of the sarpanch there was silence once again. There was no opposition from any quarter. No questions were asked. It was as though the entire atmosphere had gone dead.

The Sarpanch got up with a small round pot in his hand. Pandit Ramsaran was asked to take out a chit. Panditji got up. He chanted the gayatri mantra loudly. Then making obeisance in all the four directions, he drew out a chit from the pot.

Everyone tried to stand on his tiptoes to read the name on the chit as though those sitting far would also be able to decipher the name. Pandit Ramsaran spoke out the name on the chit loudly: 'Sukka!'

The crowd looked at Sukka. On hearing his name he started trembling. His self-confidence started getting shattered.

He entreated the Sarpanch pleading for justice: 'God lives in you, Sarpanchji, kindly do justice to me, revered sir . . . I am innocent . . . I haven't killed the cow . . . I swear by God . . . I haven't killed the cow . . . I am innocent . . . I never went to the jungle to hunt boars . . . don't accuse me of killing a cow, Sarpanchji.' His words started faltering. His voice became weak.

His entreaties produced no effect. There was a stunned silence in the assembly. Balesar, Jokhu, Ragghu and Chimra were no doubt happy at being exonerated. But they were grieved at Sukka's entrapment. Sukka hadn't done any harm to anyone. So why would he kill a cow? They knew this very well. But they didn't have the guts to oppose the panchayat. They sat silently with their head on their knees staring at the ground.

Discussions about the punishment started in the panchayat. After deliberations the sarpanch announced his decision: 'The matter relates to the killing of a cow. There is no eye-witness. So the punishment will be such that Sukka could even get saved. The ploughshare used on the plough will be heated in the fire. Sukka will clutch it with both hands saying 'mother cow', 'mother cow', and go ten steps. If Sukka hasn't killed the cow, then no harm will come to him, just as no harm had come to Mother Sita in the agnipariksha. Because Mother Sita was pure, she was honest. If Sukka is guiltless, even the iron heated in the fire will not burn Sukka. This is the decision of the panch-es.'

Pandit Ramsaran supported the Sarpanch and said the judgement accorded with dharma.

Sukka's face was wilting. He looked towards Mukhiyaji. More than the words of the Sarpanch, he heard the echo of the secret smile hidden behind Mukhiyaji's lips, which seemed to say: 'You have seen it now, bachchu, the result of meddling with me.'

The Mukhiya appeared to him to be a rakshasa with a frightening face whose long nails were piercing his neck.

Sukka tried to protest. But his words got choked and darkness appeared before his eyes. The lips drying up just quivered.

In no time there was a pile of cow dung cakes, wood, and dried grass. A match stick in the grass lighted up the fire at once. The old and the young and the children—all inched closer to the fire. Everyone tried his best to be in the front.

Flames began to rise from the pile. The ploughshare belonging to the plough of the Mukhiya was thrown into the fire.

The playful flames of fire made the faces standing by to draw back. The uproar of the crowd began to vanish in the noise made by the rustle of flames and the crackling of wood. The colour of the ploughshare slowly began to change into red, the colour which the fire had carried to the core of the iron. As the flames leapt up, every single breath of Sukka sank down. The red-yellow colour of the flames filled Sukka with terror.

In order that the cow dung fire might not get weak, dry pieces of wood were thrown in. Jumman the blacksmith was called in to heat the ploughshare. There was no one to match his workmanship in the entire area. Heating iron in the fire and moulding it into any desired shape was a child's play for him. But today he was not called upon to shape the heated iron. It was merely to heat the iron and put it into Sukka's hands.

Jumman turned over the ploughshare to check it. It had changed its colour. The colour of the glowing cinders had entered into the ploughshare. Jumman took it out of the fire. Lying on the ground, it seemed like a beam of death, which Sukka had to pick up and walk ten steps.

Sitting in his place, Sukka wanted to think about the Mukhiya's conspiracy. But being in a stupefied state, his thinking was getting disintegrated before moving in the right direction. He thought of his bride who had filled him with self-confidence. But at this moment, that confidence too had got shaken. He tried to get up but he couldn't. Then the Mukhiya's muscleman came and nudged him with the end of his lathi: 'Get up!'

He rolled over to one side. The muscleman caught hold of his arms tightly and dragging him took him to the fire. A commotion began in the crowd. People wanted to push their way to the front so that they might see the killer of the cow die from close proximity.

The flaming red ploughshare was forcibly put into his

hands. Sukka's shrieks crossing all limits of helplessness and striking against dusty streets and kuccha-pucca houses, caused the entire atmosphere to shake with fear, such shrieks that might make a dead cow get up and run. Silence pervaded the crowd, the stunned silence of the cremation ground.

Pandit Ramsaran heaved a sigh of relief, as though the entire village had been absolved of the sin of gohatya.

6

Eclipse

THE CHAUDHRI had celebrated the marriage of his only son Birampal with great affection and fondness. The bride belonged to a poor family but in beauty she was no less than Lakshmi or Parvati. Birampal too remained tied to his bride day and night. The Chaudhrain was also happy. She cherished just one more wish—that her bahu would promptly give her a lovely grandson and that the haveli would resonate with the laughter of the child.

When the daughter-in-law did not get pregnant even after two years of marriage, the Chaudhrain began to get worried. Several vows were made before gods and goddesses. Alms were given in charity to pandas and pujaris. Amulets prepared by mullas and maulvis were worn. Whatever anyone prescribed by way of spells or fasts were duly followed. Even so Biram's bahu remained unproductive like a piece of barren land. The beauty of her bahu which earlier was such a source of joy to the Chaudhrain had now started hurting her eyes.

*'Grahan' (Hindi), first published in *Kathanak*, Kanpur, May-August 1992.

'Arey, what use are these cursed good looks if one can't produce a mouse even!'

Slowly and gradually tension lodged itself in the Chaudhri's prosperous house.

The women of the neighbourhood also found a subject for gossip. 'She is just unlucky, poor woman. God had bestowed good looks on her but kept her womb empty.'

Any sympathy for Biram's bahu in the conversation of the neighbouring women was merely superficial. Actually, because of her beauty, there was an element of jealousy also, that satisfied their ego.

'What if she is beautiful! Let her produce a child . . . I gave my mother-in-law a son in the ninth month of marriage itself. "Take it, here is the son. Don't complain later that I didn't give you a grandson."' It was with sentences like these that the laughter of women sitting together started echoing in the houses of the neighbourhood.

The Chaudhri had cut down on coming to the inner quarters of the haveli. He had now started having his food served in the sitting room. He started spending most of his time in the fields. If he came home, he would find it desolate.

Instead of blessings, the Chaudhrain now started spouting abuses at the bahu. Biram too had got bored. The golden body began to appear flaccid. He also felt that there was something wrong with his wife. He would come from the fields tired and would go to sleep quietly. By the time his wife came to the room, he would be deep in sleep.

Biram's wife underwent all this tension quietly. She had suddenly become all alone. It was as if the entire household had ranged itself against her. There was so much inside her that rumbled like clouds but would dry up without raining down. She felt like crying all by herself.

One day she firmly decided to speak to Biram: 'Even you hold me guilty . . . . Let's once go to a doctor in the city. I am told, doctors can tell who is at fault. . . .'

She had not even completed her words when Biram gave her a resounding slap on her cheek. Stars began to dance before her eyes. She neither wept nor cried; she just kept staring at this incarnation of Biram. She recalled those moments when in the initial days of marriage, he would spend hours together with his head buried in her breasts like a small child. Does one forget those days so soon and that too because I haven't been able to give him a child. . . ?

The wife's drowsiness suddenly broke up when Biram shouted: 'Saali, trying to lay the blame on me! I shall cut you up in small pieces and bury them. . . . Get out of my sight. . . .'

Biram's bahu lay down in her own room quietly. She went without food or drink. No one came to ask her or persuade her either. It took her several days to get over this incident.

One day the Chaudhrain suddenly died without seeing the face of a grandson. Again it was she who was held responsible for the death of the Chaudhrain. There were only three persons left in the haveli, each wrapped up in his, or her own sheath—distant from each other, far distant, as though they had got lost in a wilderness of silence.

Biram's wife lived her life wrapped up in sad loneliness in the big haveli. Nowhere could she see anyone before whom she could unravel the knot of her mind, on whose shoulder she could rest and weep. She had already broken off contacts with her parental home quite early. She didn't feel like going to the neighbours. If she went there by mistake or out of compulsion, one question always kept haunting her:

'How sad! So beautiful, yet childless. . . !'

These words pierced her like an arrow dipped in poison.

It was full moon in the month of Bhadon. The sky was clear with no trace of clouds as far as the eye could see.

Pandit Siyaram had been going about telling people from early morning that there would be a full moon eclipse that night.

He came to the haveli in the morning itself. Biram was getting ready to go to the fields. The Pandit tried to tell Biram's bahu: 'The Chaudhrain was a virtuous woman of a generous disposition, bahuji. She observed all festivals according to shastras and distributed due charity. Now it is you who have to do everything. This time the eclipse is very inauspicious. Devilish tendencies are on the increase. It is imperative to distribute a mixture of seven grains along with salt, so that devilish disasters can be prevented. The rest of course is in God's hands.'

Biram's wife had seen her own mother in her parental home distribute grains at the time of solar eclipse to people of the so-called low castes. But she had not been able to make much of it. She didn't understand much even now but in order to follow the tradition of the haveli, she kept wheat, gram, barley, maize, pulses and salt mixed together in a large basket.

The news of the lunar eclipse filled the bhangi-basti with joy. There was hardly a house in the entire basti where food used to be cooked twice a day during the month of Bhadon. The situation would continue till the next harvest.

From the time Ramesar's father was confined to bed, they were also in the same dire straits. How much could the old mother do! He had to give up his studies also during this period. Not to speak of getting medicines for father, it was extremely difficult even to arrange for two meals a day. Ramesar's father used to work in the Chaudhri's fields. When because of his illness he stopped coming for work, Ramesar had to leave school and start working in the fields.

Things went well for a few days. But the Chaudhri kept someone else in Ramesar's place. The Chaudhri needed an experienced hand. Ramesar was completely jobless—he just did whatever odd jobs he could get. The earnings were so low that it was difficult to pull along.

Ramesar didn't like to go begging for grains from house to house. But what could he do? Even a mixture of grains and salt was all right—it would be something with which to quench the fire of hunger. The more houses he was able to cover till the completion of the eclipse, the more grains he would be able to collect.

As evening drew nearer, the people of the basti started to get together. Not only children and old men but young girls and daughters-in-law also had come out. Fasts had made everyone helpless.

The people of the basti kept looking towards that part of the sky from where the moon was about to emerge. In spite of being fractured, it was about to provide grains for them.

The disc of the moon was sighted from behind the neem tree in the backyard of Jumman. It was climbing the sky slowly. Every face showed signs of joy. Gheesu's wife said in a strange voice from behind the veil: 'This is like a full rounded thaal. Where is the cut? Wasn't the Pandit telling a lie? He wasn't taking us all for a ride. . . .'

Gheesu growled at her: 'Ari, don't make a show of your

intelligence. . . . The eclipse is not like a moneylender who can show up at your door any time and every time. The Pandit was saying that the eclipse comes at a fixed time—Rahu and Ketu will come to attack the moon on time. . . .'

Birju who had for long been eyeing Gheesu's wife from the corner of his eyes said: 'Bhabbi, Rahu and Ketu would still be sharpening their weapons on the stone. . . . This time they would come fully prepared . . . they would slice the moon with a stroke, like a sweet melon.'

Everyone laughed at what Birju had said. Gheesu's wife softly smiled in her veil. Jumman's laughter turned into a cough.

Ramesar came and joined the group. In the entire basti, he was the only one who had been able to learn to read and write a little. He recalled that the teacher had told them the causes of the lunar eclipse. He had learned them by heart. Swinging between time and circumstances, Ramesar had long since expelled all the causes from his mind. There was only one question in his mind—that he should bring home some grains, which would help them to survive for a few more days.

The conch of the temple blew at about one and a half or two. The moon had climbed high up in the sky and it seemed a little hidden from one side. The blowing of the conch was a signal for the start of the eclipse.

All the women, children and young people of the village had come within doors. Only those old women sat at their doors, who had to give away grains as a charity and save their families from disasters. There was silence all around—except in the bhangi-basti.

Groups of people, from the bhangi-basti entered the

streets of the village, shrieking and shouting, timing their entry with the blowing of the conch. After going to two or three houses, the people split themselves into four-five groups. Ramesar too was with one of these groups. He had given an old tattered dirty chadar the shape of a bag and tied it round his shoulder. There was a scuffle at every house. Everyone was struggling to receive as much grains as he could. The barking of the dogs made the atmosphere heavy. Each one tried to get past the other in dark narrow streets full of mud. The distance between one house and the other was minutely getting reduced.

Biram was already asleep in the room on the right across the corridor. The Chaudhri used to sleep in the sitting room. There was a small door on the right of the corridor, which opened into the street. Biram's bahu sat at that door with grains in the basket. There was a small lantern on the threshold. She was pouring out grains into the bags with the help of a brass bowl. She felt happy at thus giving the grains away. This was a change from the dull routine of her life. She spotted Ramesar in the crowd at the back, standing there a little shyly.

Biram's wife knew him. Several times he had brought grains from the threshing floor to the haveli. Numerous times Biram's bahu had given him roti-gur to eat. As she saw him stand silently, a slight smile spread on her lips.

She called out to Ramesar: 'Why do you stand silent at the back? . . . Come forward.' Ramesar came forward. Biram's bahu's face shone bright in the light of the lantern. The nose stud glittered brightly.

By the time Ramesar reached the threshold, there were no grains left in the basket. Ramesar started to go away empty-handed. She motioned to him to stop. Everyone else had left.

'Listen, help me lift the grains from the godown. There would be many more people who would come.'

Ramesar was in a hurry. But there was a personal touch in the bahu's request. He couldn't say no.

He spoke with his head bent low: 'From where has it to be lifted?'

'From the godown inside. . . .'

He started moving inside. Biram's bahu followed behind with lantern in hand. After crossing two or three doors, they came to a dark godown where sacks of grains were stacked at several places. There was complete silence there. A strange smell of dampness hung in the air.

Ramesar's half-naked arms and shoulders shone in the light of the lantern. All at once the smell of a male struck Biram's bahu's mind like lightning. She started breathing fast. Ramesar began to overwhelm her mind and heart. She felt as though it was not Ramesar but some jinn who stood there before whom she was left with no identity. Her body seemed to be on fire.

'Will you do something for me, Ramesar?' She stammered.

'Ji. . . !'

'Look, don't speak of it to anyone. . . .' She was trembling.

Before Ramesar could speak, she caught him tight in her grip from behind. Ramesar was bewildered. His entire body started tingling and made music. For him Biram's bahu was like the stars in the milkyway. To touch or pluck them out was beyond him.

The heat of Biram's bahu soft flesh caused Ramesar's body to melt. Freeing himself from her grip, he said: 'What is it you are doing, bahuji?. . .'

The bahu caught hold of Ramesar's wrist and wrapped herself round him. The fire of her beauty had caused the blood in Ramesar's blood vessels to flow faster. Beads of sweat appeared on his forehead.

'I have to go round to ask for grains, bahuji. . . . There is not a grain in the house. Father is ill. . . .' Ramesar's quaking voice sounded in the godown like the sighing of the waves of a river. Holding his head tight against her breasts, the bahu whispered to him: 'Don't worry about grains . . . just once . . . I need a son . . . in return I shall give you whatever you ask for. . . .'

'But . . . bahuji . . .' Ramesar's throat began to dry up.

'Don't say anything . . . no one will come to know of it . . . take pity on me. . . .'

The bahu pleaded with him. Her eyes were full of the muddy waters of a flood. Ramesar looked at the bahu. The milkyway spread on her face—white milky moonlight which had got eclipsed.

The bahu pulled him and made him lie down on the floor. The dim flame of the lantern quivered in the dark godown. And the two bodies began to fulfill the imperative need of the moment.

The rush of people was piercing the silence but it was difficult for their footfalls to reach up to the godown. The only noise there was was of the music of the rise and the fall of their breathing.

And when this music ceased, the bahu lay on the kuchcha floor with disordered clothes. Ramesar took his tattered clothes and looked at the bahu. Lying on the floor with a sense of fulfilment, Biram's bahu kept staring at him fondly with gratitude. While still on the floor, she said: 'There is a small sack of wheat near the door. Take it with you . . .'

Ramesar felt as though goddess Lakshmi herself lay on the floor—beautiful, tender, merciful, and a bestower of food. Bending down, he tried to put her hair in order with his fingers, kissed her rosy cheeks and lifting the small sack, made his way towards the basti.

The streets were deserted. The distant noise of the seekers of food came filtered from the other end of the village. The dogs were still barking. Jumman's cock had started crowing.

The moon, sick of eclipse, was making its way towards fulfillment.

7

Biram's Wife

WHILE THE sackful of wheat was successful in keeping hunger at bay for a few days, it cost Ramesar a great deal. He had acquired it after losing so much. A couple of days passed in a state of intoxication. But when the clouds of intoxication began to disperse from his memory, he began to experience the hard, rough, unfamiliar pain of reality. This experience of reality left Ramesar feeling cheated. He found everything unbelievable. He had never imagined that such a thing could ever happen to him.

He had already given up his studies because of his father's illness. In addition, he had to shoulder domestic responsibilities. Whatever he was able to earn after his back-breaking hard labour was so little that it was insufficient for three persons even. Besides, there was the begaar to be done. This was like interest on the principal amount. No logic, no law, no sentiments were able to stop it. Many times Ramesar had thought that he would break the tradition of begaar; that he would refuse to

*'Biram ki Bahu' (Hindi), first published in *Sanchetna,* Delhi, 1996.

comply whenever he was called. But this thought had got punctured like a balloon. This applied not to him alone but to everybody in the sweepers' colony. And in lieu of begaar, they received rebuke, accusation, abuse and foul language. It was as though they were not human beings, but were just commodities for use. They were put to use at will. When they got broken down, they were discarded. There was no sympathy, no compassion.

Ramesar too had started realizing that he had been made use of. Everything was becoming clearer. Even so he had not been able to forget the night of the eclipse. On that night of the lunar eclipse when the people of the sweepers' colony were roaming the streets of the village to beg for grains, he had been detained by Biram's wife on the pretext of lifting a sack of grains. Whatever had happened in the dark godown was unexpected. For Ramesar as well as for Biram's wife. Differences of poverty and prosperity, the high and the low and of caste status had disappeared in the rhythm of entwined breaths in a moment. When he regained his senses, Biram's wife had pervaded every part of his being. It was as though the parched soil of the month of Aashaad had absorbed its first showers and then given off its fragrance all around. In return what he had received was a small sack, which did provide a small relief from hunger but which led to an increase in the appetite of the heart.

After recalling the entire episode repeatedly Ramesar had let it settle deep down in the depths of his consciousness. While descending into these depths, he had always had the feeling that something was dissolving within him, as though something was melting inside. The body would become stiff and he would lose himself in a drowsiness of thoughts. He felt as though he had reached near bahuji. The drowsiness was so deep that he wasn't conscious of what was happening around him. The scent of bahuji's body had permeated Ramesar' body and mind so much that he would become restless like the musk-deer.

He wondered why the girls belonging to the sweepers' colony weren't like bahuji—how bahuji's face glows! Her lips, her eyes, her long hair, the mogra-like smell that burst from her body, everything was such that it kept Ramesar always drenched. In spite of his efforts, he wasn't able to come out of these memories.

Finding him so quiet, his mother would feel dismayed. She had started getting anxious. What was it that ailed him? Finally, one day she asked him: 'What is it, son? You are all right, aren't you? . . . Why do you keep quiet all the time?' The mother caressing his hair pressed him to her breast. The motherly touch of affection made him feel sentimental. Putting his hands round her neck, he felt a childlike thrill of delight. He just continued savouring mother's love quietly.

The mother found this love of his comforting. The threads of tenderness in relationships were still intact even amidst deprivations.

Three months after the eclipse, the news spread all over the village: Biram's wife was pregnant. Whoever heard of it asked in wonder: 'Really?' It was as if the truth was not related to the Chaudhri family but concerned the whole village. The wife of the Chaudhri's son Biram was to become a mother after so many years of marriage. The Chaudhri's wife had already passed away without seeing the face of a grandson.

The Chaudhri sent for the most experienced midwife in the village, Bhagwanti: 'There is a ray of hope in the dark haveli, chachchi. Examine her carefully. If the Chaudhrain had been alive, I wouldn't have had to worry one bit in any way. Now it's you who have to look after everything.'

'Don't you worry, Biram's father. Let me examine the bahu a little. Can one conceal anything from a midwife?'

The seal of Bhagwanti's affirmative answer produced a commotion not only in the Chaudhri family but in the entire village, as though some one had thrown a clod in a stagnant pool. The widening circular waves reached right up to the bank.

The quick-spreading news reached Ramesar's ears also. The women working in the fields were talking about it. Ramesar too was working nearby. At the mention of Biram's wife he suddenly became alert.

When he came to know that Biram's wife was pregnant, he felt overjoyed as though he had got the biggest boon of all.

He worked his hands faster and after finishing his work ran towards the village.

His feet rose as if they had grown wings.

As soon as he reached home, he shot the question at his mother: 'I am told, mother, Biram's wife . . .' The sentence remained incomplete. He realized that he wouldn't be able to ask his question.

His mother watched his face which shone as if with sunlight. Finding his mother stare at him in that manner, he felt awkward as though he had been caught red-handed. He began withdrawing into himself like a tortoise.

'Mother, Ghissu's wife and that Birma were talking—that Biram's wife . . .' He again faltered.

A smile spread over his mother's lips. She now realized that Ramesar had grown up. He should be married off. Finding his mother thus lost in her thoughts, he said:

'Where is father, ma? . . .' The tortoise had withdrawn into its shell completely.

The mother replied, wiping her face with the end of her pallu: 'He has gone to get medicine from Vaidji. . . . He should be about to come back. Go wash yourself. Look, your whole body is smeared with mud. . . . Only the high-ups know what happens among the high-ups, son. . . . It's good the Chaudhri's family name will live on. . . .'

Whereas the news about Biram's wife filled his heart with joy, he was also feeling somewhat restless. During the past two to three months, all his efforts had failed. He hadn't been able to see bahuji even once. The restrictions laid down by the code of conduct in the village and the awe inspired by the Chaudhris stood in his way. The gulf between the Chaudhri and Ramesar was very great. Two opposite poles of society.

His restlessness was increasing day by day, which he was trying to live out by himself, which he couldn't share with anyone else. Like a secret he had concealed it in the deepest chamber of his heart. It was like a spark that lay buried under ashes but which was slowly smouldering.

He had gone to the haveli several times. The desire to have a glimpse of bahuji instead of getting weakened was becoming keener. But every time he failed. The door and the window opening on the street were all shut tight. There was no chink or slit even.

That day, Biram's wife had correctly read the storm rising in Ramesar's eyes while he was taking the sack of grains away. For a moment she had felt happy. But after prolonged reflection she found it necessary. She had shut tight all the doors leading to Ramesar. Whatever had happened had happened so suddenly that Biram's wife was herself taken aback. She had never imagined that all rules of tradition and propriety would get shattered suddenly in that manner. Everything had happened so quickly that there was no time to ponder or think about anything. She had found herself drawn irresistibly to Ramesar by an invisible pull. Whatever had happened was so pleasurable that she treasured it as something invaluable.

A new life was beginning to stir inside her. Whenever it turned over, she would think of Ramesar as though he were standing at the door asking for a sack of wheat. Just this image of his in her fancy made her smile and in her thoughts she was ready to bestow herself on him. For that moment all differences of caste and status got effaced. In her imagination she felt grateful to Ramesar.

'For whatever you have bestowed on me, Ramesar, take the entire haveli for it. My life was stricken with misfortune. You liberated me from it. You are my saviour.'

Her heart began to cherish heaps of good wishes for Ramesar. Articulating them would have meant getting caught in a terrible storm and also getting Ramesar embroiled in it. Breaking the strong walls of the times and society was simply beyond her. She longed to meet Ramesar. But finding herself helpless in the face of societal restrictions, she became silent. She didn't have the courage. She wanted to provide a successor to the Chaudhri family so that she might be freed from the torture of barrenness.

She knew that if the secret came out, the pride of the Chaudhris would make them throw her out of the haveli and dump her into the dustbin, or she would forever be consigned to a dark corner of the haveli. She could bear all this for herself. But Ramesar was innocent. Why should he suffer the consequences of the fury of the Chaudhris?

Not only he but the whole basti of the sweepers could be punished for it. The basti often had to endure a lot for no rhyme or reason, which these people bore and forgot and rejoined the stream of life in the village. She had not been able to understand what barrier it was that these people were not able to smash.

Something similar had happened on that occasion also when the police beat up some ten-fifteen people belonging to the sweepers' colony with sticks on the platform of the Chaudhri's chaupal. All the women belonging to the sweepers'colony stood in the street wailing and shrieking. She had seen this herself through the window. How mercilessly were they beaten! The Chaudhri sat in his muhra smoking his hookah as usual.

When she tried to elicit the reason for this beating from her mother-in-law, she was evasive: 'This happens every-day, bahu. What can I say!'

At night when Biram came into the haveli, she had tried to find out from him also. Biram had simply said: 'This is the only remedy for these low-born people. These bastards have become very conceited.'

Biram had glared at his wife, saying: 'What have you to do with them that you seem so soft towards them? The drum, the villager, the shudra and the woman—you can control them only by beating them. . . . Don't meddle with outside matters. Mind your own business. . . .'

The red marks of devilry were beginning to be visible in Biram's eyes. Bahuji was frightened into silence.

The mere memory of that incident made her tremble. She didn't want that Ramesar should get entangled in any trouble. She decided after a great deal of thought that Ramesar's entry into the haveli would have to be prohibited so that there was no scope for suspicion of any kind.

With bahuji's pregnancy, Biram's dull life also became interesting. He began to see the same charm in his wife again. Hopes for the future brought back the same fondness and love. When he returned from the fields, he began to hang round her. He would make enquiries from Bhagwanti chaachi and sometimes from his bua. His wife heard everything quietly and tried to catch the drift of his changing thoughts.

When Biram's wife first felt the movement of the child in the womb, her eyes shone with self-pride and sparkled with tears of joy. Every part of her body, gathering together all the inner possibilities of beauty, blossomed with an invisible desire. Forgetting all the pain of her past, she began to savour the restless joy inside.

Biram watched all these changes with eyes opened wide. Once again he had begun to make merry, burying himself in her breasts. But whenever Biram played with her, a feeling of the presence of Ramesar woke up in her entire being.

Chaachi Bhagwanti began to live in the haveli itself to look after the bahu. The Chaudhri's sister had also come for some days. There was always someone or the other to keep her company. Every care was taken to provide comfort to her. The bahu who till yesterday had been barren and neglected had suddenly become important in the eyes of everyone, a kulwanti bahu.

The Chaudhri calling Pandit Siyaram gave away charity. The Pandit performed a big ceremonial in the temple. The conduit for earnings from the haveli opened up for Pandit Siyaram again. There was a talk everywhere that it was the result of Pandit Siyaram's ceremonial that a piece of barren land had become fertile once again. There was an increasing demand for him in the village.

A cyclonic storm was gathering in Ramesar's mind. He wanted to catch a glimpse of bahuji just once. It was for this that he went to the Chaudhri to ask for work so that he might be able to visit the haveli on some pretext or the other.

The Chaudhri said 'no' bluntly. This 'no' filled Ramesar with disappointment and despair. This was the last move; after losing it he returned like an exhausted bullock.

That day he kept thinking till late in the night. He was angry with himself. Why was he getting so sentimental about bahuji? He thought that bahuji had used him and that having entrapped him had robbed him of all peace. Several times he decided that he would not think of bahuji at all and that he would forget everything. But he couldn't stay firm on this resolve for long. The thought of bahuji overpowered him for one reason or the other. Whenever he saw a beautiful woman, he saw a reflection of bahuji's beauty in her.

It happened the other day. Balesar's wife had to send a letter to her parents. Ramesar was the only one who could write a letter in the sweepers' colony. Balesar's wife sat before him dictating and he was writing it down. In terms of the colony and age the relationship between them was one of consideration and respect. Balesar's wife was older than Ramesar in age. She was passable in height and build also. When while writing the letter he raised his eyes, they got fixed on Balesar's wife's face. He felt as though bahuji was sitting in front. Forgetting to write the letter, he just kept staring at her. Seeing him look at her fixedly, Balesar's wife was taken aback. The feminine eyes at once guessed the rising tide of feelings in his eyes. She said simply: 'Why do you look at me like that, lallaji. . . ?' Ramesar was confused as though he had been caught stealing. He stammered: 'No nothing. Please proceed. . . .' 'Arey, devarji. What more shall I say! You are a chhupa rustam. What is the matter? . . . I think we will have to ask chaachi to rope you into marriage. . . . These signs aren't any good.' She burst into laughter.

Ramesar became serious. He quietly tried to read out the incomplete message on the postcard. When nothing else struck him, he tried to darken whatever he had written by overwriting.

He got up after completing the letter somehow. Balesar's wife said: 'Have I offended you, lallaji?. . . I was just joking. Please have something . . . see what I have prepared for you. I had prepared it before you came. Do take something.'

Ramesar felt dejected. He didn't stop there. His inner distress grew in his eyes like a prickly pear. He went out of the village towards the canal. Sprinkling a little cold water of the canal on his face gave him some comfort and peace. He went quite far along the bank of the canal. Wherever the eyes could travel there were fields. Just a stray tree here and there, from which hung the nests of weaver birds. He felt nice seeing the nests of weaver birds. He was amazed. Such a small bird and with what application and planning it was able to make a home for itself! Sitting down on the bank, he began looking at the nests.

Evening was drawing closer. He returned home carrying his restlessness with him.

Father was again gasping for breath today. He sat near his father, stroking his back gently. The bones of his back stood out even more prominently. The skin of the body seemed to have been pasted on the bones. There was no flesh anywhere. Caressing his father's back he breathed heavily.

A small kerosene lamp was flickering in the courtyard. Everything seemed unclear, in fact quite dim, in its light. He looked towards his mother. She sat like a soiled bundle of clothes baking chapatis at the hearth. In the heat of the hearth his mother's face full of wrinkles looked even paler than it was. It seemed to him as though he was losing his identity in the midst of darkness. He had been shackled in the conspiracy of darkness. And he had lost his way. He felt as though bahuji stood smiling in a dark corner. He felt a shooting pain rise inside as though a cold wave had pierced through his entire body. The touch of his hand on his father's back felt lighter than breeze.

'Go, son, have a wash and eat something . . . where have you been since morning? . . . Balesar's wife had called. . . . Did you write her letter?'

Ramesar, rising, said softly: 'Yes, I have.' He then went and sat with his mother.

Mother's eyes were fully moist. She shuddered to see his sad face. She was not able to understand what had happened. He hadn't talked about it to anyone.

Putting two chappatis and red chilli chutnee on a twisted aluminium plate, mother pushed it towards Ramesar, saying: 'Go, give it to you father.' Ramesar took the plate and left.

It was the chilly month of Magh. Even during the day there blew a cold wind that froze every part of one's body, that defying the clothes pricked the body like thorns. The sun shone right on top. Even so the sunlight had begun to weaken.

Ramesar was returning from Latif's kolhu with his khes wound tightly round his body. The kolhu was right behind the Shiva temple. The smell of fresh gur filled the entire atmosphere. Ramesar was about to turn towards the village from near the kuchcha road when he saw a group of women going towards the temple. Ramesar, taken aback, stood a little away from the path. As they drew nearer, their faces became more and more distinct. He identified bahuji even from a distance of ten-fifteen yards. The sight of bahuji made his heart leap up for joy. Draped in a blue saree and a green dushala, she looked fetching. She was walking slowly. The women accompanying her walked so close to her as though they were carefully escorting a new bride to the temple.

Ramesar's long wait had suddenly come to an end. This was the moment for which he had been going about like mad for the past six months.

His gaze fastened itself on the graceful, modest beauty and form of bahuji. Bahuji's face shone with the glow of maternal love and self-satisfaction. Ramesar felt as though it was Parvati herself who had come walking. He was filled with gratitude. Forgetting everything, he just gazed at her unblinkingly.

He recovered himself only when bahuji passed him by without looking at him. He didn't believe that bahuji would go past him treating him with indifference. There was a commotion within him. The scene of that night of the eclipse and the pleading face of bahuji in the flickering light of the lantern in the dark godown danced before his eyes: 'I want a child, Ramesar . . . I want deliverance from the pain of being barren. . . !' Ramesar, standing surprised, was watching bahuji going into the temple.

Keeping the rising cyclone in his breast under control, he began waiting for bahuji to come out of the temple. He was not able to believe that bahuji would pass him by without recognizing him.

The women came out of the Shiva temple after quite some time. Again, bahuji came out surrounded by women as before and went past him slowly without looking at him. There was no trace of recognition on her face. Ramesar stood feeling cheated. He felt as though the sky was slowly descending and the ground under his feet was shaking.

The black pigeons sitting on the dome of the Shiva temple fluttered away. The chill in the sunlight increased.

His eyes were fixed on the retreating figure of bahuji. He still hoped that bahuji would turn back to look at him, at least once. The light blue coloured saree gradually gathering into a spot disappeared behind the screen of kuchcha-pucca houses.

In the midday brightness Ramesar's eyes were filled with the gloom of twilight. He stood silently with his gaze riveted on the way. The footprints of bahuji on the kuchcha path were riddling his body and mind like a sieve.

It was all over in a moment. It was as though someone had robbed him of his entire existence in broad daylight. He sighed heavily. Utterly exhausted and disappointed, he walked towards the basti with heavy steps.

8

Twenty-five Fours are a Hundred and Fifty

WITH HIS first salary in his hands, Sudeep was filled with the light of hope in the midst of the dense darkness of deprivations. His body exuded a kind of joy, to achieve which he had to make his way through innumerable thorny bushes and storms. The warmth of the currency notes clutched firmly in his hands had percolated down to every vein of his body. For the first time he had seen so much money at one time.

He wanted to live in the present. But the past didn't leave off pursuing him. Each moment there went on within him a tug-of-war between the present and the past. Deprivations had cheated him at every step. Even so he had tried to keep himself away from them. As a result, even the ordinary job that he had got meant such a great deal to him.

It's difficult to get leave in a new job. He too hadn't got his leave easily. He had put in overtime on Sundays and

*'Pacchis Chauka Ded Sau' (Hindi), first published in *Sahitya Sampark*, Kanpur, April 1995.

had got an off for two days by way of compensation. He wanted to share the joy of his first salary with his parents.

He couldn't of course bridge the deep gulf of time and circumstances that existed between his school days and the job. But whatever there was in the gulf, he could at least console himself and reduce its pain. Sharing moments of joy and sorrow with others helps to lessen pain. He had journeyed long in wait for this moment, a journey in which there was no difference between day and night, between honour and humiliation.

It took more than two and a half hours to reach the village from the city. So he had set out in the morning itself. He got a bus as soon as he reached the bus stand. The bus was crowded. He managed to get a seat with great difficulty.

The conductor was getting annoyed with a passenger: 'Remove this luggage, put it on the roof. It has blocked the passage. Whose luggage is it?' the conductor shouted in a harsh, loud voice.

A villager of a slight build replied in a low voice, 'It is mine, ji.' The conductor, sensing the villager's status, hardened his voice and almost thundered at him: 'If it is yours, keep it with you. Why have you blocked the way? Pick it up.'

The villager entreated him in an oddly meek voice, 'I have to get down very soon, sahib. . . .'

Whenever Sudeep saw someone beg for a favour, the image of his own father would swim before his eyes. Every part of his body would begin to crack up as though someone were sawing his body through slowly.

He looked at the conductor. The conductor's paunch was protruding out of his clothes. Like an untamed boar, his teeth red with paan were adding to his elegance.

Sudeep felt as though the wild boar had forced its way into the crowded bus. He eyed his fellow passenger with trepidation; he seemed indifferent, lost in his own thoughts. Sudeep cast a glance at the villager who hadn't yet come out of his humiliation.

The picture of his father started taking shape in his mind. The memory of the day when his father took him along to get him admitted to school knocked at his consciousness. The children from their basti didn't go to school. One doesn't know how the thought of getting him admitted to school came to his father, especially when no one in the entire basti paid any attention to education.

Father was walking with long strides; he had to run to catch up with him. He was wearing a somewhat soiled, discoloured shirt and a striped, nicker-like underwear, which he had to pull up occasionally.

When he reached the school verandah, father hesitated for a moment. Then he went slowly, peeping into one room after another. Every room was dark, with children studying there. The teachers were either sitting on their haunches smoking their bidis, or dozing. Father was looking for Master Phool Singh. After peeping into two-three rooms, he turned towards a small room. This room was even darker than the others. Master Phool Singh was sitting alone smoking a bidi.

Seeing my father, Master Phool Singh himself came out. When my father saw Masterji, he abjectly implored him: 'Kindly take this child under your care, Masterji. If he learns a bit through your kindness, he will become a man. Our life will also improve a little.'

Sudeep had not been able to erase that beggarly gesture of his father from his memory. He stood there with folded hands, his head bowed. Master Phool Singh flicked the butt of his bidi away and taking father along, went to the headmaster's room.

Sudeep was admitted to the school. Father was happy. The same attitude of imploring was evident in his joy also. He was thanking Master Phool Singh, repeatedly bowing before him.

With jolts and jerks, the bus crept along. The fellow passengers who sat near had started exhaling so much smoke from their bidis-cigarettes as though they would make all their worries disappear in the cloud of smoke. He slid a glass pane open in a nearby window. Cool breeze slowly came in.

School days started coming back to him one after the other. By the time he had reached the second standard, he was counted among the brighter boys. In spite of all the social disadvantages and discriminations, he continued going to school with full application. He was an average student in all subjects but he liked arithmetic a little more.

Master Shivnarain Mishra had asked the children of the 4th standard to learn multiplication tables up to 15. But Sudeep already knew the tables up to 24. Master Shivnarain Mishra complimented him and asked him to learn up the multiplication table of 25 also. As soon as he reached home, Sudeep started committing the table of 25 to memory loudly: 'Twenty-five ones are twenty-five, twenty-five twos are fifty, twenty-five threes are seventy-five, twenty-five fours are a hundred. . . .'

Father had returned home tired. When he heard him learn the multiplication table of 25, his face wore a look of satisfaction. Forgetting all about his weariness, he came and sat near Sudeep. He himself didn't know how to count beyond 20, but the twenty-five multiplication table was an important landmark for him, about which he had told many people individually. Whenever he mentioned it, a strange confidence shone on his face.

Sudeep repeated the table of 25. And as he said—'twenty-five fours are a hundred—', his father interrupted him.

'No, son, twenty-five fours are not a hundred, but a hundred and fifty,' he said with absolute confidence.

Sudeep looked at his father in surprise. Speaking in an explanatory tone, he said, 'No father, . . . twenty-five fours are a hundred . . . see, it is written in the arithmetic book.' 'Why do you show me your book, son? I can't even decipher the alphabet; I am totally illiterate. But this I know that twenty-five fours are a hundred and fifty,' father said with simplicity.

'The book clearly says—twenty-five fours are a hundred . . . ,' Sudeep replied innocently.

'Quite possible, your book is wrong . . . or you think that the Chaudhri would tell a lie? Chaudhriji is a much bigger man than the book. . . . He has such heavy books. That headmaster of yours, he also touches Chaudhriji's feet. Why then would he make a mistake. . . ? Tell Masterji to teach correctly . . . ,' father said somewhat annoyed.

'The book isn't wrong, father. . . .' Sudeep was nearly in tears.

'You are still a child. What do you know of the ways of the world? It happened ten years ago. Your mother had fallen ill, before you were born. There was no hope of her surviving. Big doctors from the city had treated her. The Chaudhri paid for the entire treatment. It meant a hundred rupees—a long, blue lote. The doctor's fees, the medicines, it all cost a hundred rupees. Four months after your mother had got well and had started walking about,

I went to the Chaudhri's haveli. After greetings, I said to him: 'I am a poor man, Chaudhriji. Your kindness saved the life of my wife. Otherwise my children would have been left desolate. You gave me a hundred rupees. Kindly tell me how much money I have to pay. I will pay off the entire debt in small instalments. I cannot pay back all at once.' Chaudhriji said: 'I stood by you in your time of need. Now pay back the entire amount honestly. The interest on a hundred rupees is twenty-five. Four months have gone by. The total interest comes to be—twenty-five fours are a hundred and fifty. You are my own man; I can't charge you more. From a hundred and fifty rupees, knock off twenty. I will give you a cut of twenty rupees. What remains is a hundred and thirty rupees. Pay the interest for four months—a hundred and thirty rupees—now. The principle you can pay later when you can. Keep paying the monthly interest.'

'Now tell me, son. Aren't twenty-five fours a hundred and fifty? The Chaudhri is a gentle, respectable man. So he gave me a cut of twenty rupees. Who would forego money these days? Take the case of Master Shivnarain's father, the older Mishraji. He wouldn't leave off even the fraction of a pice. In addition, he would make you do bigaar [begaar], as though it was their right. The day-long labour exhausts you completely. But nothing—by way of wages. And in addition, you get abuses. He showers abuses as though he were reciting Baid mantras.'

Sudeep repeated the multiplication table of 25—'Twenty-five ones are twenty-five, twenty-five twos are fifty, twenty-five threes are seventy-five and twenty-five fours are a hundred and fifty. . . .'

The next day Master Shivnarain Mishra asked Sudeep to stand up and say the multiplication table of 25. Sudeep stood up and started repeating the table with enthusiasm—'Twenty-five ones are twenty-five, twenty-five twos are fifty, twenty-five threes are seventy-five and twenty-five fours are a hundred and fifty. . . .'

Masterji interrupted him: 'Twenty-five fours are a hundred. . . .'

At the teacher's interruption, Sudeep suddenly became quiet and began staring at his face.

Master Shivnarain Mishra was sitting on his haunches on the chair. Smoking his bidi, he said, 'Abe, chuhre ke why don't you go on? Have you forgotten?' Sudeep again started repeating the table. He again naturally said twenty-five fours are a hundred and fifty.

Master Shivnarain Mishra rebuked him: 'Abe, kaaliye. Twenty-five fours aren't a hundred and fifty, but a hundred . . . a hundred.'

Sudeep said timidly: 'Massaheb! Father says twenty-five fours are a hundred and fifty.'

Master Shivnarain flew off the handle. He gave him a stinging slap and shouted: 'Abe, if your father is such a learned man, why do you come here? To have your mother. . . ? (a verb which 'cultured' people consider unworthy of being used in literature.), saale. However much one might try to educate you, you will remain where you were . . . so full of rubbish is your brain. The sanskaars of education are beyond you people. Come, speak correctly: "Twenty-five fours are a hundred . . ." what with the small bit of praise you have started receiving in the school, your feet don't seem to touch the ground any more. In addition, you bandy words with me, answer me back!'

Sudeep, sobbing, said: 'Twenty-five fours are a hundred' and repeated the entire table in one breath.

The incident of that day created a tangle in his mind. If Massaheb is right, then why is his father giving a wrong answer? If his father is right, why is Massaheb giving a wrong answer? Father says the Chaudhri is a big man, he doesn't tell lies. Storms began to rage in his heart.

The scratch inscribed on his tender, innocent consciousness got deepened with the passage of time. It has been said, 'A knot in the mind, once tied, is difficult to unravel.' That twenty-five fours are a hundred and fifty started haunting him day and night.

The childhood scratch had become a knot. Whenever he read or wrote the figure of twenty-five, he would think only of a hundred and fifty. Along with it came his father's confident face and Master Shivnarain Mishra's angry one, spouting abuses. With the memory of both the faces repressed in his consciousness, Sudeep kept haunting the dark inaccessible lanes of 'twenty-five fours are a hundred and fifty'. As he grew up, several questions began to trouble him, for which he had no answer.

A little before the bus stand in the village, there was a speed-breaker, which caused the sudden application of brakes and gave all the passengers a jolt. Some people barely escaped falling down. The jolt broke Sudeep's drowsiness induced by his train of thoughts. He felt his pocket. The salary was intact.

The bus stopped at the edge of the village. By way of the bus stand, there were a couple of paan-bidi shops, Badru the barber with a discoloured mirror on an old table set against a tree, a cobbler a little distance away from the barber, and a fruit-seller selling bananas and guavas. That was all.

Getting down from the bus, Sudeep looked around but there wasn't much of a bustle there. Only a few people could be seen sitting. He started straight for home. His home was in a basti of 30-40 families in the west of the village.

It was nearly noon. The sun had risen quite high up in the sky. He walked with rapid strides. He was returning to the village after almost a whole month. The memories of the time spent in those familiar streets from childhood to the present time gladdened his heart. He had not felt like this before. He was filled with an unknown joy: his own village, his own lanes, his own people. Inwardly smiling, he jumped over a mud-filled drain and turned towards the basti. Between the basti and the village was a big pond with mushrooms spread all over.

He liked the blue flowers of the mushrooms. Stray flowers had begun to appear. He started walking along the edge of the pond.

Father was busy tightening the chords of a cot in the courtyard. As he saw Sudeep, he leapt towards him.

'Suddenly. . . ! What is the matter. . . ? It seems you don't like living in the city.'

'No, nothing of the sort. Just came along,' Sudeep said simply.

Taking out his salary from his pocket and placing it in his hands, he touched his feet. Father was immensely delighted. Holding the money in both hands, he touched his forehead with it as though he were accepting the prasad of a god. He mumbled something. Then he called Sudeep's mother: 'Deepe's mother, come here and receive your darling son's salary.'

Mother came, spread out her anchal, accepted the money and clasped Sudeep to her bosom. At that time it seemed as if the entire house had been drenched in the rain of joy.

Sudeep was watching the happy faces of everyone. All were joyous. Outwardly he too was smiling, but there was turmoil inside him. He was disturbed.

He said to his mother, 'Come sit here, mother.' He took some money from her and said to his father in a serious tone, 'Father, I have something to say to you.'

'What is it, son? . . . do you need anything? Father asked out of curiosity.

'No, father, I don't need anything . . . I wish to tell you something.'

Father looked at him silently. The earlier joy had begun to get clouded. Doubts of all kinds started assailing him. He started feeling suddenly restless.

Sudeep made four piles of twenty-five rupees each and said to him: 'Please count them.'

Father looked at Sudeep. He was not able to comprehend anything. Feeling helpless, he said: 'I don't even know how to count beyond twenty. You better do the counting yourself and tell me.' Sudeep said softly: 'These are four piles of twenty-five each. Now let's count them all together . . . four piles mean—twenty-five fours are . . .' for a few moments Sudeep stopped and looked at father. Then he said: 'Now let's see if twenty-five fours are a hundred or a hundred and fifty. . . .'

Taken aback, he looked at Sudeep. The Chaudhri's face came before his eyes. The incident of thirty to thirty-five years ago got revived. The same incident, which he had related to people—one doesn't know how many times—Sudeep was narrating in a new way.

Sudeep was counting the money aloud. As he reached a hundred, he stopped and said: 'See, twenty-five fours are a hundred . . . not a hundred and fifty.'

Father snatched the money from his hands as though

he were trying to befool him. He made an effort to count but stopped at twenty. Sudeep helped him. When they reached a hundred, he looked at his father. The latter wasn't still feeling convinced. He started counting afresh but again stopped at twenty. He turned the notes over to see if the money was short. Sudeep again did the counting and showed it to him. But father still remained unconvinced. Sudeep tried to dispel his doubts in every possible way.

Finally, father believed him. Sudeep was right in saying that twenty-five fours are a hundred. Truth or falsehood, it was all before him.

It seemed as if the past had started scorching father's heart. The trust that he had cherished in his heart for thirty to thirty-five years, which had made him sing the Chaudhri's praises tirelessly lay suddenly shattered like glass and sank into his entire being. A strange repugnance came alive in his eyes, which couldn't be called defeat; the proper name for it would be the acute agony of trust betrayed.

With the help of his dirty dhoti, he cleaned the accumulated dirt from his eyes and took a deep breath. He returned the money to Sudeep. On his face had grown a ruin of anguish, from whose walls fell loosened bricks and stones and cement. A deep pain arose in his heart, which seemed to say: 'May the Chaudhri rot!. . . There would be none left to give him water even.'

9

Storm

AFTER YEARS came a letter from Veena. That too conveying a bad news. As soon as she had read the letter, she was plunged in deep sorrow. Every word of Veena's pierced her like hot iron rods: 'There is no propriety in writing to you, didi. Yet I am writing to you. A week has passed since father died. Mother isn't able to withstand this shock. Father did something or the other for everyone, but no one has had any time to come and sit for some time and console his family. . . .'

She had no courage left to read through the entire letter. She just sat on the sofa with a thud. It was as though the past was trying to make itself heard in the closed hollows of her eyes. The water reservoirs of her eyes had become full. She wanted to cry her heart out but her cries had got stifled. For long she sat on the sofa haunting the dark narrow lanes of her past.

Pinki and Sweet had come back from school together. Usually Pinki returned from school around twelve or one. Sweet came back at three. Pinki was late today.

*'Andhar' (Hindi), first published in *Hans*, Delhi, August 1996.

Finding Savita looking sad, Pinki said: 'You are feeling all right, mama?'

Savita had controlled herself. She had checked the rising tide in her consciousness: 'I'm fine . . . go change your dress. I shall serve food.'

Savita was trying to hide her mental agony, but Pinki had caught her making the effort: 'What is it, mama? You seem upset?'

'No, I'm fine . . . just a little . . .' Savita again tried to divert her attention.

She had put the letter in the almirah so that Pinki should not be able to lay her hands on it. She wanted no trouble in the absence of Mr. Lal.

Veena was her cousin—the daughter of her chacha. Veena's letter had come after a long time. Circumstances had estranged her from everyone. She was deeply shocked at the news of the death of Deepchand chacha. Veena was younger than Savita by five-six years. Even the long gap of time had not been able to break off the ties of relationship. She longed to go to her place at once, but as she thought of Mr. Lal, all her feelings started getting dissipated. After passing through mental torture for several days, Savita had decided that she would show the letter to Mr. Lal when he came back.

The memory of Deepchand chacha began to come back to her again and again. He was like an earthen lamp at night. Showing light to others while remaining in the dark himself had become a matter of habit with him. At a time when sending girls to schools made people raise their eyebrows and turn their noses, he gave education to Savita and Veena. Deepchand himself was illiterate but he knew the importance of education. It was he who had brought Mr. Lal over from the cantonment to the city. He himself lived in straitened circumstances but he gave education to his children.

It was again Deepchand who had got Mr. Lal married to Savita. At that time Mr. Lal was working as a scientist in a government institute at Poona.

Mr. Lal had returned from the South Pole after a period of almost three months. He became much busier on his return. The achievements of the expedition were being talked about everywhere. The scientists of this group had won international recognition. For Mr Lal personally it was a very significant achievement.

As soon as there was a suitable chance, Savita placed Veena's letter before Mr. Lal. The moment he read the letter his face lost colour. He read the letter several times. It was as though in spite of his best efforts to grasp the meaning hidden behind the words, the words were slipping away. Savita was silently watching the expressions on his face as they came and faded away.

Mr. Lal looked at Savita. She stood, indifferent. After deep cogitation, he broke the silence: 'We shall all go to Dehradun.'

Savita made no reply. She had kept her rising inner turmoil to herself.

'I am indebted to Deepchandji in many ways. Whatever I am today, I owe it all to him.' He was becoming sentimental.

His sentimentality startled her. She felt as though there was a stranger standing before her. It was for the first time that she was seeing the sentimental side of Mr. Lal's personality.

In Savita's thoughts emerged the day when there were sharp exchanges between them on the question of her going to her parents' home. She wanted to go to

Deepchand's house. Mr. Lal was very angry: 'You insist on going back to the same squalor from which I want to drag you out. If you go there, they will also come here. I don't want that people here should know that we belong to the Scheduled Castes. The day they come to know, all this respect will turn into hatred and envy.'

Savita was full of aversion. She felt hurt at her husband's spinelessness.

Not only Savita but a majority of members of Mr. Lal's family were also illiterate. All of them led traditional lives. Living amidst extreme deprivation, their life was no less than hellish. In spite of this, Deepchand had paid full attention to the education of the children.

Mr. Lal now avoided going back to the same atmosphere. He was of the view that the vestiges of that atmosphere would be a hurdle in his advancement. He had even started talking of the absence of good sanskaras. He was fully engaged in covering up his fear and his sense of inferiority in the web of words and reasonableness.

Savita considered these arguments to be a sign of inferiority complex, which had arisen as a reaction but which they were not prepared to accept. That day the exchanges had become so heated that they almost came to blows.

For a few days after the incident each remained withdrawn within his or her own shell. Ultimately it was Savita who gave in. Repressing her self, she made a compromise with her situation.

For sometime the relatives made complaints but later they also understood things. And, if someone chanced to come, their behaviour would deter him from coming again. All relatives had come to know things like: 'They are big people'; 'Where is the meeting ground between them and low people?'; 'They live, concealing their caste'; 'They don't now recognize their own people'; 'That is how all educated people are'; 'They even introduce their father as a servant,' etc. etc. These things had spread around very fast among the relatives. For some time this had remained a topic of conversation but gradually it started fading away from their memories.

Sometimes, if he ran into an old acquaintance by chance, he would try to avoid him. If the acquaintance was an old colleague who was an S.C., he avoided discussing topics in which there would be a reference to S.C's. He would say in bitter words: 'They are responsible for their own condition. They blame others. The government has turned them into bigger idlers by giving them the crutches of reservations. No one discriminates against us. We live on intimate terms with others. We are well-respected. . . .' He would of course mouth these sentiments, but he was familiar with his own fears. Every time he would try to gild his truth with lies.

He often saw that even in ordinary conversation, top officers and intellectuals were all prejudiced against S.C. employees and officers. Their narrow mentality would get reflected in some way or the other. The element of mockery in it was considerable. On such occasions he himself would join hands with these people; in fact he would take a lead in expressing his views.

On such occasions he would forget that his father had had a shop selling pork. He was the youngest of five brothers. All the brothers helped their father in running the shop. The business was prospering. Meanwhile he had been able to procure the contract of supplying pork to the mess in the cantonment. This led to an increase in income. They had also obtained permission to open an abattoir in the cantonment area. They had made arrangements to shift near the abattoir. They had built a piggery also, where there were some thirty-forty pigs at any given time.

No one in the family had been to school. He was the youngest of all. He was sent to a village school near the cantonment. He was short and thin. His face was entirely pock-marked. He was slightly dark in complexion. He didn't leave any favourable impression at the first meeting, but he was mentally sharp. In a short span of time he had made a place for himself in the school.

From four o'clock in the morning itself the entire courtyard was full of the noise made by pigs. The meat was loaded in the vehicle and delivered at the mess by eight-nine o'clock. Everyone in the family was busy at that time. No one had time even to breathe.

All life moving round pigs was no less than a hell. The buzzing of flies everywhere made one feel like vomiting. Pigs were rounded up and taken to the abattoir right in the morning. Killing them, roasting them and then washing the meat after cleaning it, and thereafter cutting it into small pieces—all this was quite exhausting. He too had to help the brothers. There would be small pieces of meat and blood spots not only on his clothes but also on his hands, legs and face.

As soon as he got free, he would try to rub hard to make himself clean. But he was not able to get rid of the smell of pork. That smell had become his identity. No one in the class liked to sit with him. He often remained aloof. In spite of being first in the class, he was not free from a feeling of inferiority. Several times his classmates mocked at him by calling him 'Khatik'.

He passed the High School examination in the first

division. Deepchand was a friend of his father. He was a safai karamchari in the municipality. He understood the importance of education. It was he who had said: 'Your Sukkar is very intelligent, thekedarji. Send him to a big college in the city . . . he will go far in life.'

The contractor had no time left from work. He didn't even know where the college was in the city. Even otherwise it took hours to travel from the cantonment to the city and back.

'Where would he stay in the city?' the contractor asked.

'Why . . . isn't my house there? I have two children . . . he will be the third. Don't worry. This is my responsibility.' Deepchand spoke straight.

One day he came to Deepchand with a bag containing some books and a pair of clothes. Deepchand kept him in his house for full four years. By that time he had completed his B.Sc. He had become well-known in the entire college as a good student. But he didn't receive the popularity that he deserved. This matter rankled in his chest like a thorn. The fact that his family sold pork was known to all. During those days he himself didn't conceal this information from anyone. He felt—why conceal? But as he progressed, his confidence began to slip away like dry sand.

As soon as he got admission to M.Sc., he left Deepchand's house. He began to live in a separate room. He gave tuitions to several students, which helped him to meet his expenses.

As soon as he passed his M.Sc., he got a job as a scientist in a research institute. He left the city after a year. He joined a well-known research institute at Poona. After that he never looked back. He began climbing the ladder of success quickly. Meanwhile, he got married to

Deepchand's niece Savita. They had two children—Pinki and Sweet.

By the time the children had grown up, he had entered a new world, where he had earned respect and recognition. But at times he had a lurking feeling that all this respect was nothing but mere outward show. A formal compulsion. Even so he found himself trapped in the illusionary coils of this compulsion. He was always haunted by one fear—that the truth about his caste might get revealed. He always remained very alert about it. He had instructed Savita also never ever to mention the caste even by mistake. The children didn't know much about this.

However, the journey to the South Pole had thrown the closed doors of his consciousness wide open. While collecting samples for conducting experiments of different kinds, or while making a special study of a topic, one question constantly nagged him—Why have I come here? He tried to repeat the oft-repeated answer: For human welfare and development.

This argument didn't satisfy him. Storms of questions rose in his mind again and again. Who will benefit from the scientific research activities? Those who are already developed, or those who have lagged behind by many years, or those who have got left behind, something that forms a part of his own past, those who he has begun to refuse even to recognize?

He found himself entangled in these questions. At such moments he would feel as though his veins would burst. The loneliness of the South Pole constantly pulled him towards his past.

There was a time when he had felt enraged at the mere mention of the past. He had achieved a considerable amount of success in forgetting it. But what is happening to him, suddenly, after all these years? Why is he so agitated? He was amazed. He had become lonely in a world that he had helped to create. He lacked the courage to acknowledge those who had been left behind. He could not share this mental agony with anyone. The capacity to relate to the past was getting weakened, but he longed to go back to that very past. He wasn't able to make sense of the changes taking place in his mind.

It wasn't easy for him to keep a balance sheet of the long period of twenty years. Today he lives in a splendid flat in a posh colony in the capital, where even the shadow of his past is unable to reach. The children go to an English medium school. They don't know who their maternal relations are. Who are their chacha, tau, dada and dadi? What do they do? They had always kept Pinki and Sweet away from them.

They had not taken the decision to cut off their ties from relatives all too suddenly. Instead, it was the result of all that they had suffered and experienced while going through school, college and then during the job. The awareness of his caste at every single step filled him with a sense of inferiority. At such moments his self-confidence would waver.

It appeared to him as though he were walking amidst thorns. Caste played an important part not only in ordinary things but also in the most serious decisions. Several times his merit hadn't been given its due. An effort was made to keep him away from responsible assignments.

As soon as he got transferred to the capital, he had decided to transform himself completely. The first thing that he did was to change his name—instead of Sukkar Lal, he started signing himself as S. Lal.

He had also started to practice speaking Punjabi. In a

short time he had begun to speak fluent Punjabi also along with English. If a Punjabi questioned him about his caste, he would say that he was a kayastha from U.P. If a Hindi-speaking person asked him the same question, he would say he was a Punjabi khatri. This stratagem had worked perfectly.

But Deepchand's death had jerked open the rusty doors of his memory all at once. Savita had refused to go to Dehradun: 'How do I face them . . . ? How do I explain things? Where was I all this while . . . ? I don't have the courage to give lying answers to their questions.'

She had said all this with a heavy heart. It was not as if she didn't wish to go. She deeply yearned to go and meet her brothers and sisters and her parents but before the ego of her husband, her own feelings had wilted.

Hearing about going to Dehradun, Pinki had jumped up with joy: 'I shall also go to Dehradun, mama. . . .'

'No . . . . he will go alone . . . who have we there whom we can call our own?' Savita said bitterly. Mr. Lal didn't show any reaction. If it had been some other occasion, he would probably have rebuked her. He just remained quiet.

'Dad, we're also going with you,' Pinki said in English almost with an air of finality.

He wished to protect Pinki and Sweet from his past. He feared that the children wouldn't be able to withstand that atmosphere. How would they react if they came to know where their roots were? He tried his best to dissuade Pinki, but she remained adamant. Mr. Lal, defeated, had to agree, but Sweet said plainly: 'If mama goes, I shall go too . . . even otherwise, I've joined computers. My classes would be over by then.'

From the station they straight went to Deepchand's house. Everyone was surprised to see them. Some people were not able to recognize them. When they came to know, they .exclaimed: 'Arey, Sukkar! You! You have really changed a lot. We hear you have become a big aapisar. How much do you get?'

Hearing the name Sukkar used for himself took him by surprise for a moment but gradually the sound lodged in memory began to resonate in his ears. Hearing Mr. Lal over the years, he had forgotten Sukkar.

Pinki was well nigh shocked. It seemed to her as though she had come to a primitive place. Such people, such atmosphere, she hadn't yet seen anywhere. She knew her father as Mr. S. Lal. Where did this Sukkar come from? She was getting upset at the name Sukkar. Her lips quivered to give vent to her anger but she sat suppressing it.

The family, forgetting their own sorrow, treated them very hospitably. Unmindful of the past hurts, they tried their best to show great intimacy.

Pinki had not taken the dinner the previous night properly. The very sight of the food made her turn away. She wasn't in the habit of taking food of this kind. Everything in the house, in fact everyone in the house seemed to her to give out a peculiar smell. She had even said softly to her father: 'Shall we stay here, dad?'

Mr. Lal tried to explain to her: 'It's just a matter of a night only, Pinki. We shall go to Mussoorie tomorrow. . . .'

Pinki still wasn't her normal self. Several questions were trying to rise in her mind. For quite some time she tried to make sense of the questions in her mind. Finally she let them come out in the open. She asked in English: 'Why are they calling you Sukkar? These uncultured people don't have manners. In Delhi everybody calls you Mr. Lal, and here . . . it's a pity . . . I can't tolerate, dad.' Pinki's face was getting flushed with anger.

Mr. Lal looked at Pinki as though he were doing so for the first time. Pinki's questions filled his body with a swarm of ants.

Finding her father staring at her, Pinki said: 'Why do you look at me like that, dad?' He felt a bit shaken. Controlling himself, he said: 'You shouldn't speak like this. They are all your nana and your mamas. You're calling them uncultured and dirty! It's my mistake, darling, not yours. I had considered my career to be everything. That was why I had begun to view them as you're viewing them now. But there where I am, or you are . . . they have contributed a great deal in helping us reach there. But for their help, I wouldn't have become such a big scientist. They remained in hell but the sacrifices they made in taking me out of it . . . they didn't ask anything in return, nor did I give anything; in fact considering them to be low creatures, I snapped all ties with them . . . kept you away from them. The truth is that I, Mr. Lal, am like a tree that doesn't cover its own roots with its shade. . . . My real identity is this Sukkar. Having changed it into Mr. Lal, I tried to pass off a fraudulent life for a true one. They are not uncultured, Pinki . . . you shouldn't say this. . . .' His throat was getting choked.

Pinki was looking at this incarnation of her dad. She had never seen her dad to be so emotional.

They spent a considerable length of time in silence, putting themselves together. She said very humbly: 'I am sorry, dad. That was not what I meant. But, dad, what I am not able to understand is that all these years, you didn't ever make a mention of them.'

'There were several reasons, Pinki. . . . Whatever pain I had to go through, I saw to it that you didn't get any idea of it.' Mr. Lal tried to loosen the knot of his mind. It was as if Pinki was all impatient to understand everything: 'Was it these people who gave you all that pain?'

'No. . .', Mr. Lal said firmly.

'Then?' Pinki said in surprise.

'The thinking of the society and its values', Mr Lal said with seriousness. At this reply Pinki became silent. But questions continued to sprout in her mind. She had become serious. Meditating, she said: 'I don't know what you mean by societal thinking. But, dad, running away is no solution to bring about any change. We only make things worse by running away.'

It was as if Pinki had caught Mr. Lal red-handed. Finding that he was silent, she tried to speak out: 'Even your orderly lives better than they do, dad. What did you do for them?' and then in English she added 'I think you have ignored them. You shouldn't have done that, dad. What would they be thinking about you?' Pinki said with deep aversion.

Hearing all this from Pinki was a matter of great surprise. He tried to open his mouth to say something, but the words got stuck in his throat. There was silence for some moments. Pinki again started saying: 'We shall not go to Mussoorie, dad. We'll stay here, with them. I wish to know them from close quarters. Dad, you say that these people are our maternal grandfather and maternal uncles. Why then didn't mother come here?

Mr Lal felt that Pinki had really grown up, so much that he wasn't even aware of it.

To Pinki's questions, he had no answers. It was as though his consciousness had got blunted. They both became silent. There was suddenly a big gulf between them. Pinki quietly laid herself down on the diwan. Mr. Lal also switched off the light of the room. As soon as it became dark, storms began to gather in his consciousness.

Pinki had fallen asleep, but in spite of all his efforts Mr. Lal was not able to sleep. Pinki's questions were continually making him restless. The darkness of the room had seeped into his mind. The smell of the soiled pillow had become a part of his breath. The more he tried to sleep, the more did her questions disturb him. He had shut his eyes, but Pinki's words echoed in his thoughts: 'You didn't do right by them, dad. You shouldn't have done that . . . when these are my maternal grandfather and maternal uncles, then why didn't mama come here?'

As the night advanced, Mr. Lal tried to discover an identity for himself. But it seemed to be longer than other nights.

He turned over to the other side and began to wait for the dawn but the storms that were raging in his consciousness showed not the least sign of a let-up. He felt as though he had forgotten his identity and all his efforts to retrieve it had got lost in the storm.

10

The Beast

IT WAS HOT. Jagesar straightening his neck looked towards the sky. The sun was shining right overhead. Leaving the Rajbahe bank, he came down the slope. The path was unmetalled and sandy. He was walking with long strides. Suddenly, he looked back. Birju's wife was trailing far behind. He said to her loudly: 'We will get late this way, bahuji. We still have fifteen kos more to go.' In spite of the call, bahuji didn't mend her pace. It seemed as though she was not walking but dragging herself on.

Jagesar sitting on one side of the way began to wait for her. He had a big stout lathi in one hand. With the other hand, he held a bundle of clothes on his shoulder. The bundle contained bahuji's clothes. There could be a gold ornament or two also. But this was a mere fancy on Jagesar's part. This often happens. Just as the daughters/daughters-in-law came out of the village, they would take off the ornaments and would thrust them into the bundle, or they would take them off at home itself and wrap them

*'Jinawar' (Hindi), first published in *India Today* (Hindi), Delhi, October 1996.

up in the clothes. Jagesar never tried to find out what there was in the bundle and what wasn't. His sole job was to escort the daughters/daughters-in-law to their in-laws' house or fetch them back home safely. As a matter of habit, he wasn't curious about their belongings, nor did he raise his eyes to look at them.

Even before it was morning, the Chaudhri waking him up, had flung the bundle of clothes in front of Jagesar. As usual he ordered him: 'You have to go and leave Birju's wife at her mother's home. The clothes are all in this bundle . . . come back before the evening.' Jagesar had been surprised. 'Going fifteen miles . . . coming back fifteen . . . that too before the evening!'

Jagesar didn't probe into things by habit. The Chaudhri had given the orders and he had to go. He picked up the bundle and went and stood near the door of the haveli.

They had set out very early in the morning. Birju's wife had come out of the haveli all alone. No one came outside to send her off. Birju had gone to provide fodder to the cattle in the enclosure. The bahu came out of the haveli weeping.

He started walking ahead. The bahu followed him at a considerable distance behind him. A question kept popping up in his mind—it had never happened before that some daughter or daughter-in-law should go away to her in-law's house or her mother's house and no one should even come out to send her off. There was a mother-in-law in the haveli and there were also women of the neighbourhood. Even then the bahu had come out alone.

Jagesar was in the habit of walking with long strides. He was tall in his build. The bahu walked quite slowly. They met several people on the way but no one paid any particular attention to them. Just as they came out of the village, they started walking alongside the Rajbahe. The Chaudhri's fields lay by the side of Rajbahe. There was greenery all around.

He suddenly thought of Saroj. Jagesar had seen her grow up from a child. Jagesar it was who had been sent to her in-law's place to escort her back after marriage. Saroj's sisters-in-law, her elder sister-in-law, her mother-in-law and several other women had all come out of the village with her. As soon as they left, she took off her dushala that she had put on over her heavy dress and handed it to Jagesar: 'Take this and put it in the bundle of clothes. . . . I can't walk with so many clothes on . . . and you also slow down . . . how like a bullock you run!' Jagesar had laughed at these words of hers. He replied in the same vein: 'If you ask me, Chaudhrainji, I shall carry you on my shoulders.' Saroj had run to hit him.

'So, now you will carry me on your shoulders . . . just you wait . . . I shall break your shoulders.' Saroj's childhood had returned. She had run after Jagesar. On the uneven way, Jagesar had started walking faster. Saroj had tired herself out after running some eight or ten steps. On seeing her, Jagesar had also stopped.

'You are not a child anymore . . . don't try to run.' Jagesar had tried to reason with her. 'Walk slowly . . . it's only six kos. We shall reach in time.'

They both started walking slowly. But Saroj had got tired after walking for a kos. On seeing her, Jagesar had also stopped. He did not like the sweat and other signs of exhaustion on her face. He heaved a long sigh. The same Saroj used to frisk about like a deer before marriage.

Jagesar jerked the thought of Saroj out from his mind. Birju's wife walking slowly had nearly caught up with him. She had pulled the pallu back from her head. The face was uncovered. Jagesar was seeing her uncovered face for the first time. No words burst forth from him but they certainly resonated in his mind: 'Wonderful! So very beautiful. . . .' He began to stare at her. Her eyes had got swollen a bit from weeping. She looked sad. Even so, her beauty couldn't remain hidden. Seeing her big dark deep eyes in her well-rounded face, Jagesar stood entranced.

Words seemed to get choked in his throat: 'Bahuji. . . .' Birju's bahu stood silent near him. It was as though there was a large stretch of silence between them. This silence frightened Jagesar a little. He started walking again without saying anything. As per his habit, his pace became faster. But after a while he looked back. Bahuji was coming slowly. The distance between them had again increased.

The sad face of the bahu caused several misgivings in Jagesar's mind. He didn't know why bahuji was being sent so suddenly to her mother's place, particularly when the marriage hadn't been celebrated very long ago. The more he thought about it the more confused he became. He wasn't able to get hold of any clue.

In spite of his being busy day and night with running errands for the Chaudhri, he remained unaware of the goings-on in the haveli. For him, being loyal to the Chaudhri and carrying out his orders promptly was everything. Because of the awe the Chaudhri inspired, no one dared raise his voice before him.

In a manner of speaking, Jagesar was the Chaudhri's servant. Two meals a day and clothes once or twice a year; at times he managed to do even with discarded clothes. Jagesar ate whatever he was given, wore whatever he received. His needs too were limited. He was quite small when his father had given him over to the Chaudhri. Day and night he remained in the haveli. The Chaudhri's spoilt daughter was of the same age as he was. From childhood, she was used to calling him Jaggu, she could never get into the habit of calling him Jagesar.

When his father died, he was ten. His mother also died a year later. Thereafter he belonged entirely to the Chaudhri. He could never find out what kind of money his father had borrowed that lifelong servitude had fallen to his lot. Now he wasn't ever able to think apart from the Chaudhri. Where could he go, even if he wanted to!

He reached an age when the Chaudhri put him to do jobs outside the haveli. From jobs relating to fields to those dealing with the outside world. Sometimes he had to fetch Saroj from her in-laws, at other times escort her back. Today he had the responsibility to take bahuji to her mother's place.

Placing the bundle of clothes by his side, he began to wait for bahuji. Something stirred in the adjoining field. Picking up a clod of earth, he threw it into the field. A rabbit jumped out and ran away. The sight of the rabbit sent a wave of joy through him. For a moment it seemed as though all the misgivings that had arisen in his mind had vanished. Suddenly, he said: 'Look at it, bahuji, the rabbit. . . .' The bahu walking slowly came up and sat near him. By that time the rabbit had gone out of sight. Because of exhaustion and thirst, bahuji's lips had begun to dry up and crack. Her face had become red because of the severe heat.

On seeing the bahu's condition, Jagesar became somewhat restless. Lowering his eyes he said: 'You are feeling well, aren't you, bahuji?'

The bahu was staring fixedly in the void. Jagesar seeing her thus silent began to feel even more restless. He was not able to figure out what he should say . . . what he should ask.

After remaining silent for sometime, he ventured to ask: 'I am a mere servant, bahuji, forgive me if I make a mistake . . . . finding you in this state doesn't make me feel all right about you. If there is some problem, tell me about it. It is my responsibility to take you to your mother's place. I had thought we would reach there before midday. But now it seems it will be evening. The time for taking food will also be over. If you try a little harder, we can still reach early.'

Bahuji was still staring into nothingness as though she were lost in deep thoughts. She didn't hear what Jagesar was saying.

For sometime both remained lost in their thoughts. But Jagesar wasn't able to bear the weight of this atmosphere for long. He felt that something in his strong hard hands was melting. He heaved a long sigh and getting up started to move on. The bahu still remained seated as before.

Jagesar said: 'Let's move on, bahuji. It is hot. There is an orchard at some distance. There is also a well there. We'll get water.'

After walking a few steps he looked back. The bahu was seated as before. Suppressing the simmering curiosity in him, he said: 'Come on, bahuji. . . .' His voice was full of despair.

Birju's wife got up unwillingly. She started walking slowly. On seeing her come, Jagesar also started to move on. This time he had slowed down his own pace. A storm of questions had begun to rise in his mind. What after all was the matter? Why was bahuji so very silent? No . . . he shouldn't ask.

He had been to the mother's place or to the in-law's place of the daughters/daughters-in-law several times. But such a thing hadn't happened before. The inhibitions of the women were over as soon as they came out of the village. They would start chatting and laughing. Saroj would keep talking about something or the other all through the journey. Sometimes she would say: 'I can't travel, Jaggu . . . arey, you ox . . . you could have brought a bullock cart on your shoulders. Didn't you know Saroj Chaudhrain had to come to her parents' place? You monkey.'

On one occasion she had crossed all limits. She told stories about her younger and elder sisters-in-law and her mother-in-law, laughing herself and making him laugh. At that time she didn't show that she was the Chaudhri's daughter. How delightful was Saroj's company! It was as if the springs of laughter had suddenly shot up on all sides from the fields; as if the ears of laughter had started waving in the fields. Saroj, taking off her sandals, had handed them to Jagesar: 'Wear these yourself, Jaggu. I am not able to walk a bit . . .' Jagesar picked up the sandals. But Saroj had not travelled ten steps even when she let out a shriek. She shrieked so loudly that even Jagesar got scared. A thorn had pricked her in her heel. Taking out the thorn Jagesar forced her to wear sandals. Her obstinately did she behave all along! The six-kos route would pass in the blinking of an eye. That was how Saroj was. She would become intimate with everyone, forgetting the difference between the high and the low.

It was proving extremely difficult to travel in this manner with bahuji. He again looked back. Bahuji was still walking slowly. Stopping, he waited for her. When she came near, he said: 'There is an orchard just beyond this thicket. You can rest there for a while. The water of the well is also very sweet.' Jagesar had thought that bahuji would at least say something. But she moved on without saying anything. Jagesar kept standing there, feeling cheated. The bahu was trudging in front and Jagesar behind. Every step of hers weighed a maund. It was as though she was finding it difficult to move on, as though someone was pushing her from behind and forcing her to go on. Jagesar's amazement was continuously growing. He felt that there was something wrong. What a hard expressionless face she presented!

On reaching the orchard they experienced relief from the sun. There was no one around. A rope and a bucket hung on a tree near the well. Jagesar said, taking the rope and the bucket off from the tree: 'Please sit down, bahuji . . . just rest a little. I shall come with water from the well.'

The bahu sat with her back resting against a tree near the well. Jagesar tightened the knot on the rope attached to the bucket. He threw the bucket down into the well carefully. The bucket struck the water with a splash. With the help of the rope he turned the bucket around in the water. Deftly, he pulled the bucket full of water from the well.

Carrying the full bucket, he placed it near the bahu: 'Here is the water. Drink it, bahuji.' The bahu looked up slowly. She put her fingers shaped into a receptacle near her lips. Jagesar poured the water from the bucket into the receptacle of hands slowly. Bahuji began to drink it up making a gurgling sound. The water from her hands dripped on bahuji's clothes. Without caring about the clothes getting wet, the bahu drank water as though she had been thirsty all her life.

After giving water to the bahu, Jagesar drew another bucket of water from the well. He washed himself and drank water.

The bahu sat down again resting against the tree. She shut her eyes. The sunlight filtering through the leaves of the tree fell on the bahu. Jagesar spreading the chaadar on the ground said to bahuji: 'Lie down here. Rest a while. You will recover your spirits.'

The bahu sat in the same indifferent manner with her eyes shut as though she had not heard Jagesar at all. Jagesar kept standing like a statue waiting. He hoped that the bahuji would lie down. But when she remained sitting in the same manner for a considerable length of time, he became depressed. 'Do say something, bahuji . . . have I made a mistake? . . .' His throat became hoarse.

The bahu perceived the note of pleading in his voice and opened her eyes. For a moment, it seemed as if the waters of several wells had gathered into her eyes. Jagesar could not bear to see the suffering in them. Out of confusion, he turned his eyes away.

'What shall I say! . . . Is there anything left to say. . .!' She broke her silence at last. Jagesar felt as though bells had suddenly started jingling. Taken aback, he began staring at her.

'I am not going to my mother's place of my own will. . . . I have been turned out of home by force. For all times to come. . . .' The bahu's voice seemed to come filtered out of a deep cave. The deep wells of her eyes were full to the brim. It was as if something had got stuck in her throat.

Jagesar felt a stab of pain: 'Turned out of the house!' The barrage of the bahu's tears had broken down. She had endured the sufferings of the last few months all by herself. Who could she share it with? Birju was not prepared to listen to anything: 'If you utter just one word against my father, I shall break your bones. You will lie lame and helpless in bed all your life. . . . If you are a woman, then behave like a woman.'

The mother-in-law had also said plainly that she couldn't do anything: 'This seems customary in the house. A woman is just an article of use. Traditional relationships have no meaning here, bahu. If you wish to live in peace, compromise. . . .' The mother-in-law was counselling her to compromise for a life that meant dying daily: 'Every moment of my life that I have spent has been hellish.' She burst into sobs.

The bahu, on receiving sympathy from Jagesar, could not control herself. Jagesar too was deeply disturbed. The ferocious Jagesar began to melt like ice: 'Please be quiet, bahuji . . .' he tried to comfort her. Several kinds of questions arose in his mind: 'Chaudhriji threw you out of the house . . . why?' Jagesar made bold to ask. He was not able to understand.

'Why. . . !' The bahu's face and eyes were full of deep revulsion. The inner bitterness was desperately trying to come out.

'Chaudhri . . . my father-in-law . . . instead of father-in-law, he wanted to be my husband. When I opposed, I was beaten. Different tortures were inflicted. . . . When I didn't yield, I was thrown out. . . . You were given orders. . . . go and leave her . . .' The lava, that had collected inside, suddenly burst forth.

Jagesar was in a double tangle. He wasn't able to believe. He protested: 'No, bahuji . . . Chaudhriji is a lordly person . . . he commands respect in the area. He can't do this. . . .'

'That is the problem. . . . Everyone has blindfolded himself. That is how people like you dance to his tune. . . .' The bahu was becoming vocal. The dark shadow of hatred could be seen on her face. Red threads of anger were clearly visible in her eyes.

She said after remaining silent for some moments: 'Satvir's Kisni . . . had disappeared from the Chaudhri's fields. She couldn't be found even after a long search. Her body was recovered three months later. That too, from the pond. When there were rumours in the village, people began to gather together. Then at the instigation of the Chaudhri you and Ramjivan beat them black and blue with lathis . . . you were the ones. . . .' Every single word of bahuji's pierced his chest. He was looking at bahuji with eyes aghast. Kisni had remained confined in the haveli for three months. In Chaudhri's possession. That innocent girl was ruined by the same Chaudhri. One didn't know how many days more she would have had to spend in the haveli. . . . Suddenly, Saroj's arrival at her parents' place upset everything. Just as Saroj arrived, Kisni was removed from the haveli in the night itself. So that the secret might not come out . . . she was killed and thrown into the pond. . . .' The bahu was hissing like a nagin. Jagesar, sitting opposite was nearly half-dead, as though someone had drawn out all his blood. A question arose in his mind: Why did the Chaudhri kill Kisni. . . ?'

'Go . . . go away from here . . .' the bahu said with aversion.

Jagesar was in a dilemma. He was not able to figure things out. 'If whatever the bahuji had said was true . . . no.' A scream rose inside him. A frightful page of his life was fluttering before him. His thinking inevitably began to hover round bahuji.

He swallowed a lot of spit and gathering courage said: 'I am an unlettered stupid rustic . . . whatever the master said I accepted. Never thought about things . . . , I had heard from childhood onwards that big people had their own big concerns. . . .' He heaved a deep sigh and fell silent. For some time he sat looking fixedly on the ground. Suddenly he spoke up as though he had made up his mind: 'Right, bahuji . . . please get up . . . I have to come back after leaving you at your mother's place . . . I shall have the whole thing clarified on return . . .' saying this he got up. The bahu was still sobbing.

'Trust me. Please come along. . .' Jagesar entreated her.

'Talking about coming back after leaving me—at my mother's place? If I had had such a place, would I have met with such cruel treatment like this? The mother's place, for me, is like a blind well . . . to which I do not wish to go. . . . The doors of my mother's place are already closed to me,' the bahu said with deep pain.

'Take heart, bahuji . . . the doors of a mother's place are never closed to any girl . . . you have a mother, a maternal uncle. . . .' At the mere mention of maternal uncle the bahu flared up: 'Don't ever speak to me about the maternal uncle. . . .' Her face was flushed red with rage as though Jagesar had touched a raw nerve.

For sometime both remained silent. The bahu's voice breaking the silence created a stir. It was as if a gentle breeze coming from afar and waking up the sleeping leaves was causing the branches of trees to sway about.

'I don't know when my father died. I became conscious in my maternal uncle's house . . . my maternal aunt had also died several years earlier. We were just three people at home—me, mother and the maternal uncle. I was not even ten years old when this innocent body had been ruined by the maternal uncle . . . I wailed and cried a lot . . . but there was no one to heed me. . . . Mother also tried to reason with me to accept things. Helplessness had made a coward of my mother. There was the fear of losing the shelter given by him. Though mother was tight-lipped, I wasn't. I never forgave him. I would disgrace him whenever there was a chance. Whenever he tried to come closer, I shouted and shrieked. . . .' The bahu was in full flow raking up the sparks buried in her breast.

'In name I was married to Birju . . . the truth is that the maternal uncle had borrowed a sum of five thousand rupees from the Chaudhri. When the Chaudhri didn't succeed in accomplishing his misdeeds, he threw me out. . . .' The bahu's voice was coming out as though breaking through an impenetrable wall of darkness.

Jagesar's thinking had also covered itself with the thick soiled chadar of suspicion. It occurred to him time and again that such a thing had neither been seen nor heard of in the basti. His heart was filled with hatred and anger. It seemed to him as though something was burning inside him. He was cross with himself also. He had sacrificed his entire life for the sake of a person who was not a man but a wild animal. His consciousness tried to probe the incidents from his past. Innumerable times he had wielded his lathi on his own people for the sake of the Chaudhri. He had become a beast himself. . . . He threw away his lathi violently.

The bahu, seeing him throw his lathi, became frightened but she said nothing. Jagesar got up: 'Come, bahuji . . . if you don't wish to go to your mother's place, let's go back. . . .'

'Go back, where? . . . *you* go back . . . leave me to myself. . . .' Bahuji tried to bring a touch of firmness to her voice.

'No, bahuji, I can't leave you alone in this situation . . . it is a lonely jungle . . . as soon as it is evening, it will be dark . . . I shall leave you wherever you want . . . at your mother's place or . . .', Jagesar articulated his feelings.

'Mother . . . mother's home had got ruined long back. This solitary jungle is safer than the havelis. At least, if the wolves come, they will not come in another guise. Go tell them that you have left me. . . .' The bahu tried to persuade him.

'No . . . bahuji . . . I am not Lachhman who will go back leaving Sita alone in the solitary jungle. . ..', Jagesar spoke with great self-confidence. His self-confidence startled her even. A drop of sunlight shone brightly on Jagesar's face.

The bahu got up. Full of the same self-confidence, she said: 'Let's go.' Jagesar looked at her with amazement. There was a slight smile on her face. There was still much warmth left in the sunlight on the unmetalled path outside the orchard.

11

The Web of Intrigue

IT WAS about two at night. The doorbell outside R.B.'s quarter rang. He was in deep sleep. The bell had been ringing continuously. He got up in a drowsy state. Reluctantly he opened the door. On finding an inspector with two constables he was startled. 'You are Mr. R.B.?' the inspector shot the question at him.

'Yes, sir. What is it?'

'You have to come to the police station.'

'To the police station? But why?'

'Nishikant has filed a report against you. You have forcibly entered his house and beaten him up. He is lying in the hospital.' The inspector shot out each word like a bullet.

'But inspector . . . I . . . I in fact rescued him from the goons. I myself took him to the hospital. It was not me but the goondas who beat him. I recognize one of them,' R.B. explained. His voice was full of surprise mixed with fear.

*'Kuchakra' (Hindi), first published in *Suman Lipi*, Mumbai, November 1995.

'Come to the police station, Mr. R.B. Whatever you have to say, say it at the police station,' the inspector said sternly, his eyes glaring.

On reaching the police station the inspector started interrogating him harshly. R.B. again and again said just one thing: 'I didn't pick up any quarrel with Nishikant. I had gone to rescue him. I am speaking the truth, inspector sahib.'

'Make a clean confession, Mr. R.B. Don't force us to use harsh methods.' The inspector's tone had become severe.

R.B. wasn't able to figure out why this was happening. He was shocked. It seemed to him that he had got caught in an intrigue.

Nishikant had made a statement in the presence of the doctor and V.K. that R.B. had intruded into his house and beaten him up. He had tried to kill him.

The inspector was smoking one cigarette after another and was continuously trying to frighten him. Giving him a final warning, he said: 'Confess the truth plainly, Mr. R.B. . . . or else it won't take us long to bring out the truth.'

'I am speaking the truth, inspector sahib. I have no quarrel with Nishikant. The pump attendant Ajay Singh and a companion of his were beating Nishikant. When I heard the noise, I came out to rescue him. Just as I reached there, they ran away. It was I who had taken Nishikant to the hospital. He had suffered an injury in the head. He was bleeding. Believe me, inspector sahib, I am speaking the truth . . .', R.B. entreated. He was getting desperate.

The inspector, catching hold of R.B.'s hair, gave him a wrench. R.B. winced in pain. The inspector, pushing him into a dark room in front, locked him up there.

'Cool your heels here . . . we shall see tomorrow.

Educated people like you don't understand the language of politeness. When you receive the police thrashing on your bare bottoms, all the truth will come out,' screamed the inspector. Handing the key to Munshiji, he started his motorcycle and sped away.

As soon as he left, there was utter silence in the police station. Sitting with his back against the wall in the dark room, he looked at the light scattered on the road. He felt as though the light was mocking him.

His consciousness had started falling into a deep cave of darkness. He was not able to understand why Nishikant had tried to trap him.

His mind floundered about desperately in order to reach the truth. The more he thought, the more confused he became. Suddenly there was something like an electric flash in his consciousness. The sequence of events during the past few days started coming back to him one by one

R.B. and Nishikant worked in the same section. Everything was going on well, but when the news got round that R.B.'s name also figured in the promotion list that was to come from the headquarters, there was almost the gloom of mourning in the office. It was as though the rights of others had been snatched away and were being given to R.B. Not only those who were his equals or held senior posts but those who were junior to him also began to avoid him a little.

It was not as if there had been no promotions before this, or R.B.'s name alone figured in the list. There were other names too. But as far as R.B. was concerned, everyone reacted with bitterness.

The reservation-based promotions appeared to the non-

S.C. employees to be unjust. R.B. had become somewhat isolated.

In the beginning R.B. was not able to understand the reason for this change. But one day something occurred that made everything clear.

In the absence of R.B. Nishikant was speaking to the section officer in a complaining tone: 'Why have you given this work to me, Sharmaji? . . . give it to R.B . . . his promotion is round the corner.'

'It's still a rumour . . . we don't even know whether or not the list has been drawn up at the headquarters. . . . You've all believed in what that rumour-monger, Kundu has reported . . . it's a habit with him. . . . Whenever he goes to the head office, he lets out something or the other that becomes a cause of quarrel,' Sharmaji said in his usual manner while turning over in his chair. Sharma was a chronic patient of piles. He could not sit on one side in the chair for long.

'Whatever it be, Sharmaji, there can't be worse times than these when one has to serve under R.B. I have already decided that I shall seek a transfer from this Section before his promotion orders arrive. . . . Enough is enough . . . !' Nishikant said with irritation.

'Who will let you go? You're the backbone of the Section.' Sharmaji egged Nishikant on.

'No backbone, wackbone, Sharmaji. . . . It's we who work ourselves to death but promotion goes to these sweepers-cobblers. . . . Enough, Sharmaji, there should be a change at the Centre . . . or else these people will ruin the country. . . . These illiterate and foolish people, sitting in government positions, will destroy everything. Once you get reservation in the beginning, what's the point in giving reservation in promotions? Didn't this lead to an increase in casteism? There is so much frustration among the people. Jealousy has increased. Such is the seed sown by the British that one never knows how long we'll have to suffer the consequences. . . .'

When exactly R.B. had come and stood there, neither of them could see. When their eyes lighted upon him, they were completely taken unawares. R.B. had heard the entire conversation but he kept mum. He expressed no reaction to it nor did he argue against it. He did feel the urge to reply to Nishikant's questions but keeping in mind the propriety of the office, he remained silent.

He came and sat in his chair quietly. Sharmaji too sat down, his attention riveted on to the files. Nishikant went out of the office. The other people were also quiet. Everybody was waiting expectantly for some storm to burst.

R.B. had got isolated in the office. It wasn't that there were no other members of the S.Cs. either in the office or in the Institute. There were a number of them. But on this issue they either averted their eyes in embarrassment or just slinked away. Everyone seemed to have withdrawn within his own shell. It was as though some unseen fear had enveloped them. They shrank from coming out in the open.

On several occasions R.B. had felt that while the S.Cs. employed in the Institute either as workers or officers showed great alertness in keeping a count of all the benefits accruing to them as S.Cs., they were equally socially frightened and were victims of inferiority complex. For this reason they were not able to oppose the false propaganda made against them. Several kinds of questions arose in R.B.'s mind also but the next moment they disappeared. That was the reason he was left all alone in his fight. He talked to several people in the Institute. In private discussions they seemed fairly aggressive. But soon after they all vanished like the foam of soap.

When R.B. entered his office in the morning, most of the people had come to their seats. Immediately on entering the room R.B. said in English: 'Good morning to everybody.' But no one responded. He felt very bad about it. He turned to look around but everybody acted busy.

R.B., filled with anger, abused them saying: 'Abe saalon at least some one of you could respond to my greeting. . . . Or have you all auctioned common courtesies also?'

Everyone got flustered at the abuse. Nishikant was most angry: 'R.B., it doesn't seem proper to trade abuses in the office. . . .'

'Yes, Mr. Nishikant, my abuse seems unbecoming . . . and the abuses that you were hurling yesterday standing in front of Sharmaji—those were all right. They were true and pure and beautiful,' R.B said with sarcasm.

'I . . . what . . . did I say? . . . What abuse did I give? Ask Sharmaji,' Nishikant bleated.

'Mr Nishikant . . . there's no point in asking. I only wish to ask you not to sully the atmosphere of the office. . . . If I am being promoted, I am not begging or seeking obligation from anyone . . . understand? How interested you are in office matters everyone knows. If someone doesn't speak out, it doesn't mean that he doesn't know,' R.B. said sarcastically.

'You are crossing the limit, R.B. . . . the consequences will be bad,' threatened Nishikant.

'The consequences are what I have been facing all

along, Mr Nishikant.' Saying this, R.B. sat down in his chair. He asked the orderly to bring water. The latter got up unwillingly.

The entire atmosphere of the office had got vitiated. An unknown tension had settled among the people. No one greeted R..B. any more. R.B. was beginning to understand the change.

V.K. was the most senior officer of the Section. Nishikant was his favourite. Behind the intimacy lay the important fact that both V.K. and Nishikant belonged to the same caste and the same state. After office Nishikant was often seen at V.K.'s bungalow.

Nishikant was able to get deputation assignments after every two or three months. He often used to remain out even during office hours. Because of the protection of V.K., no one was able point an accusing finger at him.

One day finding an opportunity, Nishikant started talking about R.B. Peppering his account with exaggeration, he managed to say a great deal about him—that he was a shirker, a backbiter, a problem-creator, that he was incompetent and impolite, etc. He tried to present such a picture of R.B. that V.K. started frowning. That R.B. belonged to the S.C. quota surprised V.K. He had his own caste prejudices. This bit of news added fuel to the fire.

V.K. said to Nishikant: 'Don't you bother, my son. I shall take care of that ass. A seat in the office will not change his caste. My grandmother used to say: "Don't ever be intimate with these people. If you do so, they will start biting you."'

Gratified with V.K.'s assurance, Nishikant tried to get up: 'I shall make a move, bhapaji. It is already quite late. Vimal must be waiting.'

V.K. motioned him to stop. 'Nishikant, send Vimal here tomorrow. She could give a bit of a help to Mrs.,' said V.K. 'I shall send her, bhapaji. . . . When should I send her?' Nishikant asked in an intimate tone. V.K. asked his wife sitting in an inner room: 'When should Nishikant's wife come, dear?'

'By two o'clock,' she replied from her place.

'It doesn't matter, bhapaji. I shall drop her tomorrow during the lunch time and then go back to office,' assured Nishikant.

'Right. . . . Don't you bother. . . . I shall take care of R.B. . . . ,' V.K. patted Nishikant on his back.

Nishikant, touching V.K.'s, feet, went away.

The very next week R.B. was transferred to the Stores Section. There was already a lot of confusion in the Stores. V.K. had transferred him after a great deal of careful thought. There were of course the leads supplied by Nishikant. But there had been an incident earlier also, which had got embedded in the chest like a splinter.

G. & G. Company had a very large contract to supply machine instruments to the Institute. All the work related to the contract was attended to from R.B.'s seat. In the Vendors' meeting, V.K. had done a lot of plain-speaking about a whole lot of things to the G. & G.'s manager, Bhatnagar. Apart from the failure to supply the materials on time, the materials themselves were said to be substandard in quality. The meeting had ended in quite a tense atmosphere. 'If the G. & G. Company does not improve the supply and the quality, the order will be declared null and void.' V.K. had given an ultimatum.

The next day Bhatnagar met V.K. at his bungalow. Bhatnagar, seeing an empty corner in the drawing room of the official bungalow, said: 'This corner looked somewhat bare, V.K. Saheb. There should be a refrigerator or some such other item there.'

V.K., breathing a deep sigh, said: 'When the pocket is empty, Mr Bhatnagar, how will the corner get filled up! . . . What does one earn in government jobs? And so many expenses. I had to shell out fifty thousand rupees for my elder son's admission to the engineering college. In addition, so much by way of fees every month that there is little left to save.'

Bhatnagar was constantly in touch with such officers. The company paid him a fat salary for this work. He said with excessive politeness: 'Please order us, V.K. Saheb . . . we are ready to do any service. . . .'

V.K. displayed such nonchalance as though he were a sanyasi and were about to depart for Ayodhya with his begging bowl this minute.

'All this is part of life, Mr. Bhatnagar. . . . We have a guruji . . . you may have heard of him. Swami Sahdevji . . . a divine man . . . lives in Hissar. He has built a cottage in Hissar itself. He often says: "All that you possess will remain here. . . . Nothing whatever will go with you."' Folding his hands with such fervour, V.K. touched them to his forehead as though he had just had a darshan of guruji himself.

Bhatnagar was in a hurry to return to his hotel. He had to finalize a deal with another customer.

'V.K. Saheb, Kelvinator or Voltas. . . ? Or whichever pleases madam? It will reach here tomorrow. . . . I beg leave of you for now. . . .' Bhatnagar said getting up.

V.K., motioning him to stay, went in. In a few moments Mrs. V.K. came out. . . . as soon as she came into the drawing room, she said: 'Voltas have brought out a new model. . . . It is very lovely . . . the shades are attractive too.'

Bhatnagar got up to greet her: 'The man will come tomorrow, madam. . . . I shall go now. . . .'

No one knows how the news spread all over the Institute. Sending for Nishikant, V.K. asked him: 'What's happening, bhai? . . . I am being maligned . . . O, am I corrupt? . . . As for the refrigerator, I got it from my in-laws on the occasion of rakshabandhan.' V.K. spoke after keeping quiet for a while: 'Find out the source from which all this has started, Nisikant.'

'My suspicion falls entirely on R.B., bhapaji. It is like this. Whenever the representative of the G. & G. Company comes, he always stays with R.B. What's his name, Ilyas Khan. It is my firm belief that the rumour has been spread by R.B,' Nishikant said in whispers.

Actually Nishikant had had his eyes on R.B.'s seat. In spite of his increasing closeness to V.K. he had still not been able to devise a way to ease R.B. out of it. He had made several attempts earlier also. But V.K. was impressed with R.B.'s work. He had several years' experience too.

But with the help of the refrigerator incident, Nishikant had succeeded in making R.B. look suspicious in the eyes of V.K.

It wasn't even four weeks from his taking over the stores section when a case of theft in the stores came up. The stores officer sent for R.B.: 'Do you know, Mr. R.B., what's happened in your stores? Do you ever visit the stores? Do you ever go and inspect the materials there? The matter has gone up to G.M. He has asked for the name of the people concerned. The name will have to be disclosed. What do you do sitting in the office all day?' The stores officer asked a heap of questions all at once.

R.B. was quietly trying to fathom the meaning of the stores officer's gestures and his demeanour. He seemed to him to be a spineless and cowardly person. R.B. said in his steady voice: 'I have been here in the stores for just eight days. During these eight days you have given me neither any guidelines, nor have you taken me to the stores to familiarize me with the entire procedure of keeping the materials there. My knowledge about the stores is zero. I am a technical man. I don't have any training in the stores. With such a capable officer in charge, how could there be a theft? Besides, there is the stores holder. The staff are all old and capable. So why do you threaten to send my name alone to G.M.?' Saying this R.B. stopped speaking.

After a moment's silence, R.B began again: 'Have the general maintenance and security regulations in regard to the stores ever been followed? You have been a stores officer for so many years. What have you done about it? How then can you hold only an employee responsible? Send in my name alone. V.K. Saheb, using the power of his pen transferred me to this place. Now you use your pen to send in my name to G.M. All the people in the Institute leaving me aside are capable and intelligent. . . . A man's devotion to his duties or his hard work doesn't amount to anything in your calculations. You are evaluating my abilities all right but there are other people also. Have a look at them also. . . .' A veritable sea of anger was bursting forth in R.B.

'That was not my meaning, Mr. R.B. . . . you have got me wrong'. The officer capitulated.

R.B. said with firmness: 'Send for the stores holder and ask him: "What are the security arrangements in the stores? What kind of locks are there? What is the state of the doors and windows?" You may, on the basis of paper work, be able to get someone punished, but you can't change the situation in the stores. . . . Make a spot inspection . . . is it the stores or a slaughter house . . . ?'

'O.K. Mr. R.B., you also come along. We shall see how we can improve things,' said the stores officer in agreement.

The stores officer after calling the stores holder to his cabin made enquiries. The conversation went on for an hour. R.B. remained a mute listener. The gist of the entire conversation was that the officer and the stores holder were both more interested in securing deputations and in establishing contacts with the companies supplying materials to the Institute than in the stores. The weaknesses of each other were knowingly being overlooked. The conversation went on in the same spirited manner in which it takes place between intellectuals in coffee houses and tea shops, with no results.

V.K. was fully familiar with the situation in the stores. The stores officer belonged to the same community. A deep strategy lay behind the transfer of R.B. to the stores. He knew that whoever went to the stores would get embroiled. So who could be a better candidate than R.B.!

R.B. had come to know of these calculations. He was proceeding with considerable caution. Several people loyal to the stores officer had begun to create trouble for R.B. R.B. had no hopes for any cooperation from any quarter.

Ultimately what R.B. had feared came to pass. In spite of all his precautions, V.K. gave him a bad A.C.R. (Annual Confidential Report). He was informed through a warning letter that he had been found wanting in trustworthiness, technical competence and initiative. So he was warned that he should try to bring about the desired improvement in future.

R.B. was distressed. He didn't know what he should do. He showed the letter to the General Secretary of the Staff Association. The latter's attitude also was neutral. R.B. felt as though everyone had ganged up against him.

He went straight to V.K.'s cabin with the letter. V.K. was chatting with his delicate looking steno. There was a five-inch long smile on her face.

R.B. tossed the letter on to V.K.'s table. His nerves were taut with anger. His eyes were bloodshot.

'Mr V.K., can you prove that I lack technical competence, that my trustworthiness is in doubt, that I don't take initiative in any matter?. . . You cannot prove this. . . . And if you think that by getting the promotion that I am about to get stopped you and your cronies will have some relief, you will be proved wrong. You have disturbed my mental peace. You will not remain in peace either,' R.B. said shaking with anger.

'Sit down, Mr. R.B. Let's have a quiet talk. . . . This A.C.R. will have no effect on your promotion . . . I have talked to the G.M.,' V.K. tried to explain.

'What is it that you have talked to him about? . . . I only wish to know if you can cite a single instance when there was a question mark against my technical competence; when my trustworthiness came in the way of government work; or when I didn't take initiatives. Mr. V.K., I have been in this section even before you joined the Institute. In every meeting you proceeded on the basis of *my* report and *my* data. Is this the reward you have given for my competence? . . . I am sorry, Mr. V.K., that I have become a victim of your caste prejudices. You are more interested in strengthening your caste ego than in work. . . . Here is the warning letter. Have it framed and put it alongside the photograph of Mahatma Gandhi there, so that those who come later may see what a capable officer you are. . . .' Throwing the letter R.B. came out of the cabin.

V.K. broke into sweat. The steno's face also turned pale. V.K. had seen this facet of R.B. for the first time.

R.B. came back to the stores section, livid with anger. He felt that belonging to the S.C. had kept haunting him all along. From school to college, college to job . . . he has had to bear the burden of it in some form or the other. So much so that he was reminded even in the streets and localities that however high up he might go, he would remain a low-caste person after all.

In the midst of all these pressures R.B. had not yet surrendered. But this time he felt dwarfed in the presence of V.K. V.K. had attacked him surreptitiously. He seemed to feel that he was unarmed and V.K. had attacked him equipped with all ammunition.

In the meantime an incident took place in the colony. Just opposite Nishikant's house was a pump house. Nishikant's daughter had an affair with the pump attendant. Nishikant had begun to get suspicious about the ways of his daughter. When he mentioned this to his wife, she burst upon him: Contorting her face in an odd way, she said: 'May your tongue rot! You suspect your own daughter! Your have lost your head. At first you suspected me, now you suspect your daughter. Have some sense of shame.'

Nishikant was silenced for the time being. But the seeds of suspicion had begun to sprout in his mind. The people of the colony talked about it in subdued tones, which reached Nishikant's ears.

That day Nishikant suddenly came back home. It was noon. Things were quiet in the colony at that time. There wasn't much of traffic. When he reached his quarter, the door was open. His wife was fast asleep. He looked for his daughter here and there, on the roof, in the stairs, everywhere. She wasn't to be found. He straight went to the pump house. He peeped in the pump house window. What he saw was shameful for any father to see.

He gave his daughter two or three slaps with an open hand. The girl ran towards the quarter. Nishikant swooped on the pump attendant like a hunting dog. The pump attendant was a young man of sturdy build. He got into a physical fight with Nishikant. Nishikant's clothes got torn. The women of the colony on hearing the noise started peeping out from their windows. They had seen Nishikant's daughter with dishevelled clothes running out of the pump house. Nishikant's torn clothes and screaming and shouting carried the story to a climax.

Nishikant threatening the pump attendant returned to his quarter. He gave vent to his anger and humiliation on his daughter. After thrashing her soundly, he shut her up in the room. Locking the room from outside, he then attacked his wife. The wife ran away into the other room and bolted the door.

At about ten at night the pump attendant along with three companions of his intruded into Nishikant's quarter and began giving Nishikant a sound beating.

All the doors in the neighbourhood were closed, lights were switched off, and no one came out in the open.

R.B.'s quarter was three-four blocks away. He had come out for a stroll after meals. On hearing the noise he went to Nishikant's quarter and saw some people beating him severely. He snatched the hockey stick from the hands of one of them and grappled with them. The sudden attack made them run away. Nishikant suffered many injuries. R.B. took him to the hospital. As soon as the dressing was over, he came back. On getting the news V.K. also went to the hospital.

Immured within the dark cell of the police station, R.B. was passing through a deep crisis. It seemed to him that Nishikant and V.K. had trapped him completely in the web of their intrigue. He spent the whole night sitting in this manner. He didn't close his eyes even for a moment. Every fibre of his body was shrieking in the dusty dirty cell of the police station. It was as if a ball of fire was scorching his insides.

A drop of sunlight came down in the courtyard of the police station. On a table in the verandah just opposite the cell lay the latest newspaper. The banner-line on the main page said: 'One more young man commits self-immolation in protest against reservations!'

R.B. read the headlines from behind the bars of the cell. He breathed a heavy sigh. He felt as if his head would burst. He pressed his head between his hands and sat leaning against the wall. There was darkness before his eyes, darkness in which there was not a drop of light as far as the eyes could see. The sunlight spreading in the courtyard of the police station suddenly changed into a dark shadow. Perhaps a piece of cloud had swum before the sun, which was pricking R.B.'s eyes like a lancet.

12

Amma

YOU COULD call it Amma's story—but not of one particular Amma; for you hardly know how many Ammas you would come across with broom and canister in hand early morning doing the rounds of lanes and gali-mohallas, whose decrepit bodies have wilted under the impact of time and like old trees have begun to waste away. Every moment of their lives is moving towards an unseen and uncertain future. All prophecies, intellectual acrobatics and imaginative plans about them just go to pieces or are exposed to be a lie.

I don't know what her name is—of the Amma that I am talking about. Perhaps she has forgotten her name herself. For when she came to her new house from her home, her in-laws addressed her as bahu. The younger brother-in-law and sister-in-law called her bhabhi and the old women of the neighbourhood gave her a new name after her husband's name, Sukru's wife. In the early days Sukru did not call her by her name. He doesn't call her by her name

*'Amma' (Hindi), first published in *Vasudha*, Bhopal, 1 January-15 March 1996.

even today. There was no occasion to do so in those days. The entire day she spent hemmed in by the shadow of her mother and his sister. Late at night he would go to her charpai, stealing his way like a thief, that too for a brief while. Even then, there was the haunting fear that his mother or sister might wake up. Their living 'room' consisted of the space created in the small courtyard by a tin roof and wooden pieces joined together.

During those brief moments, there was hardly any time to make conversation. She wasn't the Amma of today who walked dragging her feet slowly and whose dirty saree was thrust in near her stomach. Thick, jute-like lacklustre hair, a face criss-crossed with wrinkles, small dim eyes, one of them made smaller by time, and missing front teeth. Even the solitary tooth that remained shook like the maize seeds bobbing up and down in the baking pan of the grambaker.

Those days were altogether different: she had long thick hair, lively dark, deep eyes, beautiful dark complexion, a well-filled body whose smell had entranced Sukru. Throughout the day he yearned for those brief moments of love. Even today those were the golden moments of her life that she cherished in her memory. Their meetings, no doubt, lasted a brief while but that was the time they had lived most intensely.

When the first son was born, he was given the name of Shivcharan after great deliberation. Sukru too realized the need for calling his wife by a name and from that day on, he started calling her 'Shibbu's mother'—Shibbu's mother who was now merely Amma. Sukru of course still calls her by this name.

Amma's is now a large family that includes grandchildren. As she reaches the seventh decade of her life, her body refuses to co-operate with her. She often falls ill. Arthritis gives her a great deal of trouble. Even so she works at ten-fifteen houses before returning home.

Amma was very fond of wearing white. Even today when she stepped out for work with a broom and a broken, discoloured canister, she would still wear white. But now, because of merciless time, the whiteness of the saree has merely become an idea. The white had changed, God knows when, into dirty yellow or grey. She never realized this, not even how time has flown so fast. As a village girl who had come to the city, she had in those days looked at everything around her with deer-like eyes full of wonder.

Both her in-laws have now been dead for several years. But she distinctly remembers the time when her mother-in-law took her out to pay a 'salaam' visit to her 'clients'. At that time she had never imagined that like her mother-in-law, she too would one day take her broom and canister in hand and go from house to house.

Her mother-in-law had trained her properly—how she was to call at the house, how to enter the lavatory, how throw water there, then how many times she was to sweep on the right and how many times on the left; in which house she was to talk, to whom and how much; and how far inside the house she was to go. She wasn't to touch anything lying in the courtyard and if she was given a glass of water or a cup of tea, she knew where she was to keep it. She had learnt in which corner or alcove or branch of a tree in each courtyard her mother-in-law had securely kept her cup or glass, which came in handy later.

She had told her many, many other things, besides. She used to listen to her mother-in-law with curiosity. The ways of the village were different. There everyone, man or woman, went out in the open to answer the call of nature. Even otherwise most jobs in the village were connected with field work. But this work was utterly new for her. The moment she opened the door of a lavatory, she felt dazed. With the stench. Indians too had constructed lavatories in imitation of the West. All this seemed strange to her.

In the beginning her mother-in-law took her along on her rounds. She worked while the mother-in-law would watch and give instructions. Time had started flying on its wings. Mother-in-law had been happy with her work. She cared for her in every way and remained with her like a shadow.

One day the mother-in-law suddenly took ill. She never recovered from her sick bed. The entire responsibility for work at home and outside now fell on the shoulders of Shibbu's mother.

After Shivcharan came Bisan and then Kiran. From Shibbu's mother, the mother of three had become Amma. The sister-in-law had got married and had gone to her in-laws. There were ten members at home: the in-laws, younger brother-in-law and his wife and their daughter, Sukru and three children and of course Amma. The father-in-law did nothing but lie coughing on the bed the whole day long. The brother-in-law was supposed to be a member of a band party but except for the marriage season practically remained without work. He just spent his day roaming about. Sukru was a safai karamachari in the municipality. The salary was small. The burden of the entire household fell on his shoulders. On top of it, there was the monthly interest to be paid on the loan from Sardar Pritam Singh.

The training that her mother-in-law had given her stood the family in good stead in imes of crisis. She was able to increase the number of her clients from ten to fifteen. The additional five she had purchased from Biramdei on instalments, on the promise that she would pay back part of the money every month.

The most paying thikana of Amma's belonged to Chopra. He had a cloth shop in Bara Bazar and he earned a decent income. He used to leave early in the morning and came back home at ten at night. The children would also go to school in the morning. Mrs. Chopra remained alone throughout the day.

Amma often saw a stranger in Mrs. Chopra's house. At first she thought the man to be someone related to the family. But the mystery soon became clear. One day she was shocked to see the two in a compromising position. Mrs. Chopra had appeared to her to be a gentle and a good woman. But after what she had seen that day, she started feeling a strange kind of aversion for her.

That day Mrs. Chopra gave her an increase of five rupees. She used to get five rupees from each of her clients. Mrs. Chopra now started paying her ten rupees. She was a cheerful woman and was a good talker. She would talk to her about everything under the sun. Amma would merely listen.

Whenever Mrs. Chopra was alone, she would stop Amma for a cup of tea. Her cup hung on a guava tree in the courtyard. While taking her tea she wondered why, though she was so good otherwise, Chopra bahenji had relations with another man. She felt ashamed even to mention it.

One day, when Amma reached the Chopra house, Mrs. Chopra was in the bathroom. The visitor was sitting in the bedroom. Amma called out: 'Bhainji, please throw water . . . I've done the cleaning.' Mrs. Chopra replied from the bathroom: 'Vinod, please give the jamadaarni a bucket of water . . . I'm washing my hair . . . I'll take some time coming out. The bucket is under the tap.'

He got up and put the bucket of water in front of Amma. He smiled at her. Amma gestured to him to throw the water. In stead of throwing water in the lavatory, Vinod slipped his hand round her waist and pulled her to himself with a jerk. This misbehaviour stupefied Amma. She shouted: 'What are you doing? . . . Let me go.' And she tried to wrest herself free from his grip.

Vinod increased his pressure. He pressed her to himself by main force. Amma felt as though a man-eater had pounced upon her. She was trying her utmost to loosen his hold on her. Just as the hold got loosened a little, she jerked herself free. Her grip on the head of the broom that she had in her hand, got tightened. She struck at his temple with full force. As he was struck, he stumbled and ran towards the bedroom. Amma continued hitting him and entered the bedroom. He fell down on the floor. Amma still kept on hitting him relentlessly. A stream of abuses burst forth from her mouth.

All the shouting made Mrs. Chopra come out from the bathroom, half-naked. On seeing the scene in the bedroom, she was dumbfounded and ran to save Vinod.

'Stop it . . . what are you doing? . . . stop it . . . don't hit him. . . .' Mrs. Chopra tried to snatch the broom away from her hands. But Amma pushed her also behind and gave him two or three more blows. Then, when she had stopped, she said: 'Bhainji, tell this bastard that not every woman is a slut.' Amma's eyes were glowing red and her body was shaking with anger. Her swarthy complexion had assumed a deeper hue.

Vinod's lust had cooled down. A heavy stroke of Amma's broom had landed on his eyes. A big blue bump developed around them. He pressed his hand on it and lay sprawling on his stomach on the floor.

Amma picked up her canister and stormed out of the house. The following day she sold off the Chopra 'thikana' to Hardei cheaply. She also told her the entire story in detail.

Hardei was a foul-mouthed woman. Abuses streamed out of her mouth and no sentence of hers was complete without them. On hearing the entire episode, she said: 'You're stupid, you cursed one. You should've dragged the mother's lover into the lavatory. First, you should've stripped him naked, and made him take a walk through Mussoorie, and then made him dance. After that you should've beaten the dog with the broom and taken him to the street. That would've completed the disgrace of the mother-fucker—seeing him run with his ganpati swinging about. He would've forgotten all about romancing. . . . And that Chopree! . . . I know how to handle such women. . . . Here, take this lote. . . . From tomorrow Chopree is mine. . . . Saali! . . . imagine a mother of two still trying to seek love elsewhere!'

After selling off her Chopra thikana for twenty rupees, Amma heaved a sigh of relief.

When the news of Amma's having sold the Chopra thikana for twenty rupees reached her mother-in-law, there was a veritable storm in the house. Shouting at her loudest she created an uproarious scene in the entire mohalla. 'O cursed, unfortunate woman! You could've waited for my death before acting wilfully. This Chopree has done us, I know not, how many favours. She always came to our rescue whenever we needed help. It's not recent. It has been years that I've been going there. They belong to a respectable family. We count for nothing in comparison. And you, grand lady that you are, have become so important that you have sold off the thikana. And that too, to that bitch, Hardei. I know her very well. She must have told you a sob story. For long she had had her eyes on the thikana. Ari, you should've talked to me at least once.' The mother-in-law was weeping bitterly. Amma kept listening to her mother-in-law weep and wail but she made no mention of the incident at the Chopra household.

Mrs. Chopra helped her too—so long as the affair was known only to her. Amma had not spoken of it nor did she ever mention it to anyone else . But now that the scoundrel had attempted to molest her, she couldn't bear it.

The mother-in-law reconciled herself after weeping and wailing for a few days. But one day, it was Sukru who brought it up. That day the municipality had given him a raise in salary and he had come back home after drinking a quarter of country liquor. Placing his salary in Amma's hands, he said: 'Here is the money. But listen, Shibbu's mother, you didn't do well to hurt mother. She had cornered these thikanas after a great deal of manoeuvring. On these depends the running of the entire household. Father never did anything. Mother managed to scrape through hard times with the help of these thikanas. Bread, clothes, everything she got from these thikanas. When she was married, it was this Chopree who got us the cloth from their shop—that too on credit. And you've sold her off! That wasn't the right thing to do, Shibbu's mother. Go and apologize to her, pay twenty rupees to Hardei and get back the thikana. Why should we hurt mother in her last days? You will never find a woman like Chopree. She is as good-natured as she is beautiful.' Finding Shibu's mother unresponsive, Sukru said sharply: 'You just sit like a dumb doll . . . are you listening to me?'

Amma had been listening to Sukru quietly. There was a strange kind of uproar in her mind, which she found difficult to ignore. But she didn't want to cause trouble by talking of that incident.

Many a time she had heard the rising agitation inside her but she had remained silent. Now her heart was full of wounds without number. Whenever she tries to rake them, she trembles all over. Like her memories, she had kept all her desires locked in her discoloured tin trunk that had come from her home. She had just busied herself in the task of rearing the children without complaining. She put Shivcharan in a school in the mohalla itself. A year after she put Bisan and then Kiran in school. In imitation of baniya-brahmins, she had called her daughter Kiran Lata. Everyone at home called her Kiran but not Amma for whom she was always Kiran Lata.

As the children grew up, their expenses also increased. Even otherwise the budget had always been tight. Now there were books and notebooks to purchase in addition. Shivcharan came up with one request or the other every other day. Bisan took after his uncle—the same features and the same habits. He would spend the entire day singing film songs, dressing himself before the mirror, or playing on the dholak or the harmonium. Whenever Amma caught him playing on the dholak or the harmonium, her blood would boil.

'I have got tired of telling you. We don't want you to be a street dancer, understand? You want to go about playing on the pipe or something in the streets like your uncle!

Have you noticed the state of his health? His lungs have grown weak. He breathes like a furnace. And you wish to follow in his footsteps! Get a bit of education so that you may be a peon in an office, if not a clerk. You will at least be free from this dirty work, which doesn't get you two square meals a day properly nor any respect. We're up to the neck in debt. There is Sardar Pritam Singh at the door even before your father has come home with his salary. There is never a spell of peace anywhere, either inside the house or outside: the same miserable, harrowing routine everyday. That is how life goes—no one even lets you sit near him as if they will catch a contagious disease.'

Amma's throat had got choked. Shivcharan had opened his bag of books. Kiran Lata was preparing a cup of tea for Amma. Bisan looked about himself but finding no way to escape Amma's anger, quietly sat down to read.

Amma never scolded Kiran Lata. She always said: 'She has to leave us and go to her own house. One never knows how long she is with us. Why scold her! If she learns a little, she will at least be able to write to us about her welfare. Or else, one has to look to others to have a few words written. And then a daughter is a Lakshmi.'

Amma always kept the children away from work with the broom. Even when she fell ill, she didn't send them as a substitute. Amma was firm about this. When her in-laws or members of the community commented about this, she always said: 'No, I shall not push my children into this filth. I would make them work as labourers but I shall never hand them a broom.'

As soon as Shivcharan passed his tenth class examination, he became a temporary clerk in the municipality. He got this job through a thekedar. He had to pay twenty per cent of his salary to him. Whatever was left, he would go and put in the hands of Amma. Amma started believing that times were changing for the better.

Shivcharan had made a special place for himself in the municipality. He had become a petty leader also. There was a particular labour leader in the city who exercised much authority. Shivcharan became his henchman. Whenever there was a meeting or a procession, Shivcharan would play an active part in it. Carrying flags, distributing pamphlets, shouting slogans—Shivcharan would do all these jobs. He had also learnt to speak a little in public. All this proved advantageous to Shivcharan because he had gained a kind of foothold in the administration. He succeeded in cultivating several officers and clerks. As a result he started doing what the thekedar had done earlier, which meant an increase in his income.

When a man becomes a man-eater, he ceases to differentiate between those who are strangers and those who are his own people. He just wants blood. This is what happened with Shivcharan. Under the pretext of getting their work done, he started charging commission from all irrespective of whether or not they were relatives or persons of his community. It was said that he had a pig's hair in his eyes.

Amma didn't understand things in spite of Shivcharan's increasing income. Sukru also worked in the municipality but had never talked to her about Shivcharan. One day just as Hardei's daughter-in-law came to the street after finishing work at the Chopras, she saw Amma coming from the opposite direction. At first, she hesitated a little but later, showing great deference, she said: 'You work even now, Ammaji? What more do you need? Jethji is earning such a great deal these days. He charged three thousand rupees for a job for Ramkishan. Everyone knows this.'

'Who are you talking about, bahu? About Shivcharan? He charged three thousand rupees? Who told you this?' Amma was thunderstruck.

'Ammaji, don't pretend to be ignorant. When bundles of notes come into the house, even the neighbours come to know of it. Then, you are the mother, the mistress of the house. I'm told Shivcharan puts all his earnings into your hands. The saying comes true: 'Extort money from others, yet be known as honest.' Hardei's daughter-in-law went her way after igniting a spark.

Amma was drained of all colour. But she couldn't say anything in reply at that time.

In the evening as soon as Shivcharan came back, she said to him plainly: 'What you are doing these days, Shibbu, is not right. . . . If I had known how you are earning money, I would not have touched it. I sent you to school and married you off. . . . My task is done. . . . I haven't been able to make a good person out of you, for which I hold myself guilty. From tomorrow start cooking separately. . . . I can't share your ill-earned bread. Rob or kill . . . I shall have nothing to do with it.'

Shivcharan kept listening to his mother. He was not able to understand what his mother was saying. What has happened to her suddenly? He said: 'What's the matter, Amma? Do I bring stolen money? That thekedar had been doing just this for years. He has built such a big kothi. If I do the same thing, where is the harm? I work hard and people pay me willingly. I don't pressurize people unjustly.'

'You talk of harm, Shibbu? . . . There is no harm even in cutting someone's throat or in robbing someone, or in lending money on interest. But, son . . . do spare a thought for those who pay you out of their hard-earned money by depriving their children of food. No, son . . . no. Have you ever thought of their plight, how they live their lives?' Amma's throat was choked.

'They are responsible for their own sad condition, Amma. Instead of taking their salary home, they spend it on drinking or betting,' Shibbu argued.

'Right you are, son. If I hadn't sent you to school, you too would have been in the same situation. As for drinking, you also drink. You get it for free, so you drink. Tomorrow when you won't get it, you'll buy it. Once you get into the habit, you don't see whether the children are hungry or ill. . . . Do what you think best. I have said what I wanted to. From tomorrow live separately. . . . . I don't need this earning of yours.' Saying this Amma got up and busied herself in doing household work. It gave her endless pain that she had given birth to someone who had become a man-eater who was devouring his own kind.

When Amma looks back, everything is in a sort of mist, dim and unclear. She has passed through innumerable ups and downs.

The blister that Bisan's son Mukesh has created in her breast is the deepest. It has come as shock to her.

Mukesh had passed his M.A. But there was not even a distant prospect of a job for him. He had tried his level best but hadn't succeeded. There was a lot of tension at home because of Mukesh. For this reason he didn't come home for days together. Bisan's worries started increasing. Enquiries revealed that he had started living with a school teacher.

The teacher lived along with her two children separately

from her husband. She was young and attractive to look at. Mukesh had met her somewhere. This acquaintance changed into intimacy. There developed between the two a relationship which they had not been able to give a name to.

To escape the prevailing tension at home, he would go to the teacher, in search of peace. In the beginning, the teacher felt drawn to Mukesh because of his attractive personality. She found refuge from boredom in his arms. But after a few meetings, this attraction changed into a need. Someone was needed to look after the children. The teacher went to school at eight o'clock and Mukesh minded them throughout the day.

He never returned home before ten or ten-thirty. Once, when he reached home late, Bisan rebuked him: 'Where do you spend your time staying out late? You leave home very early and come back at night!'

Mukesh tried to sidetrack the query. But when Bisan showed firmness, all his excuses failed. Bisan had heard rumours about his relationship with the teacher. Bisan growled: 'What is this affair about the school teacher?'

At the mention of the teacher, Mukesh was nonplussed. Amma also came out on hearing Bisan's voice. Mukesh kept standing with his head held down. He didn't give a reply to any one of Bisan's questions. Bisan lost his temper. He shouted at him: 'If you have any sense of shame left, get out of the house at once' and gave him a couple of resounding slaps. Amma intervened and took Mukesh away. Bisan was still shouting. Amma sat near Mukesh and made enquiries. Mukesh admitted everything before Amma.

To Amma it seemed that it was not her grandson but

Vinod who was sitting in Mrs. Chopra's bedroom. A strange aversion filled her eyes. She didn't speak a word. She sighed deeply and lay down on the bed.

She didn't know when Mukesh had got up and gone away. Next morning Shivcharan's wife came and said: 'Ammaji, marry off Mukesh. He will get back on the track all right.'

Amma took a long breath and said: 'No, bahu, I shall not tie an innocent girl to this stud. When a person becomes used to stale flesh, he doesn't care for fresh meat. I shall not push a poor man's daughter into a pit, knowingly, not while I'm alive.' Amma took several deep breaths as though she was trying to come out of the pain.

The morning sun had descended on the roof. Amma took her broom and canister and went towards her thikanas.

That day she didn't return till the evening. She remained away the whole day.

Mukesh's leaving home had shocked her deeply.

In the evening when she returned, she was completely exhausted. She was breathing with difficulty. Everyone was anxious about her. Bisan spread out a cot for her: 'Where have you been, Amma? We looked for you everywhere. Everyone was worried.' But Amma made no reply.

On finding her quiet, Bisan said: 'Stop going to the thikanas, Amma. Where is the strength in your body? Even otherwise, there is no need for you to take all this trouble. We are managing the house somehow. It doesn't seem right—your carrying a load of shit. When people see you, it's shameful.'

'Bette Bisan, I sent you and your children to school in order that you feel ashamed. . . . That's why you were educated. I tried to take all of you away from the broom and the basket. . . . After me, not a single daughter or daughter-in-law of the house has gone to the thikanas. . . . So that you might all learn to live with dignity and not do things that might make you feel ashamed. . . . There has been something wanting, son, that Mukesh has strayed into tasting the left-overs, that too like a servant, to look after her children. He could have brought her as a bride . . . even though she was the mother of two children. That would have delighted me. I would have welcomed her as a daughter-in-law. . . . But this is not proper. He hasn't done the right thing. . . .' Amma felt choked. She started weeping.

When the tears stopped, she again said: 'With the money that I got when your father retired, I paid off Sardar Pritam Singh's debt. Now life is all up to you. . . . When Kiran Lata comes home with her children, I should have some money with me to give them. How long shall I keep asking you for it?. . . No, son. . . . If for that joy I have to work hard, I shall continue doing so till my last breath.'

A deep pool of water showed up in Amma's eyes, in which rose small waves, as though all the wounds of the past had become alive again.

Amma's broken down canister and broom lay against the wall mocking her.

13

The Homeless

THE KUCHCHI bricks made by Sukia were being placed inside the brick kiln in order to bake them. Seeing a latticed wall of kuchchi bricks in the corridor of the kiln filled him with inner joy. In no time thousands of bricks had been lined up in the kiln. The spaces between the bricks were filled in with hard coal, wood, sawdust and ears of sugar cane.

Contractor Asghar had got everything stacked systematically under his personal supervision. Before starting the fire, the kiln owner Mukhtar Singh inspected each and everything himself.

Labourers had been put on twenty-four hours' duty. They did the work of putting coal, sawdust etc in the empty spaces through the channels. Working at the channels was the most dangerous job in the entire operation. Even a slight carelessness was enough to cause death.

The kiln had started belching smoke. This smoke could be seen from miles away. Built amid lush green fields,

*'Khanabadosh' (Hindi), first published in *Pashyani*, Delhi, January-March 1996.

this deep earth-coloured kiln seemed like a blemish. Mano and Sukia had come to the kiln only a month back as daily wage labourers. After having seen him work for a week, contractor Asghar had told Sukia to take up the mould and start making bricks and take payment at the rate of a thousand bricks. There were about thirty labourers who worked at the kiln. The kiln owner Mukhtar Singh and contractor Asghar went back to the city as soon as it was evening. After the bustle of the day, the kiln, far away from the city, sank into the lap of darkness.

The flickering tiny lamps in the small cottages built in a row were unable to wrestle with this darkness. In order to enter the fowl-house cottages, one had to bend low and come out in the same manner. As soon as the work at the kiln was over, the women started attending to work in the kitchen. The hearth was a hearth only in name. In a hearth made by putting some bricks together, the crackling sound of burning pieces of wood seemed to echo the worries and hardships that occupied their mind. Everything was uncertain here.

Mano had not yet been able to adjust herself to the life of the kiln. In the face of Sukia's insistence, she had yielded. As evening fell, the whole atmosphere became utterly lonely and weird. The labourers, weary after their daylong labour, got into their fowl-house cottages. The fear of snakes and scorpions was constant. It was as though the entire jungle had come to their cottage door. In such surroundings Mano began to feel dismayed. But what could she do? Time and again she had told Sukia: 'Even the dry bread of your own place is better than delicacies in a strange land.'

Sukia's mind was preoccupied with one thing. If you have to get out of a hellish existence, you will have to sacrifice something. To every objection of Mano's, he had only one answer: 'Venerable old people used to say that the real worth of a person becomes known only when he steps out of his home. Even a mouse behaves like a warrior at his own place. Those Chaudhris who carry lathis on their shoulders aren't able to stand straight in front of government officers in the city. They bleat like old goats. . . . And they don't consider a poor man in the village worth anything. . . .'

These words of Sukia had weakened Mano. That's why one day, both of them, leaving their village, had come away to the kiln along with contractor Asghar.

Sukia had saved some money in the first month itself. They had satisfied themselves about the money after repeated counting. They had tied the money in a knot in the dhoti and tucked it inside the folds of the waistband. Mano too was pleased at the sight of the money. She had started feeling that he would now change the course of his life.

Sukia and Mano's life had begun to move along a settled course. At first both would prepare tagaari. And then Mano would bring the prepared mud to him. A third labourer had joined them in this work. His name was Jasdev. He was very young in years. Contractor Asghar had assigned him also to work with them. This speeded up their work. Sukia too had started to prepare the kuchchi bricks in the mould fast. This meant more earnings.

That day, instead of the kiln owner Mukhtar Singh, his son Sube Singh came to the kiln. The owner had gone out somewhere and during his absence the domineering manner of Sube Singh transformed the atmosphere of the kiln. During those days contractor Asghar Ahmad became timid. An orderly was posted outside the office who, squatting on his chair, smoked bidi all the day long. He kept an eye on all those who came to the office. No one could go in without his permission.

One day Sube Singh happened to notice Kisni. Kisni and Mahesh had come to the kiln only three months back. They had been married some five-six months before.

Sube Singh gave her the work of attending to the needs of the office. In the beginning no one took any notice of it. But when every day, instead of working with mud and earth, she continued to stay in the office, whispers started among the labourers.

On the third day when the labourers were coming out of their cottages to begin their work, Kisni sat bathing in the open at a handpump rubbing herself with soap vigorously. No one at the kiln had a soap. Everyone noticed the soap and the foam that arose from it. However, no one said anything. Dark clouds of suspicion gathered in everybody's mind. Soft whispers started.

Mahesh became reserved and started keeping aloof. Kisni with her swarthy complexion and a well-filled body was causing Mahesh great pain by her conduct. She remained confined to the office all the day through. Her laughter began to be heard even outside the office. Mahesh tried to bring her round. But it was difficult for her to turn back from the path that she was treading.

The life of the kiln was quite strange. The place was taking on the atmosphere of a village or a basti. The fireplaces burning outside the cottages and the smell of food being cooked produced a feeling of freshness albeit for a short time in the dull life of the kiln. Most people ate gur with their chapattis, or ate chapattis with red chilli sauce. Pulses or vegetables were seldom cooked.

As evening fell, people crowded at the handpump.

The more they tried to remove the mud sticking to their bodies, the more it entered their bodies. The smell of raw earth had entered their entire being. Apart from this smell, the kiln had no other identity.

The story of Kisni and Sube Singh had advanced considerably. Sube Singh's orderly had made Mahesh an alcohol addict. Mahesh lay drunk in his cottage. Kisni had now even acquired a transistor. Morning and evening, the silence of the kiln resounded with the music of the transistor. She would play the transistor so loudly that the atmosphere of the kiln was filled with the resonance of film songs. The musical waves had produced a clinking sound in the silent atmosphere.

When after hard work and after being on fire day and night the kiln was opened, the anxious breaths of everyone from the labourer to the owner felt relieved. The task of taking out pucca bricks from the kiln began. The joy of Sukia and Mano on seeing red bricks knew no bounds. Mano in particularly turned them over to examine them. The very colour of the brick, which she herself had prepared, had changed! It was while examining the bricks that something struck her like lightning: As soon as this thought came, several kilns started working in her mind all at once. She asked Sukia: 'How many bricks are required to build a home?'

'So many . . . several thousands . . . iron, cement, wood, sand, in addition.' This thought had occurred to her. She couldn't find a proper basis for it immediately. She became restless.

Finding her quiet, Sukia said: 'Come, we have to begin working. Jasdev must be waiting.' Mano started to follow Sukia dejectedly but the red colour of the bricks had so overwhelmed her mind that she got lost in these thoughts.

The song of the crickets and the intermittent sounds of the jackals were deepening the darkness in the dead silence of the night. The tired labourers had tumbled down into deep pits of sleep. But Mano's mind was still preoccupied with the thoughts of red bricks. A small home built of these bricks found lodgement in her mind. The more firmly this thought became entrenched, the further sleep went away from her.

The sound of the crowing of the cock coming filtered from a distant basti together with an awareness of the last spell of the night made Mano's eyes heavy with sleep.

When after attending to the necessary chores of the morning Sukia peeped into the cottage, he was surprised. Mano had never slept so late. He got worried. Feeling Mano's forehead, as she lay asleep, she found that it was cold. He heaved a sigh of relief. He woke her up: 'The day has advanced so much . . . don't you feel like getting up?'

Mano got up somewhat depressed. For sometime she kept sitting silent. Mano's sitting in this fashion began to irk Sukia: 'What's the matter today? You aren't well?'

Mano was lost in her thoughts. They were struggling to come out. Looking at Sukia, she asked: 'Suno-ji, can't we build a home with the help of these pucca bricks?'

On hearing Mano, Sukia stared at her in surprise. He had forgotten yesterday's conversation . . . Sukia said with great sadness: 'A house of pucca bricks is not built with a few rupees. . . . It needs heaps of notes to construct a house. "No money in your pocket and you set out to buy an elephant."'

'We have prepared so many bricks during the month . . . can't make bricks for ourselves?' Mano said innocently.

'This kiln belongs to the owner. We make bricks for

him. We are only labourers. We have no right over these bricks.' Sukia felt the pressure on his mind increase.

'We have no right over these bricks—why . . . ?' Mano said with bitterness mixed with surprise. There was a storm brewing in her mind. After remaining silent for some time, she said: 'If we save a little more, make more bricks every month . . . then? . . . can't we build a home even then?' Mano wanted to articulate the restless questions forming in her mind.

'Where do we get such high wages? After doing back-breaking labour for a month, how much money have we been able to save? Only eighty. Even if we are able to save money for a thousand bricks in a year, we shall spend our entire life to collect money enough for building a house. Even then it wouldn't be possible to build one,' Sukia said with a sad heart.

'Not even if we work day and night?' Mano asked eagerly.

'Have you gone crazy? . . . get up . . . we have to go for work. It is getting late. The contractor would be about to come. We have to cut the eastern chunk for preparing mud today.' Sukia was getting perplexed at Mano's questions. He got up to go out.

'Do whatever you need to . . . if you want, I shall work day and night. . . . I need a home made with pucca bricks, in our own village. . .a bright red brick house.' A thousand springs had suddenly blossomed in Mano's heart.

It seemed as if Sukia and Mano had found a goal. A home of pucca bricks had to be made—with bricks made by their own hands. They would get busy with their work right in the morning and keep on with it even after dark. Everyone from contractor Asghar to the owner was happy with their work.

Sube Singh had started taking Kisni even to the town. There was a change in Kisni's demeanour. She no longer worked with mud and earth at the kiln. Mahesh drank daily and gave vent to his anger in a drunken state. He stayed in his cottage even during the day or sat here and there. Kisni did not return from the city for several days together. When she did, she was exhausted, listless and faded. There was no dearth of clothes with her now.

The other day seeing contractor Asghar come to the kiln, Sube Singh said to him: 'Send for Mano to the office. Kisni is not feeling well today.'

Contractor Asghar tried to stop him: 'Young master, Mano. . .'

Sube Singh rebuked him even before he could complete his words: 'Do what you are told. Don't try to offer me advice. You are a Munshi at this kiln. Behave like a Munshi, or else if you try to be an owner, it will end badly for you.'

Contractor Asghar was rendered speechless. He mutely went to call Mano. He said to her aloud: 'The young master is calling you in the office, Mano.'

Mano looked at Sukia. There was timidity born of fear in her eyes. Sukia too was upset at this call. He understood things. A net was being spread to catch a fish. Anger and resentment began to stretch his nerves. Jasdev too had guessed Sukia's state of mind. He got up quickly. Scrapping away the wet mud on his hands and feet he said: 'You stay here. . . . Let me see. Come, chacha.' He followed Asghar.

Contractor Asghar knew that Sube Singh was a devil. But keeping mum had become a matter of compulsion with him. He had spent a large part of his life at the kiln. He had no identity apart from the kiln.

Seeing Jasdev come along with contractor Asghar, Sube Singh was furious: Who's called you?'

'Ji. . . Please tell me whatever work you have . . . I shall do it . . .' Jasdev said humbly.

'Why"?. . . Are you her husband? . . . Or has too much fat accumulated on her. . . . ?' Sube Singh said abusively.

'How do you talk, babuji?. . .' Before he could complete, he received a resounding slap on this cheek.

'Saale, I'll shove you into the fire of the kiln. . . . No one will ever come to know about it. . . . It will be impossible to separate bones from the ashes. . . . Understand!' Sube Singh gave him a push. As a result he fell down.

Before he could steady himself, Sube Singh thrashed him so much as to leave him half-dead. On hearing their shouts the labourers came running towards them. Finding them coming together, Sube Singh sat in his jeep. In no time the jeep was speeding away to the city. Contractor Asghar sought shelter in the office.

Sukia and Mano carried Jasdev into their cottage. He was crying with pain. Mano applied turmeric to his wounds. Sukia was shaking with anger. Countless clusters of darkness were dancing in her unconscious. She did not wish to be a Kisni. She was filled with an invincible desire to live a life of dignity. She wanted a home built with pucca bricks where she could dream about her family and children.

The entire day was spent in unseen apprehension and terror. Jasdev developed a slight fever. He was lying in his own cottage. Sukia was sitting near him. Today's incidents had frightened the labourers. They feared that Sube Singh might come back any time today. As it was evening, there was dead silence at the kiln. Everyone had shut himself up in his own sheath. The old Bilsiya who could be seen everyday sitting under the tree outside today went into his cottage as soon as it was evening. His coughing was also slightly subdued.

There was no sound even from Kisni's cottage playing on her transistor.

Intermittently the sound of the handpump was interfering with the silence around. The pump was located right opposite Jasdev's cottage. Everyone had to come to the pump to get water.

There was no arrangement for medication at the kiln. Whenever there was a bruise or a cut, earth was applied to it. In place of medicine, the wound was filled in with the ashes of burnt cloth.

Mano lighted the hearth with half a mind. After baking them, she placed the rotis before Sukia. Sukia pushed one roti down his throat reluctantly. It was as if his hunger had suddenly died down. His worries regarding Mano increased. He decided that he wouldn't let Mano become Kisni. Mano too was silently wrestling within herself. It seemed to her that she was not secure. One question kept haunting her: Is this the punishment for being born a woman? She knew that Sukia wouldn't let any untoward thing happen to her. He wasn't like Mahesh. They may have to leave the kiln. She shivered at the very thought of doing so. No . . . they shall not leave the kiln. She reassured herself. They have yet to build a home of pucca bricks.

As Mano started to go out with the rotis, Sukia interrupted her: 'Where are you going?'

'Jasdev is lying hungry and thirsty . . . I am going to give him rotis,' Mano said simply.

'A baaman will take food cooked by you! . . . Have you lost your wits?' Sukia tried to stop her.

'Is there poison in the rotis prepared by me?' Mano questioned him. Stopping for a second, she said: 'He isn't a baaman but a kiln labourer . . . as we are.'

There was dead silence all around. The small lamp in Jasdev's cottage was burning. Mano pushed the door of the cottage. As she went in, she asked: 'How are you feeling?' Jasdev tried to get up. A sigh of pain escaped his lips.

'The wretch will die rotting. His hands and feet will fall off. . . . He is an animal, not a man,' Mano said cursing Sube Singh.

Jasdev kept looking at her quietly.

'Here, eat this bread. You are hungry since morning. If you eat a little, you will gain some strength.' Mano placed rotis and gur near him. Jasdev became somewhat uneasy. He was surely hungry. But somewhere inside there was hesitation. It wasn't very long ago that he had left home. He hadn't been able to prepare anything himself. Every part of his body was aching.

'I am not hungry,' Jasdev made an excuse.

'Are you not hungry or is there something else?' It was as though Mano had caught him red-handed.

'What other thing can there be? . . .' Jasdev questioned her.

'Your brother said you were a baaman . . . so you won't eat food prepared by me. If that is so, I shall not press you. . . . It's your will . . . I am a woman . . . . If there is someone nearby who is hungry . . . no morsel of food will go down my throat. . . . And then, you work with us day and night . . . because of me you got beaten. . . . How then did this baaman come between us. . . ?' Mano came close to tears. Her throat was choked.

She turned back with the rotis. Jasdev didn't have the

courage to stop her. It was as if all the connecting threads between them had suddenly got scattered.

Mano lay down in her cottage quietly. Without eating anything. The events of the day were agitating her mind. Jasdev was hungry. This realization troubled her. There was turmoil within her because of Jasdev. She felt as though Jasdev's company had given them strength—strength that could put courage into them in their fight against Sube Singh. She had started feeling the joy of being three instead of two.

Sukia too lay in bed quietly. He was also sleepless. He wasn't able to decide what to do. It was for these very reasons that he had left the village. Those reasons confronted him again. Where could he go? It wasn't easy to plumb the depth of Sube Singh. It was a lonely place and he could attack any time. Or else Mano could . . . the very thought made him shiver. He turned over. Mano was lying awake. He drew her close and clasped her to his bosom.

Jasdev too spent the entire night lying awake. The angry face of Sube Singh struck terror in his heart. He had started feeling as though he had suddenly got entrapped in some conspiracy. He had no idea that Sube Singh would resort to hitting and kicking. He hadn't ever imagined such a thing. He got frightened. He decided that whatever happened, he wouldn't get embroiled in their affairs.

As soon as it was morning, he went to see contractor Asghar. Asghar it was who had brought him over from the city. Jasdev told contractor Asghar his inner feelings. The thekedar advised him: 'Mind your own business. Why do you get embroiled in the business of these chamars?'

Mano at once guessed Jasdev's changed attitude.

However, she made no response to it. She did her work in her usual manner. She knew that a hiatus had been created between them. But she remained silent.

Sube Singh also started realizing that it wasn't easy to seduce Mano. All his efforts had failed. So now he began to trouble Mano and Sukia. He had also told Asghar thekedar that he shouldn't pay them their wages without asking him. He wasn't to show any concession to them either.

Nothing was hidden from Mano. She kept an eye on every one of his movements. She had decided that she would resist him. There was just one thought that pre-occupied her throughout. A home of pucca bricks had got to be built. But Sube Singh was proving to be an obstacle in this.

Sukia and Mano were completely absorbed in their work day and night. Even so they weren't able to save more than the usual amount. In the past few days they had prepared double the number of bricks. There was no let-up in their enthusiasm. There was only one goal—to make a home of pucca bricks. For this reason they even bore with the excesses of Sube Singh. There was one over-riding concern with them both, however, that sustained them.

Sube Singh was able to find ever new excuses to trouble them; there was a kind of cold war between them. The mould for preparing bricks had been taken away from Sukia. Instead, he had been given work on the channels of the kiln. This was dangerous work. Mano was frightened. But Sukia tried to reassure her: 'Why be afraid to work. . . ?'

Sukia's mould had been given to Jasdev. The moment he got the mould, his attitude changed. He started ordering

Mano about. Mano remained quietly busy in her work.

'Tomorrow kuchchi bricks have to be prepared. Clear the space for it by removing these bricks.' Jasdev went towards his cottage after giving directions. Mano put the kuchchi bricks in the shape of a wall. To enable them to dry up, she had made a latticed wall with two bricks in an upright position and two placed horizontally. It was only after clearing the space for preparing bricks that Mano went to her cottage.

There was a crowd at the hand-pump. After finishing their work, all the labourers had come to the place to wash themselves.

Mano had got up even before it was morning. She was in a hurry to go to the place of work. It was dark everywhere. She didn't want to wait for the morning. She set out to finish the morning chores so that she could start work right away. The sun had not risen yet. She used to reach the place of work even before Jasdev.

Only stray labourers could be seen here and there. She reached the site of the preparation of bricks with rapid strides. The scene shocked her. All the bricks were lying about broken. It was as if someone had trampled them underfoot. On seeing the pitiable condition of the bricks, she let out a shriek. She started crying loudly. The noise brought the labourers to the scene.

There were as many stories as there were mouths. Everyone was trying to make his or her own guess. There had been no thunderstorm during the night. This could also not be the work of any wild animal. Several people said: 'This had been done deliberately.'

Mano's heart was near bursting. The sight of broken bricks drove her mad. As though some one had laid low her home of pucca bricks.

Jasdev reached there after quite sometime. He stood there silently with an impartial air as though he had nothing whatever to do with the broken bricks.

Sukia too came after hearing the uproar, leaving his work at the channels. His heart also began to sink on seeing the state of the bricks. It was as if his courage had given way. He was looking at the bricks with wild eyes. When she saw Sukia, Mano started wailing even more loudly. Sukia watched the fast flowing dust storm rising in Mano's eyes and experienced its grittiness in his consciousness. The sound of the shattering of dreams exploded in his ears.

Asghar thekedar spoke plainly: 'Of what use are the broken bricks to us? There will be no wages for them.' He destroyed all their hopes. Mano looked at Sukia with overflowing eyes. His face reflected the agony of the breaking of the dream home in the storm. She started feeling as if the entire world had become their enemies. All kinds of obstacles were being erected before them. It was now difficult for them to stay there.

He took Mano's hands in his own: 'Let's go! These people won't let us build a home for ourselves.' The dream of a home of pucca bricks was receding, going far beyond their grasp.

The rising dark smoke from the kiln spread a black sheet underneath the sky. Giving up everything, Mano and Sukia went out. Like nomads. They had needed a home . . . to live in. . . . They were leaving behind some precious moments, mirrored in sweat, which will never constitute history. Just a stage in their nomadic life, this kiln.

Before following Sukia out, Mano looked at Jasdev. Mano was certain that Jasdev would stand by them. But on finding him silent her belief got shattered. A shooting pain arose in Mano's heart which changing into icy cold breath riddled her like a sieve. Her lips fluttered to say something, but the words got choked. The glass pieces of broken dreams were hurtful in the eyes. She followed Sukia with a heavy heart, in quest of another halting place, on a journey that had no direction.

14

Shavayatra

IN A CHAMAR village there was a balhar family, which lived across the pond. The pond was like a boundary between the chamars and the balhars. During the rains when the pond became brimful with water, the balhars were completely cut off from the village. On other days, when there wasn't so much water, they managed to reach the village somehow. That meant that there was no way by which the balhars could go over to the village. No one had ever felt the need to provide for it.

Whenever any chamar needed them, he would stand on the bank of the pond and shout. It wasn't such a big pond either that he could not be heard by the balhars. On hearing the call they would come out.

There were only two members left in the balhar family now: Surja, who was getting old; and his daughter Santo, who had come back a widow from her in-laws in the third year of her marriage. Surja's wife had also died three

*'Shavayatra' (Hindi), first published in *India Today*, Delhi, 22 July 1998; in English, *Summerhill*, No. 1, 2006; in German, *SUDASIEL*, January 2006.

years ago. It was Santo who had taken over the responsibilities inside the household and outside. Even otherwise Surja had grown quite weak. His sight had also started failing. Still he somehow managed to do whatever odd work was required to be done in the village.

Surja had a son also, who had run away from home when he was ten or twelve years of age. After roaming about for a few years he had got a job in the railways. In fact it was this job that had drawn him to studies. He managed to complete his high school and then got technical training and became a fitter in the railways. From Kallu, he had become Kallan.

Kallan had borne the entire expenses on Santo's marriage. Surja didn't have a single paisa with him. Kallan had got married in the railway colony. His father-in-law also worked in the railways. He had got an educated wife, which made a noticeable difference in their living. The whole tenor of his life had changed.

He came to the village only occasionally. But whenever he did, the chamars of the village eyed him strangely. They were not able to digest the fact that Kallu had become Kallan. In their eyes he was still a balhar, lowest in the caste hierarchy, an untouchable even among the untouchables.

He felt himself isolated in the village. There was no one outside the family, with whom he could converse for a while. Even the educated persons in the village avoided him. He was a balhar after all, who lived beyond the pond. The villagers still called him Kallu balhar. He didn't like being addressed in that way. It pierced him like a sharp knife and filled him with a sense of inferiority.

This time he had come home after a long spell. As soon as he came he said to Surja: 'Come, bapu, shift with me to Delhi. We'll all live together in the government quarter.'

'No, my son, no. Why do you want us leave the village near the end of my life? At one time my ancestors had found themselves a place here. They all died here, on this very ground. I've spent my entire life living at the pond. Where shall we go now!' Surja, shutting his eyes intermittently, spoke from the heart, as though he was searching for something in his past.

Kallan looked at Santo. She of course wanted to get out of this barbarous existence. But she couldn't bring herself to contradict what her father had said, either earlier or now. She just sat scraping the earth with her big toe. It was as though her thinking was taking her far in the distance where she couldn't spot a place to rest. Kallan said firmly: 'Bapu, here there is neither respect, nor livelihood; even in the eyes of the chamars we're mere balhars. It's because of you that I have to come. My children don't want to come, they don't like it here. . . .'

Surja stopped him short saying: 'Then don't come here, son. We'll spend our life as we've done. I'm only worried about Santo . . . she will be left alone. This run-down structure will probably not survive the rains this time. If you feel concerned about us, make it a pucca house. . . .' Surja had thought of this several times but had not been able to say it. He found an opportunity to do so today.

'Bapu, I have saved up a little money, but what shall we gain by spending it on this house? I shall not stay here after you're gone. Santo will come along with me to Delhi.' Kallan spoke plainly.

On hearing this Surja burst out. He started spouting abuses. He shouted: 'You! Why even wait for me to die?. . . Take her away today itself. And listen. Don't you make a show of your money before me . . . keep it with you . . . we shall manage the rest of our life as we've done, so far.'

It appeared as though the thread of communication between the two had suddenly got snapped. Silence spread all round them.

Early next morning Kallan left for Delhi. He returned a week later after making arrangements for money. His wife Saroj and ten-year old daughter were also with him. They had left their son at the maternal grandparents' place. As Kallan came, he said to his father: 'Talk to some mistri. A truck of bricks will reach here tomorrow.' As he heard this, Surja's eyes began to shine. He didn't quite believe in what Kallan had said. But the latter assured him. That very moment he set out in search of a mistri.

Contractor Surat Ram had constructed most of the houses in the village. It was to him that Surja went: 'Thekedarji, kindly make a house for us also.'

At first Surat Ram looked at him up and down. He didn't have adequate clothing on his body and here he was, trying to have a pucca house built for himself. Surat Ram was in a hurry. He had to go somewhere. He put Surja off with a laugh: 'I've no time today. We'll talk later.'

Surja didn't lose heart. Next day he started out very early. Sabir mistri lived in the adjoining village. An old artisan. Surja told him the reason for his coming. Sabir agreed: 'All right. I shall come and see things tomorrow. But I'll take my dues in advance.'

'That is all right, mistriji. Please come tomorrow. Our house is right at the pond.' Surja wasn't able to conceal his joy. It was as if he was walking on air. His weak body too seemed to be full of energy.

By the time he reached home, the bricks had arrived. When he saw the red bricks Surja forgot all his exhaustion.

He was filled with elation. He hadn't experienced a similar joy earlier.

It was no less than a miracle for the villagers to see bricks being unloaded across the pond. There seemed a virtual earthquake in the village. Many people of the village were standing on the other side of the pond.

Ramjilal was the Pradhan of the kirtan sabha. There used to be a nightlong kirtan on the occasion of Ravidas Jayanti. He too was standing among the crowd. When he couldn't contain himself any longer, he shouted: 'Abe, o Surja, who's got these bricks?' Surja said in excitement: 'Our Kallan is getting a pucca house built for us.'

Ramjilal just looked wide-eyed, stunned. Keeping the rising jealousy and malice in control, he said: 'That is fine, Surja. But did you or did you not obtain the approval of Pradhanji before building a pucca house?'

Ramjilal's words pierced Surja's breast like an arrow. He felt as though some usurer were standing before him and threatening him. Without being able to control his anger, he growled: 'Why ask Pradhanji?'

'Still, you should've sought his approval.' Saying this Ramjilal went away but he had filled Surja's mind with doubts.

Ramjilal went straight to the Pradhan. He presented a peppered account of the goings-on across the pond before Pradhan Balram Singh. At that time Balram Singh did not make any comments. He just shook his head stroking his moustaches. The Pradhan was a cunning man. He knew Ramjilal through and through. After he had gone away he became a little downcast. That Surja balhar was getting a house built was enough to make him feel restless. Even otherwise Surja was no longer of much use to the village.

The news that the balhars across the pond were getting

a pucca house built spread throughout the village. 'It's earnings from the railways; a truckload of bricks is coming; cement, sand, gravel, steel have been ordered.' The news snowballed so much that it seemed as though it was not a house but a mansion that would be built on the chest of the village. 'Teak is coming for doors and windows. It's rumoured that coloured tiles are also arriving.' The gossip multiplied with each teller.

The next day a messenger from the Pradhan turned up across the pond. Surja, though unwilling, had to go with him.

As he saw Surja, Balram Singh shrieked: 'Now that you have made a little money, you have forgotten your limits! We didn't let the balhars settle here so that they would build a haveli on our chest. . . . The land on which you live belongs to our ancestors. Live as you have been living, no one will have any objection. But if you try and raise your head, we'll shunt you out.'

Every word of Balram Singh like a poisoned dart pierced Surja's body like a sieve. All the bittersweet days of his life began to dance before his eyes. It seemed to have happened the other day: What was it that Surja had not done for the village! How Balram had entreated him for every single vote during the elections! At that time Surja was not a balhar, but Surja uncle. Surja heaved a cold sigh and went back without giving any reply. Balram Singh tried to stop him but he didn't stop. At this Balram Singh's shrieks turned into abuses, which could be heard outside.

As he reached home, Surja said to Kallan, 'You were right, Kallu. This village is not fit to live in.' His long moustaches were quaking with anger. His eyes were wet.

'Bapu, there isn't much that's lost even now. Any one would buy the bricks. These people will not let the house be built,' Kallan tried to persuade Surja. But Surja was adamant. He wouldn't bend. He would face whatever be the situation. He repeated this to himself. 'No, my son, the house shall be built. I will lay down my life but I shall not leave this village,' said Surja with self-confidence.

Kallan was in a cleft stick. In an emotional moment he had bought the bricks but the situation in the village alarmed him. He only hoped it wouldn't lead to a clash. His wife Saroj and daughter Saloni had come with him. But Saloni had developed fever right on the first day. Saroj gave her the few pills that she had with her. But the temperature continued. She got scared and repeatedly kept insisting on Kallan going back: 'You're needlessly wasting money on the house. We'll take Santo along. Try and convince bapu.' But Kallan was unable to do so. He said to her: 'Would it to be right to cause him any distress at this stage of his life?' Saroj kept quiet.

Surja kept a nightlong vigil to guard the bricks. He didn't close his eyes even for a second. As soon as it was morning he left home to fetch Sabir mistri. He feared that someone might tutor him against them. He had no faith left in any one now.

Saloni's fever remained unabated. Surja asked Kallan to get a doctor for her.

There was only one doctor in the village and Kallan went to call him.

As the doctor saw Kallan, he declined to come. After making some general enquiries he gave him some pills. Kallan entreated the doctor several times: 'Please, doctor sahib, examine her at least once.' But the doctor remained unmoved. Kallan then said: 'I will bring the patient here to your clinic.'

'Don't bring the patient here. Or else my shop will get

shut down tomorrow. Don't forget you're a balhar,' the doctor warned him plainly. 'Give her this medicine. She'll be all right.'

Kallan came back dejected. The pills that the doctor had given also proved ineffective. Her body was burning because of high fever; because of it she was continuously delirious. Saroj was tending to her and had not moved away from her even for a minute. Her worries about her were increasing. All kinds of fears assailed her.

Surja who had left in the morning returned in the afternoon, tired and disheartened. Seeing his condition Kallan asked him: 'What's happened, bapu?' Surja spoke in a defeated voice: 'What was there to happen! The mistri has gone far away to a relative. He will come back after ten-fifteen days . . . 'son, I don't think he will come here.' Surja expressed his disappointment.

'But bapu, we were paying him all his charges in advance. Even then he's backed out,' Kallan said in surprise.

'Some one within the village must have prevented him . . . Sabir isn't a man of this kind. He too seems to have got scared of them,' Surja spoke out of deep despair. Both of them were plunged in deep worries.

'How is Saloni feeling?' asked Surja.

'Her condition has worsened a great deal. She will have to be taken to the hospital,' Kallan expressed his worry.

'Shall I send for a witch doctor? I hope it isn't some spirit or anything', Surja vocalized his inner fears.

'No, bapu, I shall take her to the town tomorrow morning. Only, if she is able to spend the night peacefully.' Kallan's voice was tinged with deep pain. Surja tried to console him.

They spent the whole night without sleep. Saloni's condition had deteriorated further. As soon it was morning

Kallan put Saloni on his back and covered her with clothes properly. Saroj was with him. They wanted to reach the town before it was noon.

The town was some eight-ten kilometres away from the village. There was no transport available. Kallan had requested the well-to-do chamars of the village for the loan of their bullock-cart, but they were not prepared to lend it to the balhars.

Carrying Saloni on his back was getting to be difficult. She kept sliding down his back repeatedly. Kallan's wife walked behind him supporting her. They wanted to reach the town as soon as possible. But the end of the journey didn't seem to be in sight.

As the sun became hotter, Saloni's body became increasingly enfeebled. Her breathing had slowed down. The town was now half a kilometre away. Suddenly Kallan felt that Saloni's burden had increased somewhat. The feverish body had become cold. He said to Saroj: 'Just see if Saloni is all right.'

There was no movement in Saloni's body. Saroj shrieked out aloud:

'What's happened to my daughter?. . . Why isn't she moving, see?' she said weeping.

Taking her off his back, Kallan laid Saloni down on the wayside. He stood there in despair, feeling cheated. There was a tumult in his mind. Her ten-year-old daughter, alive and well, had become a corpse in his own hands. Everything had happened right in front of their eyes. They were crying loudly. The path was lonely and there was no one to heed them. They sat weeping and wailing for quite sometime. They didn't know what they should do. With the dead body of Saloni lying on the unmetalled path they were in deep agony. After a long time they saw someone coming from the town. For a moment they saw a flicker of hope. The passer-by might perhaps help them.

For a moment the man stopped near them. But he walked on without saying anything. Perhaps he had recognized them. He belonged to the same village. Kallan realized that caste constituted a man's entire identity.

Eventually they got up and placing the daughter's dead body on his back started going back to the village.

The burden on Kallan's back was heavy but the burden in their heart was far heavier. Saloni's childhood shouts kept leaping up in their memory. With a heavy heart they were moving towards the village carrying her dead body. The journey seemed to be endless. It was taking them longer to reach the village than it had taken them to come near the town. Saroj's own condition was causing anxiety. She just managed to drag on. Kallan too had broken down but was somehow holding himself up. Saroj was almost half-dead. She was finding it difficult to walk.

Surja had sensed their arrival from a distance. He was able to recognize them only when they came near but he could make out from their approaching faces who they were. The manner in which they were carrying Saloni alarmed him. From his house he came out on to the road. On seeing Saloni's dead body he was not able to control himself. He felt deeply agonised. Striking his hands on the ground, he started wailing loudly. Kallan's eyes too were overflowing with tears. Hearing this hue and cry Santo also came out. There was no one to console them.

It had taken them a lot of time trudging back from the town. There was no time to call anyone. There were in no position to wait overnight. Kallan wanted the cremation to take place before it was evening. Saroj was having fits repeatedly as she saw Saloni's dead body.

The wood was a problem. They didn't have wood for the cremation. Surja and Santo went out to arrange for it. They went and beseeched the chamars but no one was prepared to help. Even after going about here and there for an hour, they were not able to get enough wood together for a proper cremation. There were dung cakes in the house. Santo suggested: 'Take these cakes instead of wood.'

The cremation ground for the chamars was near the village. But the balhars were not permitted to burn their dead there. A similar situation had arisen at the death of Kallu's mother. The chamars had refused permission point blank. They had to cremate her three-four kilometres further away. Saloni's dead body had to be carried that far. . . . Wood and dung cakes too had to be taken. There was no one other than Surja and Kallan who could help in this task.

No one from the village came to the balhars either to help carry the dead body or join in the funeral procession. Caste stood in their way. Kallan had tried hard. He had gone and met the people in the Ravidas Mandal and Doctor Ambedkar Youth Forum but no one was prepared to come. Everyone slinked away on one pretext or the other.

He started recalling the speeches made at the Ambedkar Jayanti. A deep repugnance rose up in him. He rejected all the ideas expressed there out of hand. He felt that all those speeches were hollow and unreal.

Kallan said to Surja; 'Bapu, let's not delay things any longer.' Both of them lifted Saloni's dead body wrapped in cloth. Women did not customarily go to the cremation ground among the balhars. But for Santo and Saroj there was no option but to violate this custom. Santo carried the bundle of wood on her head and also fire and a pot in her hands. Saroj came behind with a basket full of dung cakes.

Chamarins climbed up to their roofs to watch this funeral procession. Their eyes were moist. But they were helpless, each imprisoned in her ambit. These were balhars, after all. They were used to carrying not only their own dead but that of the others as well. . .

A chamar village and within it a familly of balhars!

15

Umbrella

EVERY Friday a bazaar was held, which was known as the Friday Bazaar where one could get all one's daily needs. This was a T-junction in the middle of the village from where one street went past the mosque and later branched out into several lanes. At the other end was the well of the Pradhans. The third route in contrast to these two was not straight. That route went up to the temple in front of the garhi and got divided into several lanes. It was around this T-junction that the Friday Bazaar was held. After the Friday prayers the hustle and bustle of the bazaar matched that of any fair. In one corner of this T-junction was the dispensary of Dr Ved Prakash Sharma; on the other side was the house-cum-shop of goldsmith Lajjaram. Further on there were two shops of baniyas and opposite them were those that belonged to grambakers.

A little away from Lajjaram's shop in the street outside sat Shaukat chacha. He repaired umbrellas but only a few people in the village had anything resembling an umbrella. That meant that he didn't have much umbrella repair

*'Chhatri' (Hindi), first published in *Kathadesh*, Delhi, November 2006.

work to do. So, along with repairing umbrellas, he also did the work of darning. He wrought magic with his hands. He joined torn clothes in such a manner that those who saw it were simply amazed. He was really an artist.

One Friday, instead of going to his daily work, my father took me to Shaukat chacha's shop. Actually a week ago while coming back from school all my books and note-books had got soaked in the heavy rain. This had upset my father. Since the time he came to know that I was quite a bright student, he had started taking greater interest in my studies. Even minor matters get known to everybody in the village. So when someone passing by said to father—'I hear your son is good in his studies . . . '— he would swell with pride. He would try to raise his turned-down moustaches and sharpen them. When on coming home he told this to mother, she would make me sit near her and move her fingers around in my hair. This was her way of showing her affection. At that time I felt greatly at peace.

Shaukat chacha and father were old friends. After greetings, father said: 'In spite of you, mian, this nephew of yours goes to school getting wet in the rains. In last week's rain he not only got wet himself but his books also got soiled. It took two days to dry them. If you have some old umbrella . . . at least he would be able to keep his books safe.'

Shaukat chacha looked at me. The smile through his grey beard looked gentle. 'Which class are you in, son?' Shaukat chacha asked me.

'Ji, . . . in eighth,' I replied softly.

''In eighth!' Shaukat chacha expressed surprise as though he was not able to believe it. How could he, for no son of a chuhra in those days could even think of going to school. If someone had tried doing so, no one would have permitted him to enter the school even.

'Look Sugan bhai, it's a good thing you have done that you have sent your son to school. . . . I am sure this will improve his life. . . . Don't you worry, by next Friday, he will get his umbrella. I have all the articles necessary. I have only to work them together and cover it with cloth. . . . Come next Friday, bete. . . ,' Shaukat chacha said looking at me.

'How much will it cost, mian? father asked hesitatingly.

'Cost? . . . We shall see. . .', said Shaukat chacha.

'Even so . . . I won't be able to pay you all at once . . . whatever I am able to save from my daily earnings, I shall pay in small bits,' father expressed his helplessness.

'I know everything, Sugan . . . I am not a dhanna seth myself. . . . If he is a son of yours, he is something to me too. . . . Don't you talk about money . . . just send him over next Friday. He will get his umbrella . . . come, bete . . .' Shaukat chacha looked at me with great affection.

It felt good to see Shaukat chacha to be so very affectionate. While he was talking he was engaged in his work also. It was amazing to see the speed with which the thread and the needle moved in his hands while darning. I was carefully watching how the needle moved in his fingers from one side to the other. Half the place where he sat was lighted by the sun; the other half was shaded. He sat in the shade and the articles were in the sun. His beard was constantly shaking.

Shaukat chacha, taking out a bidi from the bundle, offered it to father: 'Here, have a smoke. . . .' Father lighted the bidi; Shaukat chacha, lighting his, held it between his teeth and continued darning with the same concentration as before.

The radio in the dispensary of Dr Ved Prakash Sharma was broadcasting the news. Several people stood outside listening to it.

'You know, Sugan, that China has attacked our country and that thousands of people have been killed. Nehru was speaking about this yesterday over the radio. The slogan—Hindi-Chinee bhai bhai—has just remained a slogan. . . .'

Father heard this in silence. He wasn't able to understand much. Even so he enquired: 'How many kos would it be to Chin from here?'

'Arey, it's just there behind the Himala parbat . . . ,' Shaukat said pointing towards the north with his hand.

'That means? . . .' father asked in surprise.

'He has positioned such machine guns on the Himala parbat that their bombs would straight hit Delhi. . . .' Shaukat chacha said with emphasis. Father began looking at the chacha wide-eyed. His face registered the combined emotions of surprise and fear. Lines of worry appeared on it.

'In that case the bombs could fall here also . . . in our village . . . on the Chaudhri's garhi . . . ,' father asked in alarm.

'Yes, they could. . . . ,' Shaukat chacha said in the same vein.

'In that case there is danger to everyone's life here?' Drops of sweat started appearing on father's face.

'Of course there is danger. . . . When there is a war, it's always the poor people like us who suffer . . . ,' Shaukat chacha said becoming serious.

Father was sunk in his thoughts. Taking several puffs of the bidi rapidly, he threw it into the drain and got up to go.

'Why are you scared? Don't worry, our army is also fighting bravely . . . it won't let their bombs reach us here . . .,' Shaukat chacha said to father laughing.

'Is that so? . . .' Father tried to be carefree.

The crowd of people buying their needs had added to the bustle of the bazaar. Customers from nearby villages also flocked to it.

Seeing father stand at Shaukat chacha's shop, Chaudhri Mamraj said: 'Abe, Sugan, what are you doing here?'

As soon as he saw the Chaudhri, father, bending his head down, tried to withdraw into himself, so that he could escape from the cross eye of the Chaudhri. He would often behave in this manner whenever he was face to face with a bully. I don't know why father behaved like that. Perhaps the Chaudhris occupied such a dominant position in the village that everyone felt compelled to bow before them.

Father replied to the Chaudhri's question timidly: 'Nothing Chaudhriji . . . I had some work with Shaukat bhai.'

'Is this your son who is studying in school?' The Chaudhri, eyeing me, shot out the question.

'Ji . . .,' father said softly with his head bent, as though he had committed a crime in sending me to school.

'Oh, yes, send him to school, send him. It's you who are the "bosses" these days. . . . The rest won't get any jobs. . . . Chairs and tables have been laid out for you in government departments. . . . You have become the jamaais of the government . . . I guess I should also get a Harijan certificate for my Mahendra. There is a tehsildar from our own community at the tehsil.' The Chaudhri said all this at one breath.

Father sat with his head bent low. He was not able to

understand much of what the Chaudhri had said. He said softly: 'It will be good, Chaudhriji, if with your blessings he is able to learn a little.'

The Chaudhri's temper changed suddenly. 'Don't talk nonsense. Put him to work in some trade . . . he'll be able to earn something . . . what'll he get after education? He'll be neither here nor there.'

Father's face also started changing its colour. But he controlled himself. He was well-acquainted with the Chaudhri's nature. To contradict him was to annoy him. And annoyance led him to use abusive language. So father tried to evade the issue.

Shaukat chacha tried to change the drift of conversation: 'Please give me also a chance to serve you, Chaudhriji. . . . I also wish to be audacious enough to try to show you my skill.'

'Come to the haveli . . . the bandi needs to be darned . . . .', said the Chaudhri.

'Ji . . . I'll surely come . . . ,' Shaukat chacha said with humility.

On return from Shaukat chacha I started waiting for the coming Friday. That I shall get an umbrella to go to school—was a matter of great joy for me. Every moment the umbrella kept revolving in my mind. The thought of what kind of umbrella it would be came to me again and again. Till now all the people who I had seen with umbrellas—their umbrellas started coming to my mind one by one. . . . These seven days seemed very long, which passed in great excitement. Several times I had asked father: 'What kind of umbrella will chacha make for me?'

Father understood the state of my mind. That was why he didn't rebuke me for asking the same question again and again. He would only say smiling: 'See it when it comes.'

That day I had got up early. Father was already up. He was drawing at the hookah on the platform outside. Rubbing my eyes, I said to him: 'It's Friday today, father.'

Father said laughing: 'I remember . . . the umbrella has to be brought from Shaukat chacha. When you come back from iskool [school], the umbrella will be in your hands.'

I wanted to say: 'I won't go to school today, father . . . I shall also accompany you to Shaukat chacha to get the umbrella.'—But I couldn't bring myself to say it. Father might lose his temper—this fear made me keep quiet.

The umbrella kept revolving in my mind in the school also. I wasn't able to concentrate in any class. I was just waiting for the final bell to ring. But the day seemed unusually long.

As soon as the bell rang, I ran out and crossed the school boundary. Behind me was Anirudh Sharma who ran to catch up with me. He said: 'What's the matter today, Jai? . . . Why are you in such a hurry? . . . You were quiet in the class also and now you are running like a horse.'

'Yes, it's something special,' I said.

'What's it?' he asked out of curiosity.

'I shall tell you tomorrow. . . . Now you also come along quick,' I said.

Both of us used to sit on adjacent seats in the class and also go home from school together. Seeing me run he also started running. That day instead of the main road, we took to the footpath in the fields. This route was shorter. When I reached home, my heart started beating fast. I was about to get an umbrella!

Father was smoking the hookah sitting on the cot in

front. The umbrella lay near him. When I saw it, my joy knew no bounds. Mother was also standing there. I just kept staring at the umbrella. Father said nothing, neither did mother.

Finally it was I who asked: 'Is this the umbrella chacha has given?' My curiosity was aroused. Only father's moustaches were shaking. He just looked at me from the corner of his eye. It seemed to me as though he hadn't heard my question. Mother said laughing: 'Put down your bag first. Then you can see your umbrella. It will stay with you now.'

Truly speaking, the day had brought me such joy for which I had been waiting for a whole week. The umbrella that permeated my thoughts every moment, that always remained in my mind's eyes—that umbrella was now in my hands. It was quite a big umbrella with a wooden rod and a handle. The cloth was no doubt old but seemed quite strong. In spite of being old the umbrella was precious for me at that time, a veritable gift. Possessing it made me happy beyond measure.

The next day I went to school with the umbrella. I was full of elation. My pace had automatically become faster. Self-confidence filled the core of my being. I wished to tell my friends that I too had an umbrella. Henceforth my books wouldn't get wet. As I was leaving home for school, father said by way of instruction: 'Take care. Don't lose it.'

My heart was filled with greater reverence for Shaukat chacha. In my mind I said to him repeatedly: 'You have given me such a good umbrella, chacha. I am so happy.' I don't know if my words reached him. But seeing the shape of my umbrella caused my friends to whisper among themselves. Lakshmikant from my own class said to provoke me: 'Abe, chuhre ke, where did you pick up the umbrella from?'

His words pierced me to my core. Tears began to well up in my eyes. A shooting pain arose in my heart but at that time I didn't have the courage to express it. For a moment the joy of getting the umbrella vanished. Finding me quiet he burst out into a loud laughter and sat down in his seat. But there was something hot inside me that had started simmering.

On Saturdays there was a school assembly in the afternoon. This assembly used to be held in the verandah in front of the office of the Principal. The Principal and teachers sat on the chairs on one side; the students sat on the floor on the other. Speeches, songs and poems etc. were presented at the assembly. India-China war was on, so the theme of this Saturday was patriotism. For this reason a twelfth class student Vikas was to present Makhan Lal Chaturvedi's poem 'The Yearning of a Flower' and an eleventh class student Shivraj Singh was to present a song entitled 'Love of one's country'. Thereafter the teachers and the Principal were to make speeches.

As the bell rang, students started assembling in the verandah. Some students, who were in a carefree mood, were deeply engrossed in talking loudly to one another. The P.T. Master Gulab Singh asked them to keep quiet several times but it had had no effect on them. After a while they again started shouting. The Principal hadn't yet reached the assembly. The students' loud noise changed into an uproar. Soon they came to blows.

Master Ishwarchandra taught the eleventh and twelfth classes. He was fat and flabby, his complexion dark, eyes narrow like a crab. Whenever he spoke, he shrieked, as though those standing before him were deaf and dumb.

He often seemed excitable. People called him patriotic. Whenever I saw him, I found him to be speaking loudly and deeply distressed at the dying patriotic spirit among the people. Whenever he was alone, there was an air of restlessness about him.

In order to quell the students' noise, he shouted at the top of his voice: 'Abe, mother f. . . keep quiet, or else I'll come there and. . . .' This 'monkey's threat' proved ineffective. They remained as engrossed in their talk as before. Master Ishwarchandra's anger shot up to the seventh heaven. His temples also began to change colour. His nostrils began to swell. He stood up. Anirudh Sharma and I were sitting close against the wall. Master Ishwarchandra went past us towards the boys. Suddenly he turned back. He saw the umbrella resting on my shoulders. He swiftly grabbed my umbrella and started thrashing them like an army commander swooping down on the enemy. After only two or three strokes the umbrella broke in the middle, which rent my heart. I was shocked. I didn't have the courage to look at the mess the Master had made of my umbrella. It seemed as though the entire blood in my body had frozen.

Master Ishwarchandra threw the broken umbrella outside the verandah and sat down in his chair gasping for breath. The boys who had received the thrashing also became quiet.

I started weeping loudly. Anirudh Sharma was trying to quieten me down. As soon as the Principal came, the programme started. Vikas of the twelfth standard began to recite Makhan Lal Chaturvedi's poem but not a word of it was audible to me. I was only looking at my broken umbrella. While the entire assembly was drenched in patriotism, I was mourning the loss of my umbrella. For the assembly the breaking of the umbrella was meaningless. Compared to the love for one' country, an umbrella was a negligible object. But for me the breaking of it was like the shattering of dreams. I looked at Master Ishwarchandra. He sat swaying with the poem in silent enjoyment.

I felt a deep desire rise up in me and I came out of the assembly. Picking up my broken umbrella I swiftly went and threw it down before Master Ishwarchandra. My entire being was shackled by numbness and deep sadness. Seeing me stand before him, he was taken aback. His nostrils began to flutter in anger.

However, his angry demeanour had no effect on me whatsoever. I kept standing there as before. Master Yogendra Singh Mishra was speaking about the India-China relationship. But I was not able to hear a word of his speech. My ears had shut themselves up, as though someone had poured mercury into them.

Master Ishwarchandra's ferocious eyes seemed impatient to throw the remnants of my pride after mutilating it further outside the verandah. Darkness started appearing before my eyes. Ishwarchandra's eyes seemed to glare at me steadily like the eyes of a wild animal hidden in the bushes, which could swoop down on me any moment. I was waiting for my consciousness to dissolve.

Glossary

aanchal	:	the end of a sari
aapisar	:	officer
Aashaad	:	name of Indian month corresponding to June-July
abe, abey	:	interjection used pejoratively with undue familiarity, disrespectfully or rudely
agnipariksha	:	fire ordeal such as the one through which Sita had to pass.
almirah	:	cupboard
arey	:	an interjection used for men to attract attention
ari	:	used for women
ashram	:	a refuge
Ayodhya	:	place associated with Lord Rama
baaman	:	Brahmin
babuji	:	used for an educated/well-dressed person from the city
bachchu	:	a variation of bachcha, a child
Bahu, bahuji	:	young wife; a term used in formal address
Baba Saheb	:	Dr Bhimrao Ambedkar
baalister	:	barrister
Baid mantra	:	sacred verses from the Vedas
balhaar	:	lowliest of the low dalits
bandi	:	a home-made vest
baniyas	:	traders

Bapu	:	Mahatma Gandhi
baraat, baraati	:	marriage party; a member of it
basti	:	a settlement
bataashas	:	puffed small sugar-cakes
bazaar	:	market
bete, bette	:	son
bhai	:	brother
Bhadon	:	name of Indian month corresponding to the period from mid-August to mid-September
Bhainji [bahenji]	:	a respectful term of address for a woman
bhang	:	an intoxicating drink
bhangi	:	see Chuhra
bhapaji	:	a Punjabi term of respect for a father-figure
bigaar [begaar]	:	forced labour
biri, bidi	:	a twist of tobacco rolled into a tobacco leaf
bua	:	father's sister
chacha	:	uncle; also used as a mark of respect to one's elders
chachi	:	aunt; also used for an older woman to show respect
chadar, chaadar	:	a sheet; a woman's light shawl
chakravyuha	:	a ring-shaped formation of troops from which it is difficult to come out
chapatti	:	a thin cake of unleavened bread
charpai	:	cot
chutnee	:	spicy sauce

chaupal	:	an assembly room in a village
Chaudhri	:	the headman of a village; an honorific title
Chaudhrain	:	wife of a Chaudhri
Chin	:	China
Chhupa rustam	:	Rustam is the name of a Persian hero. The term means someone who hides his light under a bushel.
chhutku	:	an affectionate term for a small child
chowkidar	:	a watchman
chuhra	:	a sweeper
chuhra-chamars	:	sweeper-cobblers
chuhre ke	:	son of a chuhra, sweeper; used pejoratively
dada/dadi	:	paternal grandfather/grandmother
daroga	:	a police inspector or superintendent
darshan	:	visiting a respectable, venerable, holy person
devarji	:	a term used to address husband's younger brother
dhanna seth	:	a wealthy or moneyed man
dholak	:	a small drum
dhoti	:	a piece of cloth worn round the lower part of the body, one end of which passes through the legs and is tucked behind
didi	:	elder sister
dom	:	sweeper; also name of a community of musicians and dancers
dushala	:	a shawl
gadiya lohars	:	roving blacksmiths

gangajal : pure holy water from the river Ganga
ganpati : name of the elephant god, Ganesh; used here humorously
gara : a pejorative term used for Muslims to indicate that they bury their dead
garhi : a small fort
gayatri mantra : name of a sacred verse from the *Rig Veda* recited on auspicious occasions.
ghee : clarified butter
gur : raw brown sugar
guruji : a venerable teacher, spiritual guide
halwa-puree : pudding and fried chapattis
harijan : a term used for untouchables made popular by Mahatma Gandhi
haveli : an imposing house or building
Hemtee.Otmat : H.M.T. Automatic; a well-known brand of Indian watches
himala parbat : the Himalaya mountain
huzoor : a term of respect
insalate : insult
iskool : school
jalkhumbi : water mushrooms
jamaais : sons-in-law
jamadaarni : a female sweeper
jayanti : a birthday celebration
jinn : demon
jot : jyoti, light, flame of a lamp or candle lighted before an idol
kabaari shop : a dealer in old or broken furniture, etc.
kaaliye : here a boy with a swarthy complextion.
kaliyug : the name of the last and the worst of

		the four yugas or ages according to Hindu beliefs
kanjars	:	an itinerant community, the members of which make and sell trinkets; used pejoratively for dirty, uncouth person of low origin
kayastha	:	an upper caste Hindu community of mixed origin; writer caste.
khatik	:	a keeper of pigs, butcher
khatri	:	an upper caste Hindu community of merchants and traders
khes	:	a kind of heavy cloth
kirtan mandli	:	a group singing religious songs
kohlu	:	a press mill for sugar cane or oil-seeds
kos	:	a measure of distance, about 2 miles
kothi	:	a big house.
kuchcha/pucca	:	(of houses) built partly of baked bricks and partly of mud
kulwanti bahu	:	a daughter-in-law from a good or noble family
Lala	:	baniya, trader
lallaji	:	an affectionate term of address used for someone (a male) who is younger
lathi	:	club
Lachhman [Lakshman]	:	Lord Rama's younger brother who left Sita alone in the forest in search of his brother
Lakshmi	:	goddess of wealth; beauty. The reference is to the belief that a woman's presence in the household will bring luck.
litchi	:	a fruit

lote	:	note, that is currency note
Magh	:	January-February
mai-baap	:	used for a master, overlord
Mai Madaran	:	one of the deities worshipped by the dalits
mama, mamaji	:	maternal uncle
mandap	:	a temporary pavilion or structure erected for marriage
massahib	:	master sahib, term of respect for teacher
maund	:	Indian measure of weight
mian	:	term of respectful or affectionate address used by Muslims
mistri	:	mason
mogra	:	jasmine flower
mohalla	:	a quarter of a town
muhra	:	an indigenous chair
Mukhiya, Mukhiyaji	:	head of the village
mullas and maulvis	:	Muslim religious scholars, functionaries
naan	:	bread
nagin	:	a female cobra
namaaz	:	Muslim prayer
nana, nani	:	maternal grandfather, grandmother
nandini	:	A cow of plenty belonging to sage Vasishtha in Hindu Mythology much envied for its beauty
neem	:	tree known for its bitter fruit and leaves with medicinal value
pallu	:	edge of a garment
paan	:	betel leaf

paan-biri shops	: shops selling betel leaves and biris
palki	: palanquin
panch	: member of a panchayat
panch parmeswar	: five members of a panchayat who in their impartiality and justice are supposed to be divine
panda	: a brahmin superintending religious functions at a place of pilgrimage
pandat	: pandit
paratha	: a fried chapatti
Parvati	: Lord Shiva's consort
pheras	: rounds of the sacred fire done by the bride and the groom for marriage
pice	: the lowest unit of Indian currency at one time
pradhan	: chief
prasad	: food offered to an idol; the remnants of the food given back to the devotee for distribution.
puja	: worship
pujari	: priest of a temple.
Rahu and Ketu	: Rahu is the demon who along with Ketu is supposed to seize the sun and moon in his mouth and cause eclipses.
rakshabandhan	: a festival during which sisters tie a knot round the wrists of their brothers seeking a pledge of protection from them.
rakhi	: a piece of thread with a rosette tied by a sister round the wrist of a brother who promises to protect her
rakshasa	: a demon

ramnami	:	a garment with Lord Ram's name printed all over
Ravidas jayanti	:	birth anniversary of saint Ravidas, particularly venerated by dalits
roti	:	bread
saale	:	wife's brother; by transference a term of abuse
saali	:	wife's sister, by transference a term of abuse
safai karamchari	:	a municipal employee who attends to scavenging work
salaam	:	a practice that required the dalit groom or bride to go on a round of the houses of their upper caste clients to receive clothes and utensils
sanskaras	:	inherited values that are conducive to refinement and perfection
sanyasi	:	one who has renounced the world
sarpanch	:	head of the panchayat
shastras	:	religious texts
shavayatra	:	funeral procession
S.C.s	:	Scheduled Castes listed in the Constitution. That is how dalits are referred to in legal terms
shloka	:	Sanskrit verse
shudra	:	a member of the fourth and the lowest division of the Hindu caste system
Sita	:	Lord Rama's wife who had to pass through the fire ordeal in order to prove her chastity
sohra	:	an abuse; a variation of *saale,* wife's brother

suno-ji	:	please listen
tagaari	:	a tub containing a mason's mud
taim	:	time
tau, tauji	:	father's elder brother. The term is also used as a marker of respect for an elderly male
tehsil	:	part of a district
tehsildar	:	a revenue officer-in-charge of a part of a district
thaal	:	a big flat metal plate
thakur	:	landed proprietor
thekedarji	:	contractor
thikana	:	here, a place, a house where a dalit did the cleaning
tika	:	a ceremony connected with Hindu marriage
vaanar sena	:	an army of monkeys—a reference to an important component of King Rama's army
Vaidji	:	an Ayurvedic doctor
vidai	:	farewell; the ceremonial departure of the bride for the groom's place
zarda	:	tobacco for chewing with betel leaf or otherwise